Janet Morris Belvin

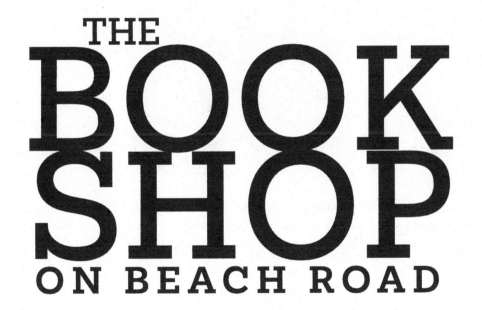

THE BOOKSHOP ON BEACH ROAD

The Bookshop on Beach Road
A Novel

A heartwarming WWII romance set amidst Operation Drumbeat
Off the Outer Banks coast

This is a work of fiction. Names, characters, places, and incidents are products of the author's imagination or are used fictitiously and are not to be construed as real. Any resemblance to actual events, locales, organizations, or persons, living or dead, is entirely coincidental.

Title page art by Martha Jean

Printed in the United States of America

ISBN 978-1-66786-351-1 eBook 978-1-66786-352-8

JOURNALIST TOM BROKAW named the generation of Americans born between 1901 and 1927 "The Greatest Generation." My parents Frank and Theodosia Morris were members of that generation and maybe your parents or grandparents were too. They came of age during the Great Depression and many of them fought unimaginable horrors in the Second World War. While the soldiers and sailors were at the battlefront, the women left behind stepped up and filled the empty spots in factories, stores and farms, all the while taking care of their homes and children. This generation embodied courage, sacrifice, patriotism and integrity. Members of this age group are being lost daily, and when they go, they take whole encyclopedias of knowledge and experiences with them – rich stories that are lost to time. To their memory and to honor those few remaining, this book is dedicated.

From "For the Fallen" by Robert Laurence Binyon (1869-1943)

"They went with songs to the battle, they were young,
Straight of limb, true of eye, steady and aglow.
They were staunch to the end against odds uncounted,
They fell with their faces to the foe.
They shall grow not old, as we that are left grow old:
Age shall not weary them, nor the years condemn.
At the going down of the sun and in the morning
We will remember them."

A *NOTE* FROM THE AUTHOR

WRITING A NOVEL is a wonderful way to create your own world and that's exactly what I have done in The Bookshop on Beach Road. I've written the town of Nags Head, North Carolina and the Outer Banks the way I remember them or at the very least the way I wish they could have been. The events in this book are based on some very real and terrifying happenings. There really were U-Boats terrorizing the Outer banks during 1942. Many lives were lost during that time. Some of the people mentioned here were real – Admiral Karl Dönitz, for example, really was the head of the Nazi U-Boat operation. There really was a Trading Post and an Oasis Restaurant. There really is an Owens' Restaurant. But there never was an R & R or a Raleigh Theater. There never was a Colony Books or Coastal Real Estate Company. (At least I don't think so!) Another one of the privileges of creating my own world is the ability to time shift. So while some of these things I've written about actually occurred at the proper time, others I have moved around for the purposes of my story. We'll all be happier if we just go along with my little "creations."

Finally, I want to say that this book is not nor should it be taken to be historically accurate. Though I am very interested in World War II and I appreciate the sacrifices made by so many during that time, this book is also a love story and should be enjoyed as such. I've had some remarkable assistance from some wonderful friends and family, who've made it easy to write during a worldwide pandemic.

Thanks go to my friend **Johnny Roach** for valuable assistance in the workings of a plane. Thanks also to **Jerry and Larry Hester** for the use of their Outer Banks condo while I did research for this book. Thank you, too, **Jerry**, for the inestimable gift of your thoughts on design. Thanks to **Martha Jean Adams** for her artwork which represents Astrid's art in the book. **Louise Purdy**, thanks for the use of your name for one of the main characters. I hope you like her. My favorite librarian **Pat Familar** encouraged me with her excitement. The staff of the Outer Banks History Center at Festival Park in Manteo, NC gave helpful assistance as did the staff of the Graveyard of the Atlantic Museum in Hatteras, NC. Here's a sincere thank you to booksellers everywhere! I have to give supreme credit to my better half for the use of his massive World War II lending library, his editing skills, and his belief in me. To all of my friends (too many to name) and family who have cheered me on, telling me that they were eagerly awaiting this book, I really could not have done it without your supporting "Yays!"

And, finally, this book is for you, **Paul**, and, of course, for **Mama, Daddy**, and **Camden**, always in my heart.

XXXX

Janet

PREFACE

In an office in a waterside villa in December of 1941, the chief of U-boat operations for Nazi Germany, a fifty-year old, balding man was studying maps tacked onto his wall. Karl Dönitz's headquarters for U-Boat operations was located near the U-Boat pens at Lorient, a town in northwestern France, and later moved to Paris. Just days before, on December 7th, the nation of Japan had perpetrated a surprise attack on the United States Naval Base at Pearl Harbor. Four days later, Germany declared war on the United States of America. And Karl Dönitz learned from Naval High Command that all restrictions on attacks against American vessels had been lifted by Germany's Fuhrer, Adolf Hitler. Dönitz, seizing an opportunity for assault, requested the release of twelve U-Boats from the Command. Early in 1942, he'd learned that the United States had only one Coast Guard cutter out spotting for German subs. So night after night, tankers and supply ships were targeted and sunk. It was not an uncommon sight for Outer Banks residents to see ships on fire offshore, their positions marked by thick plumes of dark smoke.

Dönitz was a slight man, about 5 feet, 8 inches tall and weighing barely 142 pounds, but his subordinates referred to him as the Lion and loved working for him. He was born in Berlin in 1891 and had commanded a U Boat in World War I. He was ruthless, a strong supporter of Adolf Hitler and, after Hitler's suicide at the end of the war, would be made president of Germany, a position he held for just 23 days. But in the 1930s, Dönitz was chosen to put Germany's submarine force back in action, in defiance of the Treaty of Versailles which had expressly prohibited any German submarines.

The U-Boat named U-47 had sunk the British battleship *Royal Oak* in 1939 causing the death of more than 1,200 sailors. The U-47 captain Gunther Prien was lauded nationally and decorated by Hitler himself. But Dönitz took credit for the attack although it had been planned by his subordinate Victor Oehrn. After the *Royal Oak* sinking, Oerhn focused his attention on the east coast of the United States, knowing that it was completely defenseless. And along that coast, cargo ships, tankers, and merchant marine vessels travelled daily, headed for the port of Norfolk and the shipping lanes beyond toward Europe. By January of 1942, Germany had ninety-one U-Boats in good working order. Of these, only six were given to Dönitz for use off the coast of North Carolina, the rest being in service in other locations. Later one of these boats developed an oil leak, so only five were delivered to Dönitz for his use.

At this time, Britain had desperate need of American ships and oil, food and war materiel since the German "wolf-packs" (groups of German submarines) had sunk so many of Britain's ships and supplies. It had occurred to Victor Oehrn that a U-boat attack somewhere along the American east coast would render Great Britain empty of oil, the oil that was necessary for the war effort. Destroying the more than fifty ships that passed along that corridor daily would sever the Allied lifeline to Europe.

On the Marine navigational maps tacked on his wall, Dönitz noticed that at one location the ocean depth was six hundred feet not far off the coastline, a perfect place to position one of Hitler's feared U-Boats. The ocean bottom dropped off very quickly in this location close to the shoreline, allowing the subs to avoid being trapped on a shallow bottom. Dönitz put his finger on the tack marking the spot

– Cape Hatteras, North Carolina – at the southern tip of the Outer Banks. With few American military having been sent to the area up to this point, Dönitz knew that the Atlantic coast would now be a death trap for shipping.

He immediately notified his small staff of seven that he was holding an office meeting the next day to outline his thoughts. The staff was composed of seasoned U-boat commanders who were extremely loyal to Dönitz. He and his team came up with a name for his plan – *Operation Paukenschlag* – Operation Drumbeat. The Outer Banks were squarely in Dönitz's crosshairs.

CHAPTER ONE

1994

Della Gates looked down at her expensive leather sandals and shook the sand from them. Shading her eyes because of the brightness of the noonday sun, she got out of her late model Audi to have a look east toward the Atlantic Ocean. Walking to the sands bordering the ocean, Della looked at the houses there. Along the road that paralleled the narrow sandy beach, fifteen or twenty gray shingled beach cottages of ancient age reigned over the beige sands of Nags Head Beach. The houses, referred to locally as the "Unpainted Aristocracy" of Old Nags Head, had been built during the years following the War Between the States, as summer getaways for family members of northeastern North Carolina planters, merchants and professionals. Della thought of how many hundreds of thousands of people had watched the sunrise from the porches of these simple, stately cottages.

Nags Head was one of several beach towns located along a string of islands on North Carolina's easternmost coastline. The coastline shifted constantly over the years as the ocean's strong winds and high tides beat upon the sand dunes. Occasionally some of the houses had had to be moved back as the ocean encroached upon the cottages. But the owners refused for the most part to leave the area, claiming the sea air offered a healthy alternative to the stifling air of cities or the malaria which wreaked havoc upon those living near the Great Dismal Swamp.

Now over one hundred years since the "Unpainted Aristocracy" had been built, the spot was a popular destination for tourists and sun-worshippers year-round. The beaches up and down the coastline had been changed over the years with the destruction of early small houses which were replaced by McMansions, painted in garish pastels and planted with palm trees and other tropical landscaping that, to the eyes of most Nags Head natives, just didn't belong.

Development of the area surrounding the "Unpainted Aristocracy" seemed imminent, and Della worried about that very thing, wishing the area could stay as she remembered it from her childhood vacations there. She surveyed the long line of cottages, most built upon pilings and covered in unpainted wood siding or wood shingles. Their oceanfront sides sported long porches with benches and rocking chairs. Della shook her long chestnut hair, worrying about the changes she was seeing.

How much longer before these are all gone, she wondered.

She turned back from the ocean's waves and headed to her car. Crossing the wooden boardwalk over the dunes, she ran her hand over the tops of the sea oats, the wind tossing her hair.

Well, I can't worry about that right now, she told herself. *I've got other things to worry about.*

CHAPTER TWO

1994

D ella really wasn't in the mood to look for a place to stay. In fact, she would have been just as happy to stay in her parents' house. But she knew it was unfair to them and given that she had lost her steady income, she needed to find a job.

It was an early May afternoon and the rain of the previous day had washed away the humidity. The weather forecasters gleefully predicted more rain for the next couple of days; not great for the Memorial Day Weekend, they noted. Normally it would have been a perfect time to find a rental, but right now, Della Gates wanted no part of it. She'd just lost her job as part of the most recent cost-cutting measures that malls and retail stores everywhere were taking. She had been the book buyer for a large book store chain based in Raleigh and had been focused primarily on revamping the children's sections in the chain stores. So it came as a total shock when she was called into her supervisor's office and told that she'd been "let go." Last hired, first fired, he'd said, and that included Della.

To add to her mounting list of problems, she'd just broken up with her fiancé of two years, Dylan Metcalfe. Della and Dylan had started in the same company, Colony Books, at the same time but Dylan, the son of the head of the company, was on the fast track to advancement while her career was stalled. On the evening after she'd been released from her job, Della had taken herself out solo for a farewell meal at a tony restaurant in Crabtree Mall. Imagine her surprise when she walked in and saw Dylan enjoying a cozy candlelight meal with a voluptuous redhead. Her shock registered on her face as she drew in her breath. At the same moment, Dylan happened to turn toward the door, making an expansive gesture in his conversation with the redhead. Seeing Della there, he jumped up and ran toward her.

"Wait, Della. This isn't what it looks like," he'd said as she turned on her heel and walked out the door. "She's just a coworker."

Yeah, right, Della thought. *And I'm the Easter Bunny.*

And that was the end of that romance. She drove back to her apartment and had a good cry. After a restless night, she packed up a few of her belongings, preparing to go home to her parents, Roy and Maxine Gates. Luckily, she was at the end of her one-year lease, so the dreaded meeting with Emery, the apartment manager went better than she expected. Three weeks later, Della had transferred her clothes and the few pieces of furniture she owned back to the Outer Banks, where her parents lived. Defeat covering her like a blanket, she moved into a guest bedroom in her parents' house in Kitty Hawk where she'd been, licking her wounds, for about a month. The cheery pink walls and lacy canopy on her twin bed did nothing to improve her mood. So her usually joyful demeanor was pretty much non-existent.

Her Great Aunt Louise Gates, who owned a local bookshop, had come to the house one day for a visit, and upon learning of her niece's situation, mentioned the "Help Wanted" sign in the window of the local grocery store. Louise also mentioned that her shed apartment was available in case Della needed a place of her own.

Della, recognizing that she needed some immediate financial relief, thanked her Aunt Louise profusely and called the grocery store to set up an appointment.

Nevertheless, just in case she might find a better, more private place than living with her aunt, the next day found her at a rental office on Beach Road looking for a house to rent, just as every other college student and international worker on a visa was doing. She sat in her car, buttoning and unbuttoning the clasp on the straw purse she'd bought herself as an early birthday present, (before she knew she would be out of a job.) Then she stepped out of the car, shielding her eyes from the bright sun, and entered the Coastal Real Estate office. She looked around at the rental houses displayed on cards in a showcase, not one looking a fraction different from another, not one looking remotely like a house she'd care about. She decided she'd take up her Aunt Louise's earlier offer of her shed apartment and was on her way out of the office. Della walked carelessly down the aisle, not really paying attention to where she was headed when suddenly, she felt something nudging her thigh.

She looked down and saw the most beautiful yellow Labrador retriever she'd ever seen – with a big, blocky head and eyes that looked right at her. Without thinking, she leaned down, grabbed the leash that was dragging the floor and began scratching him behind his ears. She looked up a minute later when she heard a man walking around the end of the aisle whispering, "Biscuit! Come here, boy."

Biscuit, whose gorgeous head Della held in her hands, obviously heard the voice of his master because he turned his head to the side and went bounding off in the direction of the voice. Unfortunately for Della, in dashing off, Biscuit pulled on his leash, knocking her to the floor.

"That's great – one more piece of bad luck for me. You're on a roll, Della. Now I'll have to get these white jeans to the cleaners," she mumbled to herself.

Just about that moment, the owner of the Lab came rushing up to her, reaching out his hand to help her up. Della was in no mood to be gracious – In fact, she was pretty grumpy. Never mind that she had dust and dog paw prints all over her jeans and her hair was a mess. She was sure she looked a fright.

"I am so sorry," the dog's owner said. "Let me help you up. My dog got away from me and ran into the office before I could catch him. My name is Lucas Howard – Luke. I am so sorry. Biscuit here is still just a pup. He doesn't really know how strong he is."

"What's he doing in here, anyway?" Della snapped.

"Dogs are allowed as long as they are leashed. It seems Biscuit didn't get that memo," Lucas chuckled.

Della was trying to maintain her bad mood, but she was having a difficult time. She was not sure she had ever seen such a handsome guy in her life – broad shoulders, tall, dark hair with just a hint of curl, gray eyes, killer dimples – one on each cheek, and a hint of a five o'clock shadow. And that smile that went all the way up to his eyes. Meanwhile, Della was silent, realizing how terrible she must look.

"So are you ok?" Lucas said. "You seem kind of dazed."

"Errrr, no, I mean yeah, I'm ok. Just a little stunned." She was busy brushing off her jeans, trying not to look into those eyes. And Biscuit at the same time had discovered that he liked the smell of her, so he reached his muddy paws up on Della's jeans, adding yet another stain.

"Biscuit, NO!" Lucas said. "Oh, no, I can't believe he did that. I really insist on taking care of the cleaning, Miss…um, I don't even know your name."

"It's Della. Della Gates. Thank you. That's quite all right."

"No, really, I insist. And let me buy you a cup of coffee and a piece of pie. I know a cafe just across Beach Road that's really good. It's the least I can do until I can get your jeans cleaned."

So Della said OK. They walked over to the diner. And that's how they met. But really that was just the beginning of it all.

CHAPTER THREE

1942

E arly 1942 brought World War II to the shores of the Outer Banks. After the US declared war on Japan, Germany's Axis partner, on December 8, 1941, Germany began a devastating U-Boat assault on American vessels. Just hours after Germany had declared war on the United States, the United States responded, declaring war on Germany. These U-boats which Hitler launched were so called from the German name for them (*Unterseeboot*, the German word for "undersea boat.") They had the ability to strike ships 20 times their size both above and below the surface of the ocean with deck guns and torpedoes. Kitty Hawk, Nags Head, and Hatteras residents were, for a period of about seven months, witness to the explosions of ships being sunk off their coasts, followed by huge oil fires racing across the top of the ocean waters. During these early days of 1942, more than fifty ships, many of them carrying necessary supplies of fuel and gas for the Allied forces, were sunk off the coast of North Carolina.

In early 1942, the Outer Banks only had a few full time residents. Men of the right age for military service had been called to the war leaving only a few women and children as well as the elderly. So from January of 1942 until the summer of that year, the residents of the small towns and villages along the coastline saw ships fired upon by German U-Boats almost daily. Several hundred crewmen on these ships were lost over the first few months of that year, some of their bodies washing up on shore along with oil and other debris from the wrecks.

One of the casualties of the U-boat attacks on the Outer Banks was the *Esso Houston* tanker owned by the Standard Oil Company. The 7,699-ton ship carried some 81,701 barrels of crude oil bound for Hampton Roads, Virginia. At 2:34 AM on May 13, 1942, the captain and most of the 42-man crew of the *Houston* were asleep in their bunks. Meanwhile, a few miles east of the tanker, aboard *U-162, Kommandant* Jürgen Wattenberg waited on the Atlantic Ocean's surface. The *Houston*, ablaze with lights, would be easy pickings.

U-162 had its emblem of a white sword upon a black ground painted on the side of the conning tower. Inside, the interior was damp and confining but the men who were not on watch were snoring in their racks. The crews on duty were constantly moving about the narrow confines of the U-Boat, checking gauges, obeying orders, or listening to the hydrophone. At 0234 hours, one torpedo was fired, striking the port side of the *Houston*. The captain of the *Houston* realized immediately that repair was impossible and ordered the crew to abandon ship, which they did in three lifeboats and one raft.

Twenty minutes later, *U-162* fired a second torpedo, hitting the *Houston* amidships, causing a fire bright enough to be seen up and down the coast. The ship, splitting in two, immediately began sinking to the ocean floor. In a matter of a few moments, the ship and all its contents were lost. Of the forty-two souls on-board the *Houston*, eight officers, thirty men and four armed guards, all but one were saved, picked up out of the roiling waters of the Atlantic by a Norwegian tanker. They, like future survivors of these attacks, were brought to hospitals in cities along the coastline to be treated for the second and third degree burns they suffered from their plunge into the fiery oil slicks.

Kommandant Wattenberg immediately directed his radioman to send a message to a nearby U-Boat that his crew had scored a direct hit. He smiled to himself, confident that Herr Hitler would personally decorate him for this, and, leaning into the speaker tube, directed his crew to submerge.

Over the next several months, the waters off the beaches of the Outer Banks of North Carolina became the grave sites of over three hundred ninety merchant vessels, one of which was the *Houston*. At one point, U-Boats torpedoed at least one merchant vessel per night. Their oil slicks covered the ocean waves, the fires from the torpedoed ships creating infernos and taking the lives of hundreds of crewmen. Those who lived along the coast felt the tremendous blasts from these explosions, often strong enough to splinter the windows in their cottages. Walking along the beaches the day after the explosions, Outer Banks residents frequently discovered the debris from the wreckages, occasionally including body parts or actual dead bodies.

In a small office in the Coast Guard Air Station in Dare County, a young flight operations officer sat at his desk looking over the flight plan for the evening's operations. The base was a major maintenance depot for the flying boats the Coast Guard used in search and rescue operations. It had been built in 1939 as part of the military buildup for the coming war. Now that Germany had declared war on the United States, the Air Station was responsible for antisubmarine searches as well as search and rescue operations for vessels entering the domestic shipping lanes off the coast of North Carolina from Norfolk, Virginia. Norfolk, of course, was the location of the largest naval base on the east coast. Finn Ingram, tall and blonde with a slim build, had been newly transferred to this post from Norfolk, as worry began to build concerning the presence of U-boats in the area. The youngest son of immigrants from Norway, Finn and his family had come to the United States during the early 1930s and had become full citizens. Finn had taken great comfort in the fact that his family was safe in the United States from the war in their home country. As a Coast Guardsman, he regularly flew spotter planes over the Outer Banks, then out over the Atlantic Ocean, searching for trouble spots, as they called Nazi U-Boats. These "trouble spots" were important for the German war effort to sink potential supply ships carrying ammunition, fuel, and supplies for the Allied campaigns in Africa and Europe. Night after night, merchant marine ships, cargo ships and the occasional Navy ship were torpedoed and sunk. These vessels were coming regularly out of the port of Hampton Roads.

After turning off his radio, Finn walked up the stairs to the watch tower to see if any enemy ships, submarines or aircraft had been identified. On the wall of the stairway, Finn saw, as he did every day, the poster reading "Loose Lips Sink Ships." It was a slogan that had become newly popular as worry began to build that people would inadvertently drop information into their conversations that might help the enemy. The slogan also helped to dispel the rumors that were rampant in the days following the Pearl Harbor attack.

Finn checked to see if it was a C day to buy gas. Gas rationing had just recently begun in seventeen eastern states to help the war effort. By the end of the year, gas would be rationed in all 48 states. The rationing provided each owner of a vehicle with a lettered sticker denoting on which day he or she could buy gas. Coast Guard members like Finn received a "C" sticker, issued to professional people: physicians, nurses, dentists, ministers, priests, mail delivery, embalmers, farm workers, construction or maintenance workers, soldiers and armed forces heading to duty. Ordinary civilians received the "A" sticker. In addition to conserving gasoline, the rationing also helped to preserve tires as rubber was no longer readily available.

Finn exited the Coast Guard station and started his Willy's-Overland Jeep driving to the beach just beside the pier. He had not eaten lunch yet and planned to get a fish sandwich at the Jennette's Pier Café. The pier and pier house had been built in 1939 and extended nearly 750 feet out into the ocean, making it a perfect place for fishing. On the beach near where the pier had been constructed, grass and sea oats had been planted and sand dunes had been fortified by the Civilian Conservation Corps during the Great Depression.

Ducking his head as he entered the café, Finn stood inside the door. He waited at the café counter until he was approached by a young girl. The waitress was a beautiful eighteen year old teenager, her brunette hair rolled tightly behind her head. Wearing a blue striped uniform with a white linen apron tied around her neat little waist, she smiled and approached the young officer. She grabbed a plastic-clad menu and led him to a booth with a window facing the Atlantic Ocean. Finn followed her, his mouth watering from the smells of fried seafood which the kitchen produced.

"Is this OK?" the waitress asked.

"It's perfect," Finn told her. "Now what do you suggest? I'm awfully hungry."

The waitress recited a list of the day's specials and told him she'd be right back with some water. Finn opened the menu and ran his finger down the list of sandwiches. He found the catfish filet sandwich he was looking for and closed the menu, waiting for the return of the waitress.

The waitress had gone back to the kitchen to check on the delivery of certain items they'd ordered from the R & R, the local grocery store. She noted the delivery of barrels of ice and fresh vegetables. A teenaged boy who worked on one of the local fishing boats brought in a box of fresh crabs, fish and shrimp. The waitress checked off the items on her list, then received the bill of lading from the delivery boy and handed it to the cook.

She washed her hands in the kitchen sink, and then reappeared at Finn's table, setting a glass of ice water in front of him. Her order pad in her hand, she pulled a pencil from behind her ear and looked down at Finn.

"Have you decided?" she asked with a smile.

"You know, I don't think I've seen you here before. Are you new at the restaurant?"

"Well, I'm new at the restaurant but I grew up here. I just started working here and my mother and I live with my grandparents. My dad is in Norfolk working for the War Department. He comes home on the weekends. My brother is in the Navy in the Pacific."

"Thought I had never seen you around! I think I'll take the catfish filet sandwich with fries and make the fries extra crispy. And I'll have a Pepsi-Cola. You know, I eat here about once a week and I knew I would have recognized you. My name is Finn Ingram, by the way."

The waitress wrote down Finn's order, and placed her pad and pencil in her apron pocket as she headed to the kitchen. Looking over her shoulder at Finn, she smiled and said, "My name's Louise, by the way. Louise Gates."

CHAPTER FOUR

1994

After Lucas helped Della up from her fall, they walked across the road to the tiny diner. The Ocean Tide Café was a white cement block affair, one story with red shutters and window boxes containing a profusion of red geraniums. It had been run as a café for more years than Lucas could recall. As they walked in, Lucas seemed to know everybody and hailed them with a friendly wave or a few words of greeting. He directed Della to a table in front of the window. Biscuit walked right through the diner to a room in the back like he owned the place.

"Hey, Lucas, honey. What're you up to?"

The petite woman with salt and pepper hair and a broad smile was Luke's grandmother.

"Hey, Nana. This is Della Gates. Biscuit just knocked her off her feet in the realty office across the road. I was looking to see whose houses are renting these days and Biscuit got away from me. Della kind of found him."

"Well, hey, Della. So you've met the Biscuit, huh. Looks like your jeans got the worst of the deal. I'm Eunice Howard and Lucas here is my grandson."

"Hello, Mrs. Howard," Della said, half rising from her seat.

"Now you sit right down, Della. I'm gonna bring you a piece of pie and a cup of coffee that'll change your life. What'll it be – apple, blueberry, pecan, egg custard, coconut custard…"

"Whoa – that's a lot to choose from. I'll just have a cup of coffee for now."

Lucas spoke up and ordered coffee and a piece of apple pie with a wink for his grandmother. Della didn't realize it was a secret signal until Eunice brought out two slabs of the most gorgeous Dutch apple crumb pies you've ever seen. She set them down on the table and handed each a paper napkin-wrapped fork, knife and spoon and smiled.

"Now just enjoy that, honey. It'll pull you right out of yourself."

Lucas cocked his head to the side and shook it a little bit as though to say 'there's nothing you can do about it so you may as well dig in.' So she did. Of course Eunice was right. That was a pie that would change your life. It was all Della could do to keep from licking the plate. In between finishing the pie and having her coffee cup refilled by Eunice, Lucas and Della started talking.

Have you ever met somebody that you just automatically feel comfortable with? Della thought to herself. Well, that was Lucas, who said again to call him Luke.

"OK, Luke, what's your story?" Della said.

Luke was the youngest of three sons of Eunice's son Sam and his wife May. Luke was the last to live at home with his parents. His dad, Sam Howard, ran the local single screen Raleigh Theater in Nags Head.

Luke was a fireman with the Outer Banks Fire and Rescue Squad and helped his dad when he wasn't at the firehouse. His brother Matt was married with a child and lived in a nearby town. Gideon was single but dating. Luke had graduated from North Carolina State University and was a big supporter of the Wolfpack. When Luke and Della had exhausted Luke's life history, they moved on to Della's.

Luke looked at Della with her windblown hair and muddy jeans and said, "So tell me about yourself, Della Gates." So she did.

"I'm an only child. My dad Roy Gates and my mother Maxine Gates didn't marry until they were in their late twenties and I was a little surprise. Actually a big surprise – I weighed 9 lbs. at birth. They live here on the Outer Banks– moved here last year. "

Della told Luke (reluctantly) that she'd lost her job and had come home to her Mama and Daddy's house to regain her confidence. Her parents had moved to Kitty Hawk the year before after closing their small grocery store in Pennsylvania. Della admitted to feeling humiliated - a twenty-seven year old woman having to run home to her parents. On top of that, she'd caught her fiancé Dylan having a very cozy dinner with another woman instead of what he'd told her he'd be doing - early birthday shopping for a present for Della. Anyhow, she'd been home for about a month when her daddy said, "Honey, you've got to stop moping around and find something to do besides eating." (She'd put on four pounds since she'd been home and her Daddy was beginning to be annoyed that his stash of choc- olate chip cookies was always low.)

So one week before meeting Biscuit and Luke, her Aunt Louise had offered the free use of her shed apartment and told Della of the job at the grocery store. Della moved her few belongings into Louise's apartment and began to feel a little better about herself, though she still hoped to find a place of her own. She had applied for and gotten a temporary job at the Robbins & Richards grocery store (known locally as the R&R) checking groceries, but really hated it. It was nothing like the efficient, modern grocery store her parents had owned. Nevertheless, having a job and income gave her some measure of confidence again.

Aunt Louise Gates' one-room apartment was in the shed addition attached to the west side of Louise's oceanfront cottage. It had a bed, chair (with a saggy cushion), small table, sink, two-burner stove, tiny icebox, shower, and toilet. There was one salt-crusted window which looked out on the parking pad outside. Aunt Louise let her stay there rent-free. And it was one block away from the grocery store so she didn't have to use her car, a positive because she couldn't afford the gas on the poor paycheck she brought home.

"You cannot believe the navy blue polyester vest I have to wear," she'd told her mother Maxine after the first day on the job. "And I am so slow on the cash register, a fact which doesn't make my supervisor very happy."

Louis Murdock, Della's supervisor at the grocery, was a bantam rooster of a man, always strutting about, looking self – important. His glasses continually slipped down his nose as he pushed back the limp brown forelock that never seemed to stay in place. Working for him did not present a very promising scenario for a bright future. All the people she went to college with had started exciting careers in big cities. Several of her very best girlfriends had even begun having babies. Sharing this news with Aunt Louise and her parents did nothing to help her self-esteem.

Nevertheless, Luke seemed not to care, or maybe he was just embarrassed that Biscuit had knocked her down. Anyhow, they finished their pie and coffee, said goodbye to Eunice and walked out onto the sandy street. An unexpected breeze blew sand into Della's eyes which made her next move fairly clumsy (and a little bit laughable.).

She turned to take another look at the diner and lost her footing on a piece of broken curb. Down she went again on the pavement. She'd hit the sidewalk so hard that she was sure she could hear concrete crack beneath her. She got up quickly, wiping her seat off as much as she could. Luke looked concerned and asked several times if she was ok, but Della could tell he was holding back a grin.

She decided there was nothing to do but laugh it off, so she did and told him she had to go back to her apartment to get ready for work. Being the Southern gentleman that he obviously was, Luke offered to walk the three blocks back to her apartment with her. And having apparently no shame about the way she looked and the clumsiness of her recent behavior, Della accepted.

They walked the three blocks back to Della's apartment and climbed the wooden stairs. The apartment was in the single story shed addition on the back side of Louise's cedar-shingled cottage. It had been added on, so Louise told her, for the grown son of the builder and his wife back in the 1880s and had been also used as a maid's room. The apartment was only one room and had no ocean view. And since it was on the road side, she heard road noise whenever she was in there. But it had a broad porch, a continuation of the porch which wrapped around Louise's cottage on the east, south and west elevations. Set upon wood pilings, Louise's cottage was a four-bedroom house with interior walls of heart pine. It was composed of a mix of gables and rectangles and had weathered to a lovely silvery-gray color. Sitting atop the roof of Louise's cottage was an old brass weathervane containing large and small brass balls, the letters N, S, E and W speared onto the four directionals and a rod which ended in an arrowhead. Louise loved to check the weathervane each morning to see what the day would bring.

Like many of the other old cottages on the beach, it had originally been located on the opposite side of the road facing the Roanoke Sound. Vacationers in the 1880s approached the ocean waters by means of a wooden boardwalk laid atop the dunes. But when it became fashionable to live on the ocean side, the cottage had been placed on rollers and moved across the island to its current ocean-front location. The east face of Louise's cottage looked out upon the ocean. Entry to the house from the porch was through a screen door which bore a large, old wooden spool in place of a door knob. Four comfortable rocking chairs faced the railings which were painted a glossy white. The porch's railings contained lean-out benches, one on either side of the steps. At one end of the porch a hammock invited afternoon naps. The south side of the house had an outdoor shower and storage room underneath the back porch. Each of the many windows in the house and shed addition was framed with green painted shutters, hinged on the sides. The second story win-dows on the ocean side were shaded by wood batten shutters hinged at the top and propped open by wooden sticks. This cottage had stood beside the Atlantic Ocean for over a hundred years and looked ready to stand for a hundred more. So all in all, Della felt very for-tunate. She unlocked the door and opened it for Luke. He stepped in and looked around, which only took a minute, obviously.

"Nice place you've got here," he said. "Very convenient."

Luke mentioned again that he wanted to take care of cleaning her jeans, but she said that it wasn't necessary.

"There's a good dry cleaner in town," he said. "If I can take it there early tomorrow, they can have it for you by tomorrow night."

Della thanked him saying again that he didn't need to do that. She said goodbye as he walked down the outdoor steps from her apartment. She closed the door, and then ran to look at herself in the mirror. Her hair was a fright, and her jeans were torn at the knee from her fall.

"Oh, Della, really?" she said, shaking her head at her reflection.

CHAPTER FIVE

1942

Finn Ingram sat at his desk in the Coast Guard Air Station, constantly stretching a rubber band between his thumb and forefinger. He looked out the salt-covered window above his desk at the hangar nearby. Mechanics were going over the Vought OS2U Kingfisher he'd be flying that night. His buddy Hawk Hawkins would be riding along as his observer and it felt good to know that the mechanics were checking everything – the two .30 caliber machine guns and the bomb and depth charge mounts. He'd been ordered to fly a spotter plane that night, searching for German submarines offshore. He knew that he needed to focus all his energy and thoughts on the success of that mission, but he couldn't get Louise Gates out of his mind. He'd been back to the pier restaurant several times since meeting her, every time requesting to be seated at her table. When he'd eaten there the previous day, he'd mustered the nerve to ask her on a date for the weekend and he'd been surprised when she'd said yes.

Louise had said she wanted to see the Jack Benny movie "George Washington Slept Here" which was playing at the Raleigh Theater in Nags Head. The theater had been open since 1920 and was a local treasure. So they made plans for the Friday matinee showing.

When Friday afternoon arrived, Louise was nervous and excited. While Louise's mother was in Norfolk recently, she'd bought Louise a green frock sprigged with yellow flowers and white linen cuffs on the short sleeves. Donning the new dress, she added white gloves and a pair of saddle oxfords with white socks to complete her look. She checked her appearance in the looking glass time and again until she heard a knock on her grandmother's front door. Quickly looking in the mirror one last time, she patted an imaginary hair back in place and smoothed non-existent wrinkles from her skirt.

"I've got it, Granny," she called.

She walked through the hall and opened the door. There on the porch stood Finn Ingram, wearing a sharply creased pair of gray slacks and a white shirt, open at the neck. He wore a broad smile as soon as he saw Louise and asked if she was ready to go. She smiled and said yes, grabbing her sweater from a hook on the wall near the door. Finn took it from her and draped it across her shoulders, and then guided her down the steps toward his Jeep.

Finn had borrowed a Jeep from the Coast Guard station. The Willys MB Jeep was a newly produced vehicle for the US military and it quickly became a favorite for all the Coast Guardsmen (the "Coasties" as they were known to the Outer Bankers.) It had a handbrake, a steering column-mounted gear shift and rounded cutouts instead of doors. The headlights were halfway painted black as required by law during wartime. Finn helped Louise over the cutout and started the engine. The ride to the theater was a short one and they arrived just in time. Finn bought the tickets at the outside ticket window, and then guided her to the concession stand.

"What would you like, sir?" the girl behind the concession counter asked.

Louise scanned the candy boxes inside the glass counter, pausing to make her choice. The counter girl pointed out the M&Ms, 5th Avenues, 3 Musketeers, and Snickers bars. But none of those seemed just right for Louise.

"You know, I think I'll just have a box of popcorn, Finn."

"You sure? Let me get you a candy bar to go with it."

"No thanks, just the popcorn."

"Make it two," he told the counter girl who formed two red and white striped boxes and scooped popcorn into them. She handed them to Finn, accepting his quarters in exchange. Finn tucked a couple of nickels from his change into Louise's hands, puzzling Louise. Finn whispered that he always liked Buffalo nickels and he hoped Louise would think of him every time she saw one. Louise deposited them in her pocket and patted them to make sure they were safe.

The two young people smiled at each other and walked into the darkened theater. Finding a pair of seats near the middle of the small theater, they settled down as the United News reel came on the screen. Finn's arm touched Louise's by accident, bringing a shy smile to Louise's face. Finn looked over at her in the darkened theater feeling a spark from his nearness to her. There on the screen, in glorious black and white, Finn and Louise watched a war bond drive, a parade of British soldiers returning from battle, and a horse race to benefit the Army-Navy Relief Fund. Following the newsreel was a Looney Tunes cartoon featuring a duck bearing a strong resemblance to Adolf Hitler. After an ad for United States Savings Bonds to end the war, the movie started and the theater lights dimmed even further. And for the next hour and a half, all thoughts of war and trouble disappeared. Louise occasionally looked over at Finn's strong and handsome profile, causing her heart to do flip flops. Meanwhile, Finn occasionally stole a glance at Louise as she was laughing at Jack Benny's antics on screen.

Oh wow! She's beautiful, he thought.

When the movie was over, Louise looked at Finn and smiled.

"That was a terrific movie!" she said. "I think there's a Captain Midnight serial starting next Saturday. Maybe we can go? For a little while during the movie, I didn't have to think about the war at all."

"I'd love to go. I've wanted to see the Captain Midnight serial. I'll see you at the café and we can set a time to go. I wish I didn't have to think about the war," he replied. "Have you got your blackout curtains installed on your windows? You know the government has begun to order what they are calling 'dim-outs' for all communities within 16 miles of the ocean. All those lights allow enemy subs to silhouette commercial and military vessels going along the coastline, increasing the chance that they could be hit. You know that means no streetlights as well as lights from your home. And you've got to black out your automobile headlamps at least halfway."

"Yes, Granny was at her Singer for days sewing the blackout curtains. She had me hang them after I got off work at the café. We had a hard time finding black fabric at the R&R. They had to special order a bolt for us. And my grandfather put black tape across most of the headlamps on his car. "

"Well, just make sure your windows are completely covered as soon as the sun goes down."

Louise gave a little shiver as she thought of what that meant. Finn asked if he could hold her hand as they walked back to the Jeep.

Louise nodded a shy okay and accepted his help into the seat. By then, it was nearly five o'clock and the sun hung low over the western sky. The two gazed up at the sky, wanting the day to last forever. But Finn's shift would soon begin, so, reluctantly, he had to take Louise back to her grandparents' cottage.

He drove slowly, and soon he turned into the gravel driveway of the cottage, the tires crunching on the sand. Behind the house, Louise could hear the constant crashing of the waves on the beach below. There was no other sound as Finn pulled the handbrake to stop the vehicle. Emerging from the Jeep, he walked around to Louise's side and took her hand to help her over the cutout. She warmed a bit inside as Finn held onto her hand as he walked her up the steps. He looked down into her brown eyes and held his gaze. She wondered if he was going to kiss her, but just then her grandfather coughed inside. Louise and Finn giggled a bit at the signal for her to come inside. Finn squeezed her hand meaningfully.

"I had a grand time, Louise," he whispered.

"Me, too, Finn. See you at the café?"

"Definitely. But I'm on duty for the next couple of days. So I'll see you after that. "

Finn fairly sauntered back to the Jeep, a song in his heart. But as he backed out onto the road, he knew that within an hour or two, he'd be behind the steering yoke of his spotter plane, looking for Nazi U-Boats.

CHAPTER SIX

1994

The next morning dawned bright, sunny, and warm. So Della was able to walk to her job at the grocery store wearing just a light sweater over her tacky polyester vest and pants. The sweater was a necessity because Louis always kept the air conditioning turned all the way down to 65. The R & R was the closest grocery store in Nags Head. At one time it was the center of life in the town and sold most anything people needed. The shelves back in the early days had groaned under the weight of groceries, lard in big wooden tubs (dipped out with a wooden paddle and put in cardboard cartons to sell,) animal liniments (a big seller was Pinee, made from the tar of North Carolina pine trees,) big glass jars of Tootsie Rolls, lye soap, hard candy and soft drinks. Under a red coffee grinder giving off the heady aroma of coffee beans, small brown paper bags of roasted peanuts waited for buyers. A small notions department in a corner carried bolts of cheesecloth, oilcloth and muslin, along with thread and scissors. Nearby was a rack of overalls in sizes from toddler to men's XXL. A woman from the Nags Head Woods came once a week to pick up and deliver laundry which she'd washed at her home.

Attached to the back of the store was an ice house. The first owner of the store delivered ice to all the cottages along the beach every week along with larger grocery orders. The ice box in the ice house carried milk, ice cream, fresh eggs, butter, fresh fish and crabs.

The older generation of Nags Head's inhabitants could still buy Carter's Little Liver Pills and Musterole at the 1994 version of the R & R. Also available was gas (from a single pump out front) and oil. Signs in the front windows of the frame store advertised revival services in nearby churches, Lions Club glasses drives and notices of lost hunting dogs. Behind the signs, tall pyramids of colorful canned goods sat in the window wells. Wooden floors ran the length of the store with five aisles divided by five-foot-high shelves. To the left was a cold case filled with cheeses and meats. A big glass jar filled with dill pickles floating in brine sat atop the case. Behind that was a large walk-in freezer. In the rear of the store was a small hardware and appliance section with a sign stating "If we don't carry it, you don't need it." It was a store past its prime but it was the only general store within the town limits, so it was usually busy.

Louis was at work already, of course, his white folded paper hat set jauntily over his forehead. . He met Della at the door of the store, unlocking it at the top and bottom and scowling as she entered.

"You're awfully close to being late, you know. I've already had my bag boy call to tell me he was not coming in today."

"I know, Louis. I'm still getting settled in. Where do you want me today?"

Louis looked at his clipboard, his glasses slipping again.

"Hmm. I think I want you blocking the canned goods today."

Blocking the canned goods was an easy job – it just meant making sure that all the cans of the same brand and variety were neatly aligned on the shelves.

That shouldn't take too long to do, Della thought.

"And after that, you can clean the bathrooms."

Ugh! She knew it had been too good to be true. Cleaning the bathrooms was a disgusting job, especially the men's room.

Why couldn't they hit the hole? she thought.

Della spent the next hour and a half blocking the canned goods, stretching the job out for as long as she could. She tried to hide from Louis and the bathroom job by blocking the cookie aisle next without being asked. But halfway through the job, Louis found her and pointed toward the restrooms with a mop and bucket.

Two hours later, the men's and ladies' restrooms were sparkling and Della was not. She was exhausted and she still had an hour to go before her shift was over. Louis, seeing that she was through with the restrooms, sent her over to the trainer cash register.

"You were so slow yesterday, Della. You need to practice here."

Louis would probably never transition to bar code scanning at the checkout station, so clerks had to ring up groceries the old fashioned way. For the last hour of the day, Della rang up grocery items as they appeared on a screen, Louis's one update to the store. Each time Della was supposed to beat the previous time shown on the screen, but she was so exhausted that she seemed to be slowing down. Soon, thankfully, it was time for her to clock out, so she pulled her clerk's vest over her head, walked to the office area in the back room and signed out on her time sheet. Louis followed her into the back room where she was retrieving her purse.

"Don't let me see you take off that vest in the store ever again, Della. We have an image to project here," he said, glaring up at her.

"OK, sorry, Louis. It's been a tough coupla days. I'll remember."

Sheesh, Della – is it possible for you to get fired from two jobs in a month? I'm going home, getting in bed and pulling the covers over my head.

CHAPTER SEVEN

1942

Off the coast of Cape Hatteras, the swells were huge on a night in early June. The white-capped waves rolled and furiously tossed any vessel in the ocean. The crescent moon was hidden behind clouds leaving the ocean in nearly complete darkness, a perfect night to go hunting, the U-Boat crewmen thought. Aboard the U-Boat nicknamed *Seewolf, Kommandant* Jürgen Wattenberg sat at his desk, templing his fingers and remembering the success of the last week – torpedoing the *Houston* had been a major triumph. He'd radioed Karl Dönitz, the chief of U-Boat operations for Nazi Germany, after the hit. Wattenberg had been pacing back and forth in his tiny cabin waiting for word from his radioman about any potential targets on this night.

Finally a young officer stood at the entrance to Wattenberg's cabin. Upon being recognized, the officer thrust into Wattenberg's hands a piece of paper with the coordinates for the evening's target. The officer said that he'd received the message from Paris just moments before. (U-Boat commanders received their instructions by radio through the Eiffel Tower.)

"*Danke*," Wattenberg said curtly. The officer stood at attention, waiting for instructions. Wattenberg read over the paper hurriedly and looked up at the officer.

"*Gleich weitermachen!*" he barked. "Proceed at once."

The young naval officer saluted and turned on his heel to go.

"*Heil Hitler!*" he said. The officer was proud to be on one of the five U-Boats sent to patrol the area between New York and Hatteras. They'd sunk four ships since February, an American tanker, a Swedish freighter, a Venezuelan freighter and a Brazilian tramp freighter. Each of the ships they'd sunk had crews ranging from twenty-eight to seventy souls, nearly all of them lost at sea. Wattenberg and his young officer were feeling more confident with each sinking. Wattenberg felt certain the Knights Cross would be pinned on his chest soon.

Meanwhile, from the Coast Guard station, Flight Officer Finn Ingram was zipping up his flight suit, preparing to take his spotter plane up for a look around. His Coast Guard station had received the usual 1700 hours position report of any German submarines in the area. His commanding officer had then plotted their positions, represented by tiny red oval pins on a magnetic board in the office. Finn's commanding officer then instructed him that he would be spotting that night to check the accuracy of the report. Finn had saluted and left the office. He paused in the narrow hall for a moment, bowed his head and prayed for safety and the success of his mission.

As darkness covered the beaches, Finn stepped out hurriedly toward the hangar where his observation plane, a Vought OS2U Kingfisher, waited. The Kingfisher had been built by the Vought and Sikorsky companies and carried two men, a pilot and an observer. The plane was armed with a .30 caliber machine gun in the nose and a machine gun for the observer as well as having the ability to carry two 100-lb bombs or one 325-lb depth charge. The Kingfisher's slow but steady reputation was a comfort to Finn. Before the war, Finn had been responsible for routine search and rescues in this plane for fishermen and duck hunters in trouble on the water. But with the acceleration of the war, such duties were almost completely halted and Finn and the rest of his company were charged with supporting the Navy in convoy coverage, search and rescue or recovery and antisubmarine warfare. Navy destroyers were now tasked with escorting convoys of merchant ships using new inventions like radar and sonar which helped spot enemy subs.

Finn's friend, David Hawkins, known to all as "Hawk," was a small man with a ready smile. He was already in the rear seat, prepared for his observer position. Finn climbed into the cockpit, belted himself in and went through the procedure for starting the airplane. He advanced the mixture lever a few times to build up fuel pressure, primed the engine, pushed the power lever forward and back once to get fuel into the carburetor, stepped on the starter pedal in the floor and turned the magnetos to the "on" position. When the engine fired, he advanced the throttle so the engine could idle. At that point he turned on the radios and navigational aids, and fastened his leather helmet, watching as the propeller turned. After transmitting his readiness for takeoff, Finn received clearance to do so. Taxiing and taking off smoothly, he headed east over the Atlantic.

On the Outer Banks beaches, the surf continued to pound the sandy shore. Within fifteen minutes Hawk located a tanker nearing Cape Lookout. It was 2200 hours and the crew inside the freighter, a 5,700 ton Venezuelan tanker, *Impulse*, was headed from Texas with a load of crude oil. The crew felt confident that they had made it past the Diamond Shoals and were traveling at a speed of about twelve knots an hour.

Finn noted the tanker's location about 100 miles offshore by radio and was headed back to the station when he spotted a U-Boat surfacing about eight hundred yards away from his plane. Upon surfacing, the U-Boat was preparing to fire its torpedoes. The waves above the deep water were gathering strength, tossing the ship to and fro. Finn quickly radioed the U-Boat's coordinates but was too late with the information. He watched in horror as a torpedo fired from the U-Boat sped toward the starboard side of the tanker and tore apart the bow. Immediately the ship began to take on water. A second torpedo was fired from the water's surface a minute or two after the first hit, but it was a dud. After firing the second torpedo and seeing the damage he'd inflicted upon the tanker, *Kommandant* Wattenberg decided to retire to his cabin and headed his sub out into deeper water. Before submerging, he broke radio silence, sending a brief message to his superior officer about his hit. Wattenberg ordered his U-Boat to dive telling his crew to go below and take them deep. He leaned back against the periscope in the control room, satisfied with his achievement.

The Venezuelan tanker didn't go under right away and sent a distress signal which was acknowledged by the Coast Guard station. Finn, piloting the closest plane to the *Impulse*, noted the burning oil on the water. There was a limited amount of time to rescue any of the crew, he knew. Beads of sweat pooled on his brow as he and Hawk searched frantically for survivors. Looking through the cockpit glass, Hawk spotted a single rubber lifeboat aft of the tanker, which was rapidly taking on water from the tremendous swells of the ocean.

The crude oil which had been carried by the tanker began to spread atop the water and had been ignited by the explosions from the torpedo. Finn assessed the area near the life raft and, seeing that the fuel spill and flames had not travelled around to the area of the raft, he brought the amphibious craft to a landing atop the rolling waves, not an easy task to accomplish in the best of circumstances. He lifted the cockpit window and tossed a rope to the man in the raft.

"Is there anybody else from the ship?" Finn yelled. "Where's the rest of the crew?"

The crewman was alert enough to grab the rope and hook it onto his Mae West. But he was clearly in shock and couldn't answer. Each wave that passed over the lifeboat lifted and dropped it precariously. The downed sailor was able to move to the rear of the aircraft, and after several missed attempts, climb up onto the float.

Hawk hurriedly pulled him into the plane, deposited him onto his lap in the second seat of the cockpit and Finn flew them back to the station. He was on his wireless immediately informing the radioman at the Coast Guard station of what he had seen.

Within minutes, Finn landed the Kingfisher at the station. Several Coast Guardsmen rushed toward the plane as Finn opened the cockpit. He and Hawk took off their helmets and looked down at the scene of chaos below the plane. An ambulance crew dashed to the plane to gently lift the injured sailor to the stretcher they'd carried. Within minutes, the ambulance crew was speeding toward the hospital in Manteo, the injured crewman aboard.

Almost immediately after receiving the message from Finn that a U-Boat had torpedoed a tanker, a US Navy destroyer in the general area headed to the location of the torpedoed tanker. A young seaman, barely 20 years old, sat in front of the newly installed green radar screen on the destroyer watching the beam sweep around and around. Suddenly he recognized a solid shape a nautical mile ahead off the port bow – a U-Boat! Sailors on board ship raced about the deck in response to the voice over the loudspeaker saying, "All

Hands! Man your battle stations. This is NOT a drill!" After ascertaining that there were no survivors from the tanker anywhere, the commander of the destroyer headed to the location of the *Seewolf* at flank speed. After extensive searches with sonar, the destroyer located the U-Boat on the bottom and deployed multiple depth charges. The U-Boat suffered hydrostatic shocks that disrupted power, and lighting inside the sub.

The depth charges destroyed the periscope, killing two crewmen in the conning tower. Pipes cracked and bolts unscrewed from their holes, flying out and striking any crewmen who were in their path. The glass fronts of gauges shattered. Dishes and cooking utensils flew about the interior of the sub. Water began issuing from the cracks into the interior of the sub, where the German crews were working frantically to rid their sub of water. However, it was difficult for the men to accomplish their tasks as only the red emergency lights were working. Suddenly inside the U-Boat, the crews were unable to see and had no power to run pumps. The U-Boat began flooding, with fires breaking out in various areas of the sub. The crush of the ocean's water ruptured the center of the U-Boat's hull as a result of the shock waves from the depth charges and the crewmen were subjected to a deafening sound as they realized their fate. *Kommandant* Jurgen Wattenberg would never receive his Knight's Cross.

At the Lorient, France headquarters of the U-Boat operation, Admiral Dönitz gave instructions repeatedly to contact *Kommandant* Wattenberg over his shortwave radio. He was practically fanatical about knowing where his U-Boats and their commanders were at any given time, ordering his commanders to check in with him frequently. He ordered the radiomen to make their communiques short to keep the enemy unaware of their location.

"Reply at once with your position," he ordered, but there would be no reply.

No crewmen of the U-Boat survived the hit. Several of their bodies, wearing life preservers, floated in the ten-foot high waves, amidst debris from the U-Boat. The German sailors' bodies were picked up by the Navy crew aboard the destroyer and later flown to Norfolk. Their pockets and clothing were examined by Naval Intelligence for any clues as to their identities. The intelligence gained from previous recoveries like this one or captures of survivors had led the Navy to install Direction Finder Stations all along the Outer Banks. As soon as a U-Boat broke radio silence, the Navy was able to pinpoint its exact location.

Back at the Coast Guard Station, Finn saw to it that his plane was refueled and serviced. He checked in with his superior officer on the condition of the sailor from the tanker he had rescued and learned that there had been no other survivors of the attack. Rubbing his eyes and wiping away a tear, he offered another prayer of thanks for his safety and for the souls of the lost crew. Back in the locker room, Finn unzipped his flight suit and headed for the shower.

He let the water from the shower head run over his hair and body for a longer time than normal, thinking back on all the ships that had been sunk in the first few months of the year – nearly four hundred by June. He soaped up and rinsed off, shaking the water from his hair. Emerging from the shower, he toweled off, slipped into a pair of briefs and headed for his rack. He was off duty for the rest of the night but would try to catch a nap until he was called out again.

Finn laid his head on the thin pillow, closed his eyes and willed his brain to slow down. As a general rule, that was practically impossible for him after a spotter run, and that night was no different. His mind raced, following his route from the station to the ship rescue, playing over and over what he did and what he could have done differently. Finally after about thirty minutes, his brain decelerated and a sweeter image played on the corners of his mind.

He remembered his movie date with Louise Gates. He remembered her soft brown hair and brown eyes. He thought of her enticing figure and sweet Southern accent. He remembered the almost-kiss they'd shared and soon he fell into a blissful, dreamless sleep.

CHAPTER EIGHT

1994

Della walked the block back to her apartment and climbed the outside steps. She unlocked the door and entered the small apartment, wiping the perspiration from her forehead. She shuffled through the mail she'd collected from her mailbox and was just about to hang up her sweater when she heard her cellphone ringing in her purse. She scrambled to find it.

Why does my phone always hide in the far recesses of my purse?

She looked at the screen and saw a number she didn't recognize but decided to answer it anyway. It could be Louis telling her she didn't have to work tomorrow!

"Della? It's Luke. Luke Howard. I got your number from Louis at the R & R. I was feeling bad about how Biscuit destroyed your jeans and wanted to make it up to you. I was wondering if you'd have time to see me tonight. "

"That'd be great, Luke but I'm just getting in from work and I look a mess. What time were you thinking?"

"Well, I was wondering if you wouldn't like to go out for a bite? You haven't had supper yet, have you?"

"No, I'd like that very much. Where are we going?"

Luke told her about a new seafood restaurant in town and Della agreed immediately. She asked for a half hour to change and Luke agreed.

She disconnected the call and went to her closet to see what might be appropriate.

I should have asked how fancy this place is, she thought.

Nevertheless, she decided on a jersey knit crew neck tee in peach, a pair of khaki slacks and tan flats.

This is not a date. It's too early to call this a date. I don't date anymore after Dylan. This is definitely NOT a date, she told herself.

Thirty minutes later, a knock on her door told her that Luke was there. She opened the door to see him standing on the porch and looking out across the road. She invited him in and Luke looked around.

"Your place is looking nice."

"Well, it's mostly Aunt Louise's stuff but I've put a few of my things around. I had to stop setting up things to go to work. Maybe I can finish organizing this weekend."

"Well, it looks good so far. You ready to go?" he said. "You might want to get a sweater. Sometimes the air conditioning is pretty strong in these restaurants. I'll try not to mess up your clothes this time. I left Biscuit back at the house," he grinned.

Della lifted a sweater from her dresser drawer and threw it over her arm. Luke pulled his keys from his pants pocket and turned to follow Della out the door. Leaving the apartment, Della turned and locked the door, then stopped.

"Oh, Luke, I forgot – I had a piece of mail delivered to me that should have gone to Aunt Louise. It looks like a bill or something. Do you mind if I hand it off to her before we go?"

"Not at all. I'd love to see her."

Della unlocked the door, and retrieved the letter from the table by the door. Then, relocking the door, Della, with Luke in front of her, walked across the porch to Louise's back door. Della knocked softly and called out, "Aunt Louise? It's Della. May I come in?"

Della opened the front door gently and walked into the center hall with Luke following behind on the creaking heart pine floors. The hall led to the family room which spanned the entire ocean side of the house. Four large windows looked out upon the gentle waves of the Atlantic Ocean. A huge brick fireplace was centered along the north wall; two easy chairs faced the fireplace from across the room where Louise Gates sat. The room itself was brimful of well-used furniture and photos going back to the late 1800s. A bookcase beside Louise's easy chair held three shelves of beautifully bound hardback books. Resting in the easy chair, Louise Gates, a slim woman in her seventies wore a loose housedress and bedroom slippers. Her gray hair was pulled back into a messy bun on top of her head. She had removed her glasses and placed them on the table by a book she'd been reading. An opened envelope lay on top of the book. Immediately Della and Luke noticed her face was flushed and damp with perspiration.

"Aunt Louise, what's wrong?"

"Oh, child, I'm just not feeling great today. I was a little woozy earlier when I was trying to sweep these sandy floors. And I have just got to get around to washing these windows. You can hardly see out of them because of the salt air. But I'll be okay with a little rest."

Luke rushed to her side and picked up her wrist, taking her pulse.

"Miss Gates, your heart is really racing. How about if I call my buddies at the fire station? I think you need to be seen by a doctor."

Kneeling on the other side of the chair, Della took her aunt's hand. "Aunt Louise, you remember Lucas Howard. He's a volunteer fireman."

"Of course I do, Della. He comes in to see me at the shop every once in a while."

Smiling at the older woman, Luke stood and pulled his cellphone out of his back pocket. He punched in the number for the fire station and waited impatiently for an answer.

"Hey, Buck, I've got an elderly woman with an elevated heart rate, possible heart attack. I need a bus right away. Address is …?"

"135 Beach Road," Della said quickly and Luke repeated the address into his phone.

"Elderly woman? Thunderation! I'll have you know I'm not elderly in the least! I just turned 70 and I can run circles around you two," Louise huffed.

"Yes, ma'am, I have no doubt about that, Miss Louise. I just said that to get the rescue squad to get here a little faster. It's pretty easy to see you are not elderly."

In a matter of five minutes, an ambulance came screaming down the street and pulled up in front of the cottage. Two emergency medical technicians raced out of the cab of the ambulance and hurried to the door where Della was standing. She ushered them in through the hallway and into the family room. They knelt immediately around Louise's chair while Della and Luke stepped back. Taking her pulse and checking for stroke signs, they stood and relayed some information to the dispatcher at the fire station.

"Miss Louise, we think we better take you over to the hospital for a check-up. How does that sound?" one of the EMTs said.

"I think it sounds terrible, young man. I don't want to go to any hospital. I'm just fine. It's just that I got up a little fast. Now you all just go on about your business and let me rest."

The EMT who'd dared to suggest a hospital visit shook his head. "Now, Miss Louise. You be nice. We're just gonna make sure you're ok."

Della stepped in at this point and insisted to Louise that she be seen by a doctor. Slipping an arm around her aunt's shoulders, she lifted her gently from the chair and helped her over to the door.

"I'll go," Louise said with a sniff," but I won't ride in that contraption. Lucas Howard, have you got a car?"

"Yes, ma'am. I'll drive you right over if that's ok with the EMTs."

"Well, get me my coat and shoes and purse at least. I can't go out in this weather dressed like I'm going to bed!"

Della raced to the bedroom for the purse, shoes and coat and, after retrieving them, slipped them on her aunt. Then, seeing that Louise was in the care of one of their coworkers at the fire station, the EMTs agreed to Louise's decision. They watched guardedly as Luke and Della walked Louise over to Luke's small sedan. She settled herself in the front seat of the car and buckled the seat belt around her as Luke and Della watched with concern. Then they got in the car and began the trip to the hospital, following behind the racing ambulance.

The Outer Banks Hospital was nothing more than a small brick building located in the tiny town of Manteo. It had been established in the 1930s just after the Depression and was funded by subscriptions from local residents and a large donation from an anonymous donor. Patients came from Hatteras to Kitty Hawk to have their babies, and see the doctor for heart attacks and head colds. Though it was small, the hospital was a Godsend for the residents of the Outer Banks. The doctors and nurses who staffed the hospital worked hard to make sure it was as up to date as possible.

The EMTs traveling just ahead of Luke's car, their siren blaring, radioed their information to the emergency room as they traveled. Arriving at the door which led to the emergency room, they were met by a nurse bearing a wheelchair. Luke and Della brought Louise to the hospital door as quickly as possible.

"Oh, no, young man! I'm not riding in that contraption. I can walk just fine," Louise declared loudly when she saw the wheelchair.

But the nurse with an orderly beside her wouldn't take no for an answer and guided her gently into the chair. Louise was wheeled up to an exam room where a young doctor checked her heart and blood pressure while Luke and Della sat in the waiting room. Two hours later, they emerged from the hospital's emergency room area and headed for his car.

"I'm really sorry, Luke," Della said. "I know this really messed up our plans for dinner tonight."

"Hey, don't worry about that. I'm just glad we were there when she needed us." Luke said, shaking his head. "Let's go back to your aunt's house and get the things she needs.

A ten-minute conversation with the attending physician in the emergency room had confirmed what Luke had suspected. Louise had suffered a minor heart attack and was being kept overnight in the hospital for observation, an outcome that she disagreed with completely.

A few minutes later in Louise's house, Della and Luke walked back to Louise's bedroom. Against one wall was a simple white-painted iron bedstead made up with a white ribbed cotton bedspread. Two small tables sat on either side of the bed with small glass lamps atop them. In a white painted oak bureau between two windows, Della found the things Louise needed – her robe, a nightgown, and, in a small closet, her make-up case and slippers. She packed them carefully into her aunt's overnight bag and handed it to Luke. Della smiled seeing the Duke's mayonnaise jar of Buffalo nickels on her aunt's dresser.

"Look at this, Luke. I guess Aunt Louise is a coin collector, so she saves every Buffalo nickel she finds."

They packed up all of their finds and drove back to the hospital, entering by the admissions desk. A silver haired woman behind the desk got up when she saw Luke entering and came around the desk to hug him.

"Luke Howard, is the hospital on fire?"

"No ma'am, Miss Rita. We just brought Miss Louise Gates in. She was having a little difficulty with her heart. This is her niece, by the way – Della Gates.

Rita Johnson, the admissions clerk at the hospital, was a long-time fixture in the front hall of the hospital and knew most everyone in town.

"Well, hey, Della. Nice to meet you although I wish it were under better circumstances. It's been real busy around here today," Rita said. Now don't you worry. We'll take good care of Louise. She's a real character."

"Thanks, Miss Rita. Now, Della, if it's not too late, let's deliver these things to your aunt and see about that dinner."

CHAPTER NINE

1994

Della stood back as far as possible from the tiny wreath on the back of her apartment door. She squinted her eyes to see if there were any bare spots that needed fluffing. She was relieved to see none, because she was out of shells with which to decorate. She'd been trying to give her small apartment a beach vibe and decorated it with as many beach items as she could find – seashells, sand dollars, bits of sea glass and fishnet.

All these nautical items reminded her of the dinner she'd had with Luke the night before. She and Luke had taken Aunt Louise's necessaries to her in the hospital, and then agreed that it was not too late for dinner at the seafood restaurant. So they'd gone at 8:00 PM to Captain Billy's Sea Shanty, a kitschy restaurant if ever she'd seen one.

Still, you had to give Captain Billy points for trying. Colorful wooden oars hung everywhere on the walls interspersed with portholes. Heavy ropes were coiled around the bottoms of each of the columns and glass floats nestled in coils of rope by the cash register. Brass lanterns sat on each table and booth and a long tank filled with fish swimming about greeted diners as they entered.

Luke and Della had been guided to a booth, tufted in blue leather. The waitress handed them tall menus and brought glasses of ice water. They'd looked over the offerings, finally settling on crab cakes and salads for both.

The food had been delicious. Della hadn't realized how hungry she was and embarrassed herself with how many hush puppies she ate. Luke smiled and offered to order another basket when their hands touched reaching for the last one. Della had declined, saying she couldn't eat another bite. She'd blushed charmingly and Luke signaled for the waitress to bring the check. He left a generous tip, paid the bill at the cash register and thanked the cashier, stepping outside with Della.

The temperature had gone down a bit while they'd been in the restaurant and Luke had held Della's sweater for her. She'd told him what a delightful meal it had been, truly meaning it. She thanked Luke for a nice evening and for helping her with her aunt. As she looked up at him, her green eyes looked into his gray ones and her heart melted. All these things she was recalling a day later as she finished her meager decorations.

But it was definitely not a date, she told herself firmly. *Now I've got to get to Aunt Louise's kitchen. I've got work to do.*

Meanwhile, at the hospital, Louise Gates had been given the all-clear to be released from the hospital, armed with a plastic bag full of new medicines and typed instructions on her new health regimen. She'd harrumphed to her physician, telling him that she'd lived seventy years quite successfully and didn't really need any whippersnapper of a doctor telling her how to live. A nurse entered the room and handed Louise an appointment card with instructions for her next visit.

The doctor smiled, patted her on the shoulder and asked the nurse to bring the wheelchair. That was another indignity Louise had no intention of suffering, but the nurse told her, "Sorry, Miss Louise. It's hospital policy. But at least, you're getting home in time for Memorial Day. "

So Louise had been wheeled down to the admitting area, complaining all the way. There her nephew and his wife Roy and Maxine were waiting to bring her home. Della's parents had gone to the hospital to fetch his aunt who'd asked to be picked up as soon as she could be released. Roy was a tall, thin man with gray at the temples and a permanent tan from the yard work he enjoyed. His wife Maxine was nearly as tall as her husband, with a carriage as straight as an arrow and a smile for everyone she met.

Roy loaded Louise's few belongings into the back of his sedan. Then he walked around to the passenger side of the car. He offered his arm to Louise, planning to put her in the front seat, an offer she refused with firmness.

"I'm your aunt, Roy Gates, and you will not tell me where I can ride. Maxine belongs up there with you in the front. Now close this door and let's get me home."

Maxine chuckled and shook her head. She'd seen this scene between those two many times before. So she shooed Roy around to the driver's seat and handed Louise her purse. Then she closed Louise's door and got into the front seat beside her husband.

A few minutes later, Roy pulled into the driveway of Louise's cottage and parked beside the shed apartment in the back. Inside, Della heard the approach of her father's car and opened the door to welcome her family. She'd been cooking all morning to prepare for her aunt's arrival.

Louise Gates stepped cautiously out of her nephew's car, her pocketbook clutched in her hands. Maxine emerged from the front seat carrying a plastic bag labeled "Patient's Belongings." Roy opened the trunk of his sedan, pulled out his aunt's overnight bag and put his hand under her arm.

"Now don't you start treating me like an old woman, Roy Gates." Louise said sharply. "I'm just fine."

The trio walked slowly up the steps to Louise's cottage and settled her in her chair. Maxine proceeded to the kitchen to help Della with the meal. Shortly after Roy had settled Louise, Della went out on the front porch and pulled the rope attached to the farm bell on the railing. Inside, Louise cocked her head and smiled.

"That girl," she said. "She knows all my stories, doesn't she?"

Roy and Maxine accompanied Louise to the dining room where the table was set for four. The dining room furnishings had changed little since Louise's grandparents had first decorated it decades ago. Eight mismatched ladder-back chairs surrounded the oak farm table in the center of the room. A bowl of seashells sat in the center of the table. A sideboard bought by Louise's mother at a second hand store in Manteo held the family's set of white china. Underneath the table a woven grass rug covered the pine floor boards. On the wall, a large piece of driftwood, collected by Louise when she was a young girl, hung on the wall over the sideboard.

Louise, Roy and Maxine seated themselves at their accustomed places. Meanwhile, Della came rushing in, grinning from ear to ear.

"I remembered, Aunt Louise."

Louise had once told Della that when she was a child visiting her grandparents who had owned the cottage, she spent most of the day playing on the hot sandy beach or in the ocean's waves, sometimes straying a quarter mile or more from the house. So the only way to call her in for meals was to ring the farm bell. All the neighbor children knew then to bid their playmates goodbye until after lunch, usually eaten on the porch, and the requisite nap which followed.

"We never wanted to come in and definitely didn't want to take a nap. But after one of our cook Miss Mattie's delicious meals, I'd strip off my swimsuit and hang it on the clothesline on the porch, or hammer a nail into the wall and hang it there. Then I'd put on a playsuit and go upstairs to my bedroom. I'd lie down on top of the sandy cotton bedspread and Mama would close the curtains. She'd pull the light string from the overhead light bulb, turn on the old rickety electric fan and I'd lie there looking at the knotholes in the ceiling, trying to make faces out of them. After a while I was fast asleep. She'd tiptoe out quietly, and shut my bedroom door with the wooden spool which served as a doorknob. Before I knew it, Mama was coming upstairs to wake me up for the afternoon fun. Then I'd put my swimsuit back on, still full of beach grit from the morning's adventures, and head down to the sandy shore with my metal buckets and pails. I'd fish in the surf or go crabbing in the sound. My friends and I would build sand castles, and go exploring the shipwreck up towards Kill Devil Hill. Every day was magic. That's why I wanted you to stay with me in this house, Della. I want you to love it the way I always have."

Maxine reached across the table and gave Louise's hand a squeeze.

"We're just glad you're feeling better, Louise," she said. "And I know how much Della appreciates your offer of the shed apartment for her. Now then, there'll be lots of time to tell more stories. Let's ask the blessing and tuck into this beautiful salmon salad Della made for us."

CHAPTER TEN

1994

In a sleek office in Raleigh, North Carolina, a thirty-something man of above average height and handsome demeanor sat behind a desk of ebony wood and heavy glass. On the taupe wall opposite his desk, a sign announced "Colony Books – Bringing literature to everyone." Dylan Metcalfe's office was filled with expensive furniture. A tan leather tufted couch lined one wall and was fronted by a mahogany English tea table. Behind the grand desk on the opposite side of the room, a bookcase and hutch carved with elaborate scrollwork sat behind Metcalfe's tall leather chair.

Dylan Metcalfe was a persuasive talker and had been born into wealth. His father Alton Metcalfe had built an empire of large bookstores in big cities across the Southeast. Alton bought fading businesses for a song, closed them down and eventually razed them to be replaced by new, modern stores. His son Dylan was looking to inherit the company and was trying hard to impress his father by replicating his business plans in a couple of smaller areas on the east coast. Dylan's plan was to visit the towns, hang around a few locations and get the local 411 on what businesses were having difficulty surviving. Then he'd pass a little money under the table to a supervisor at the Department of Occupational Regulation who would then declare the building unsafe. The reasons could be anything from asbestos contamination to the presence of lead paint. It didn't matter. It was always a lie. Another one of Metcalfe's tricks was to grease the palm of a shady Internal Revenue Service agent who would then shut down a business for any number of bogus reasons – failing to pay taxes on time or failing to file tax returns at all, for example. If Metcalfe was behind it, the accusations were always false.

A stack of brochures on the table by the door heralded in bright colors the younger Metcalfe's plans. They promised great things ahead for the towns Colony Books chose to shower with prosperity. One of the towns he had zeroed in on was Nags Head. He had seen the expanded housing construction there as well as the great increase in summer tourists on the Outer Banks.

Dylan was filing his nails when his secretary walked into the office to let her boss know that it was time to leave for his 1:00 appointment across town. He looked up, saw that his secretary was there and smiled.

"Did you get my taxi?" he asked.

"Yes, it's outside waiting for you."

Dylan held up his index finger when his cellphone began to ring. The call was from one of his employees, apparently seeking instructions on the next transaction. Dylan provided directives for his employee as he shooed his secretary out of his office.

Finishing his call, Dylan walked over to the plate glass window of his corner office and peered outside. The morning sunshine on this early spring day was being overtaken by clouds that promised rain. He had on a brand new pair of Church's leather shoes and he didn't like the idea of soaking the soles in a downpour. So he grabbed his raincoat from a wooden hanger in the closet, and spied a box on the closet floor. Inside the box was a photo of his former fiancée, Della Gates. He picked it up, looked at it for a minute and tossed it back in the box. Thrusting his arms in his raincoat, he hurried out of his office toward the elevator, bent on making it to his taxi before the rain started. In the elevator, Metcalfe pushed the down button, and began mentally listing business places he'd seen in Nags Head – Robbins & Richards Grocery, the Ocean Tide Café, the old theater, L. Gates, Bookseller, and Soundside Shells.

Yes, he told himself. *That just might be the perfect next spot for Colony Books.*

Dylan exited the elevator, and walked outside, thankful for the over-hanging awning that reached to the curb. His ride was by the front door of the office building and Dylan smiled to himself. He liked efficiency.

CHAPTER ELEVEN

1942

The next day, Finn was off-duty, having been granted a 24-hour liberty. He'd hoped to sleep later than usual, but he'd tossed and turned all night. So at 7:00 AM, he got up and dressed. Just to make sure, he checked the assignments listed on the bulletin board by the office door. Not seeing his name anywhere, he signed out, started up his Jeep, and headed up the beach road toward the Jennette's Pier Café.

The road was empty of other cars and the sun was beaming. But it did nothing to improve Finn's mood. Try as he might, he couldn't stop replaying in his mind the sight of the tanker going down and the agony of the single survivor he'd rescued the night before. So many families were affected by the downing of the tanker. Just minutes before the sinking, the ship's crews were going about their business, maybe eating, or playing cards, or sleeping, unaware that they were minutes away from their death. All he could think about was the lives lost. What if he'd gotten there sooner? Could he have saved another life?

He pulled into a parking spot at the pier, the gravel spraying under the tires of the Jeep. He killed the motor, and got out, walking up the pier and heading for the café door. As he pulled the screen door open, he was surprised by the appearance of the very one he'd been thinking of as he fell asleep the night before. Louise Gates, holding a broom, had been in the process of sweeping the sand off the floor of the café and out the screen door. She'd backed into the door to hold it open as she swept and when Finn opened the door, she practically fell onto the cement stoop. Finn reacted quickly, stopping her from hitting her head on the stoop by catching her in his arms. She took a few breaths and righted herself, enjoying momentarily the feel of Finn's arms around her.

"Whew! Thanks, Finn. You're kind of early, aren't you? What brings you by the café this morning? I thought you were on duty today."

"No, I'm off duty. I just needed some breakfast, OK?" Finn retorted gloomily, looking down and setting her aright.

Louise seemed taken aback by Finn's rude response and stepped aside to let him enter the café. He took a seat in one of the pine booths under a window. Outside, the ocean waves gently caressed the sands, a far cry from the angry whitecaps Finn had fought the night before. Fishermen at the end of the pier were baiting their hooks and casting their lines for their supper. Finn looked out of the window at the ocean, trying not to think about the souls lost there the night before.

Wearing a sweet smile, Louise approached the booth, a mug of coffee in her hand. She set the coffee down in front of Finn, and pulled a napkin-wrapped trio of utensils from the pocket of her apron.

"Here you go, Finn. Would you like sugar and cream?"

"No, just black."

"So what's going on today?"

"I just want some peace and quiet, OK?"

Louise's mouth dropped open at the harshness of Finn's answer. She stepped back from the table and wiped her hand across her mouth.

"Got it. No problem."

Sensing that Finn was in a foul mood, she pulled a plastic-clad menu from a stand nearby and placed it in front of Finn. She mentioned the morning's special and said she'd be back in a minute. Finn glanced at the menu, closed it and took a sip of his coffee. Soon Louise approached the booth tentatively and asked if he was ready to order.

"Yes, Louise, I am. I'll have a glass of water, two eggs sunny side up, bacon, biscuits and grits with red-eye gravy. And keep the coffee coming. My head is killing me."

Louise took Finn's order back to the kitchen and busied herself making fresh coffee, bussing the table of a group of fishermen who'd come in at dawn. She wiped off the tabletop and looked occasionally in Finn's direction, seeing him with his head in his hands.

What could possibly be wrong with him this morning, she thought.

Soon, the cook called out "Order up!" and Louise rushed to the kitchen window to pick up Finn's order. She carried the plate to Finn's booth and set it down carefully.

"Will there be anything else?" she asked cautiously.

"Yes, can you sit down for a minute and talk? I could use a friend."

"I've got one more table order to bring up and then I'm due a break. Is that ok?"

Finn nodded and reached for her hand, squeezing it gently. He looked tentatively into her eyes. Louise smiled and squeezed back.

She turned and headed for the kitchen, scooping up a paper napkin that had fallen on the floor. Finn picked up his fork and began to eat. The more he ate, the better he felt, especially with the prospect of talking with Louise. Moments later, Louise returned and sat down across from Finn. He proceeded to unburden himself, telling Louise about the tanker's sinking and the lives that had been lost. Tears came to his eyes as he told her that he'd only been able to save one crewmember. Louise reached across the table with both hands for Finn's forearms.

"I want to apologize for the way I was just now," Finn said, looking down and shaking his head. "I haven't been on too many of these U-Boat spotter plane missions and this is the first one I've been on where I wasn't able to help save multiple lives. It just got to me."

"No need to apologize, Finn, and you did save one life. Just imagine if you hadn't been there for that man. I can't imagine what you saw and went through. The last thing you should be doing is putting yourself down. Maybe you might like to talk to my pastor. Would you like to join my family at church tomorrow? "

Finn nodded his head slowly and gave Louise a weak smile. He pushed his coffee cup toward her, signaling an end to the conversation. As she reached for the cup, he put his hand around her wrist.

"Thanks, Louise. I'd like that."

On the other side of the world, at this very same moment, Admiral Karl Dönitz was pacing in his Paris office, a scowl on his face. He'd received word of the latest sinking of one of his U-Boats and was furious. He'd met with members of his staff early that morning and decided to use a previously prepared plan to place naval personnel with excellent cultural and English-speaking skills on the Outer Banks beaches. They'd pretend to be fishermen, go ashore and gather intelligence that might be useful in future U-Boat attacks. Admiral Dönitz was certain that with the addition of the spies to his U-Boat program, his U-Boat operation would ultimately be successful.

CHAPTER TWELVE

1994

Asatisfied sigh escaped Roy Gates as he patted his stomach.

"Della, where in the world did you learn to cook like that?" he asked his daughter.

Della smiled shyly and pointed to Maxine, who took the compliment with her usual smile. Della began clearing the table, assisted by her mom. Louise pushed her chair back from the table and started to get up. Roy stood at her side, taking her arm gently. He walked her to her easy chair, knelt beside his aunt and took her hand.

"Lou," he said, tenderly, "I'm not sure you ought to hold onto the bookshop anymore. You've had more than one scare and I don't want anything to happen to you."

"It's a good thing I don't need to depend on you for bright ideas, nephew," Louise replied. "I've already thought about that."

"Oh, yeah? What's your plan?"

"That daughter of yours – she lost her job, right? And her fiancé decided to step out on her, right? So she won't be going back to Raleigh for a bit, will she? And she has a nothing job at the R&R,

right? Well, then...what about asking her to step in for me, get the bookshop up and running until I get back on my feet? What do you think she'll say?"

There was no time for Roy to answer because Della walked in at that very moment, a cup of hot tea in her hands and a stack of new magazines for her aunt. She set the teacup down for her aunt and fanned out the magazines on the table by Louise's chair.

"There's the lady of the hour," Della said cheerfully. "How are you feeling now? I wish I could have been at the hospital to help Mom and Dad take you home, but Louis called a staff meeting for early morning before the store opened. And I worked my shift until 2:00," she groaned. Della knelt beside her aunt's chair opposite her dad. Maxine came in, wiping her hands on a tea towel.

"What can I do to help?" Maxine asked.

Louise looked at Della with a grin.

"How nice of you to ask, but I'm more interested in your daughter's help, Maxine," she said with a twinkle in her eye. "I've got a little something in mind."

Louise put her feet up on the stool in front of her easy chair and took Della's hand in hers. She closed her eyes for a minute, remembering, and then looked into her niece's eyes.

"You know, Della. That bookshop of mine has been a part of Nags Head life and my life for several decades now. When I opened it during the war years, a lot of people felt that a woman alone in business couldn't make a go of things. But I needed a purpose back then and I've always felt that every village should have a bookshop. So I worked hard and, although it hasn't always been easy, I DID make a go of it for a lot of years.

"But let's be honest – I have not updated things in the last several years. I should probably have computerized things long ago. And there are boxes of books in the back room that should be entered into the account books and shelved. It just seems like I've been pretty tired lately so I just haven't gotten around to it. What I'm leading up to, in this roundabout way, is asking you if you'd take over and reopen the bookshop for me – at least until I'm back on my feet."

Della was momentarily taken aback at the enormity of the request. After all, she had thought all along that she'd go back to Raleigh some day after the hurt from Dylan's betrayal had faded. But then, she began to consider the possibilities of settling permanently at the beach and working at the bookshop. There was the proximity of her family; the certainty of a job with a future, though the financial reward would be much less than she had before but she wouldn't have to see Dylan Metcalfe. She wouldn't have to deal with Louis and the R & R. And then, there was Luke Howard, the thought of whom brought an unwilling smile to her face. Luke – with those gray eyes, those dimples and that kind smile of his.

"Child, what are you smiling at," Louise said, shaking her head.

"Oh, it's nothing, Aunt Louise. I was just considering the possibilities. And yes. I say yes to reopening the bookstore until your doctor gives you the okay to go back to work. I'll just have to let Louis know at the R & R."

"You may want to have a look at the bookshop before you say yes, Honey," Louise said. "It's not like that big company where you were working in Raleigh."

"Don't worry, Aunt Louise. I like a challenge. You can count on me."

Della patted her aunt's hand and left to walk the one block to the R & R. It was time for Louis's usual break and she wanted to speak to him privately. He was in the employees' snack room having a Payday bar and a Yoo Hoo, when Della confronted him. He looked surprised and concerned that his employee might be trying to get overtime pay.

"No, Louis," Della told him with a sly smile. "I'm not here to work overtime, as appealing as that sounds. I need to take some time off. One person I know at my former job went to lunch and left a note taped to her chair that said, 'I'm not coming back – ever.' I'm not doing that. My Aunt Louise just had a heart spell and asked me to take over and reopen her bookshop. So I need to have some time off, if that's ok."

Louis drew himself up to his full five feet, four inches and said, "It most certainly is NOT OK. I'm already short-staffed and anyway. Why doesn't your aunt just get rid of that dusty old bookstore anyway? Nobody reads anymore. Everything you ever need is on television. That store and your aunt are just dinosaurs. She needs to come into the present!"

Della stood for a minute, her mouth agape with incredulity.

Did he really just say that, she wondered?

Soon she came to her senses, turned on her heels and rushed back to her apartment where she gathered up the navy blue polyester uniform with Robbins and Richards embroidered in gold thread on the chest. Going back to the R& R, she sought out Louis, who was behind the meat counter talking to a customer.

"Here you go, Louis. Here's your uniform. I quit. Oh and by the way, my aunt is not a dinosaur and neither is the bookshop! And you need to clean your meat counter," she said looking hard at the customer.

Turning on her heel, she walked proudly out the front door and headed back to her aunt's house.

CHAPTER THIRTEEN

1994

Memorial Day in Nags Head each year was an epic day and this year was no different. The town had hung the usual flags on light poles throughout the town. The stores put on their red, white and blue decorations – patriotic displays interspersed with the usual mix of sea side décor. And patriotic wreaths and American flags were hung on store doors and mailboxes all down the Beach Road. Shops advertised holiday sales and a few shoppers could be seen in each store.

One who was not planning to celebrate was Louise Gates. She'd received a notice of Colony Books' plan to consider opening a branch in Nags Head. The letter had arrived the day before her recent heart attack, though she hadn't mentioned it to anyone. It would have humiliated her to have anyone else know that her shop was in danger of being outclassed the way a store like Colony Books would do. So she'd just put the letter away and decided not to think about it anymore.

Louise Gates hadn't bothered to tell Della about the letter she'd received, so Della felt free on this holiday to attend the annual Memorial Day parade. Starting at 10:00 AM, the local high school band led the parade with patriotic songs followed by groups from various organizations on the Outer Banks – Boys and Girls Scouts, equestrian clubs, churches, and at the very end, several ladder and tanker trucks from the local volunteer fire department.

Della had stepped out of her apartment and walked to the edge of Beach Road, waiting for the parade to come by. She was scanning the fire trucks looking for Luke's face when suddenly she spotted him at the wheel of an antique fire engine. He was wearing a navy blue tee shirt with the fire department logo, uniform pants and a navy blue uniform cap with the department logo in the front. He smiled when he saw Della and motioned her to walk beside the slow moving truck for a minute.

"Hey, Della," Luke shouted over the noise of the crowd. "Louis doesn't have you bagging groceries today?"

"No, the store is closed for Memorial Day, believe it or not. And anyway, I quit. Aunt Louise needs my help at the bookshop. "

"Well, then, if you're free for the rest of the day, how about getting together for a bit? I know a great place to get some steamed shrimp."

"That sounds wonderful. What time?"

"Call me at the fire station in a bit after I park Old Betsy here."

Della gave him a "thumbs up" and fell away from the parade line. She could hardly believe she'd walked three blocks as she talked with Luke. She turned back and headed toward her Aunt Louise's cottage, the ocean breezes tossing her hair and cooling her face. As she entered the driveway to her aunt's cottage, she paused to look at the sign by the road. Most of the older cottages had wooden signs with the name and location of the owner. Aunt Louise's sign was a cypress board with "Louise Gates, Nags Head, N.C." painted in green. Over her shoulder the roaring and crashing of the breakers on the sand brought a smile to Della's face. In the sky above, a bright May sun was shining on the beach below. She was beginning to feel more at home here on the Outer Banks than she ever did in Raleigh.

Before going into her apartment, Della went up the steps to check on her aunt. She tapped on the door, and then stepped inside, singing out her aunt's name.

"Come on back, girl," Louise called.

Louise was on the wide back porch, in Capri pants and a red tee shirt, one leg up on one of the two lean-out benches built into the railings and eating parched peanuts. She looked over her shoulder at the surf beyond and smiled back at Della.

"Now who couldn't feel better just looking at this view?" she said. "I remember seeing a whale out there once during the war. I thought it was a German submarine."

Della sat down in one of the rocking chairs facing the ocean and leaned back, closing her eyes for a minute. Damp towels and dish cloths were pinned to the clothesline at one end of the porch. One of Louise's old fashioned bathing suits hung on a nail banged into the wall nearby. She looked at the wall behind her, reading for the hundredth time several pencil inscriptions – dates and the names of several storms which the cottage had weathered. May 8, 1945 was scribbled in another location along with the words "VE Day!"

Della pointed this out to Louise who told her, "We had to put up blackout curtains during the war and we weren't allowed out of the cottage after dark. Mama started locking our door at night. We'd never done that before. I remember once looking out of my bed-room window when all the lights were out. I saw tracer bullets going across the sky from a Navy destroyer. We'd see smoky explosions and fireballs at night out over the ocean and knew that some ship had been torpedoed. The window lights would rattle and Mama's dishes would shake around in the Hoosier cabinet. Sometimes the windows would even break. It was a scary time, I tell you. But during the day, children played under the porches of all the cottages nearby. One of their games was war with their friends. Can you imagine? The littlest one was always the Nazi and the rest were the good guys.

"And we used to have to keep turpentine on the back porch steps, because of all the ships sunk off the Nags Head coast during the war - almost 400! Some of them are in water right now less than 300 feet deep! Their bilges leaked oil into the ocean for many years and it would get on the sand and then onto our feet when we walked on the sands. We'd have to clean the tar off our feet with a brush and turpentine. Sometimes the wind would blow the sand over the tar and we'd step in it again before we knew what was happening. Shew! What a mess. We almost quit swimming in the ocean back then.

"Another thing - we used to see all the ghastly relics of the sunken ships and downed planes – bodies and body parts, clothing, parachutes and life rafts, debris of all kinds. Once a boy I knew found a life raft peppered with bullet holes. Everybody thought the Germans on the U-Boats were shooting any survivors of the ships they sank. We heard later that the Navy was trying to sink the lifeboats so that other boats would not have to keep finding them. Who knows?

"The local fishermen were always complaining of the oil slicks on the ocean which played havoc with their catches. If we could ever get any fresh fish, we had to have ice delivered to our storage room below in big blocks from an ice house in Edenton. We'd chip off bits to keep the croaker and spot fresh until they could be cleaned and cooked. The wall down there is just full of little holes where we stuck the ice pick when we were through with it. "

"Aunt Louise, you've had some fine times here at the cottage, haven't you?"

"Yes, child, so many memories. Before the war, we used to take a dip in the ocean just after rising, then have fish for breakfast – fried herring, which Daddy got at the herring fishery on the Chowan River. In the afternoons, we'd go over to the pier where the fishermen had pulled in their catch. We carried a dishpan and bought a mess of fish for that night's dinner. Sometimes they'd already be cleaned, but most of the time we'd have to clean them. That was my job with my daddy. All the neighborhood cats would come around looking for fish heads to eat. After supper, there would be dances on the pier and fishing contests in the surf. That's one reason I wanted you to live here with me – I want you to love this place the way I have. It's always been kind of an anchor for our family.

"You know my great grandfather built this cottage shortly after the War Between the States. He sailed from the Perquimans River to the Nags Head sound side. The first version of the cottage was built on the sound side of the road on a lot he bought for $20.00. Later when the ocean became more popular, the cottage was placed on logs and rolled across the road to its present location."

"I can't imagine how difficult that must have been, Aunt Louise."

"Yes, but those were people who never gave up. They'd been through hard times after the Civil War and they saw this place as next door to Heaven. The earliest people who came here were in search of a place to escape the yellow fever and what they called the 'miasma' of the inland towns like Elizabeth City and Edenton. So they just kept on fixing the place up, even after the hurricanes, nor'easters and hard times. This cottage may not have fancy things like hot tubs or swimming pools, but I think it's perfect the way it is. "

Louise was in good spirits and told Della that she felt well. So when Della mentioned that Luke had asked her out for lunch, Louise shooed her out the door. But Della insisted on fixing her aunt a tomato sandwich before she left. She put the sandwich on a tray with some chips and a glass of sweet tea and brought it outside to her aunt. Lunch on the back porch was a family tradition, so Louise was happy. After making sure that her aunt had everything she needed, Della practically skipped to her apartment to freshen up for her date. And yes, she thought to herself, it definitely was a date!

Meanwhile, Louise spent the remainder of the afternoon on the back porch watching dolphins cavorting in the ocean waves. After a while, her eyes began to get heavy and she napped in the hammock. She thought again about the handsome officer from so long ago. Every so often, his face came to her in dreams. He had a shock of blonde hair that persisted in falling over his forehead and a dimple in both cheeks that sent her heart racing. Just before the sun set behind Jockey's Ridge, Louise woke up and watched the sunset, something which always brought a tear to her eye. *I wonder what became of him,* she thought, as she did each time the young Coast Guardsman came to her in a dream. She slipped out carefully from the hammock and walked inside.

CHAPTER FOURTEEN

1942

Louise reached over to her Bakelite alarm clock and hit the top, shutting off the annoying noise. She squinted at the clock face to see how late she was. Then, remembering that it was Sunday, she got out of bed and pulled the covers up, promising herself to finish the job later. Still in her blue striped pajama shorts and white tee shirt, she went downstairs to the kitchen, poured herself a glass of orange juice and popped a piece of bread in the toaster. When the toast popped up, she buttered it, grabbed her juice and went out on the back porch to eat. One or two cars drove by, but for the most part, the beach road was quiet. It was a peaceful morning with clear skies over the ocean. Louise loved the morning ocean breeze and ate on the porch whenever the weather allowed. Sea gulls glided overhead, searching for their own breakfast. Louise watched as the tide ebbed. Soon her mother called out to her to come upstairs and get ready.

Louise swallowed the last bite of her toast, then took her dishes in to the sink and headed to her room. She washed her face, then put on a robe, and sat down at her dresser to apply the light rouge and lipstick which constituted her makeup regimen. She selected a navy polka dot dress with padded shoulders, and A-line skirt that came down to the knee. Because of the shortage of silk during the war, Louise went bare-legged and slipped her feet into a pair of navy sling back shoes with a chunky heel and a peep toe. She gave herself one last glance in her mirror, and then skipped downstairs to wait for Finn. She'd told her parents that he would be joining them for church this morning; she wondered if he was a regular church goer before the war. She wondered if her parents would like him. Suddenly there was no more time to wonder because a knock came at the front door.

Louise took a deep breath, and then stepped slowly to answer the door. She opened it to see Finn on the other side of the door and ushered him into the family room. He wore his dress blue uniform and carried his cap under his arm.

"Morning, Louise. Am I too early?"

"Not a bit, Finn. Come in. My parents and grandparents are just coming downstairs now."

They sat down on the green davenport and looked out at the ocean beyond the windows, a feeling of calm enveloping them. Almost immediately they heard the sounds of the four adults meandering down the stairs. Finn stood up immediately and gave a little bow when they entered the room.

"Mama, Daddy, Nana and Grandpa, I'd like to introduce Finn Ingram. He's a flight operations officer with the US Coast Guard. Finn, these are my parents, Miles and Rhonda Gates and my grandparents, Arthur and Emily Hudson."

"Pleased to meet you," Finn said and shook hands with the men. Louise's mother and grandmother both gave him a big smile.

"Well, Finn, you've had breakfast, I assume," said Louise's dad, looking the boy over carefully.

"Yessir, I ate at the station earlier," Finn replied.

"Then let's get going. It's about time for the service to start."

The four adults followed Louise and Finn through the hall and out to the porch. Then Louise's parents and grandparents got into Arthur's 1936 Ford Woody. Finn escorted Louise to his Jeep and started the engine. A few minutes later, they arrived at St. Andrews-by-the-Sea.

Built in 1915, the church was clad in gray shingles, its door a bright red. It had been moved to its present location after 1929 upon the construction of the Beach Road. The church custodian was ringing the steeple bell as they exited their vehicles. The bell, which had been preserved in a barn in Pasquotank County, came from the original church building of Civil War times. The bell was given back to the church and installed when a new belfry was constructed atop the roof of the church. Mothers were calling their barefoot children from underneath the church. The recent rains had made puddles everywhere and the children sailed their hand-carved boats in the muddy water before church.

An elderly gentleman stood at the door of the church greeting the congregants as they entered the sanctuary. The small chapel, with its interior walls of unpainted pine, was filled this morning, everyone talking quietly to their neighbors before the start of the service. At the altar table between two pillar candles, a brass vase held a bouquet of sea oats.

"This is the day the Lord has made. Let us rejoice and be glad in it," began the service. Reverend Hill used as his text that morning the story of the Disciples and Jesus in the boat during a storm.

"Water surrounds us," the pastor Reverend Hill noted. "Our children play in it and wade in it. We fish in it. We get food from it. This place of worship is mere yards from the ocean's waves. The Scriptures mention water 722 times. The Disciples were terribly frightened but Jesus told them to be calm. His words are good for us today as well."

He told the congregation how Christ spoke to the storm, saying "Peace, Be Still" and the winds and the water obeyed him. Comparing the storm the Disciples faced to the storm of war their country was facing, Reverend Hill prayed for the safety of all those in the military, both at home and abroad.

"We've needed faith in days past when we lived through hurricanes and nor'easters. We'll need faith in the days ahead," the pastor noted.

He asked if there were any military personnel in the congregation. Finn stood humbly along with three other men and received the applause of the church. The closing hymn was "Eternal Father, Strong to Save," the Navy hymn. The organist played a brief introduction and then the forty or fifty congregants sang out loudly. Louise looked up from under the brim of her hat to see Finn wiping away a tear from his eye. He noticed her looking at him and gave her a sad smile.

Reverend Hill closed the service with a prayer for the blessings of each new day and for the safety of the President and all in the military. After the Amen, he walked to the front of the church to receive handshakes from all his parishioners. He gave a special greeting to Finn as he was a visitor and said, "We're praying daily for you boys. You come and talk to me any time you need anything."

"Thank you, sir," Finn replied, looking the minister in the eye. "I will."

They got back into their cars and headed back to the Gates cottage. Rhonda Gates invited Finn to stay for Sunday dinner but he had to say no as he was soon to go on duty at the Coast Guard station.

So Louise walked with him back to his Jeep and thanked him for accompanying her to church.

"I should thank you, Louise," Finn admitted. "I'm afraid I haven't been as regular in my church attendance as I should have been. I can see it's what I should be doing."

"Good, maybe you can come back with me next Sunday if you're not on duty."

"I'd like that," Finn answered. "And pray for me. I'm flying a spotter again tonight."

Louise gave his hand a squeeze and looked deep into his eyes.

"You just take care of yourself. And I'll see you at the café this week, OK?"

"You bet! That's a date."

CHAPTER FIFTEEN

1994

Della walked back across the porch to her one-room apartment and freshened up her make-up. She put on a pair of white French sailor pants adorned with two rows of brass buttons. She topped them with a navy and white striped tee shirt and slipped into white flat sandals. Soon her cellphone buzzed and she looked down at it. It was Luke and he was a couple of miles away. She took one more pass at her hair and straightened her apartment while she waited for Luke's knock. She soon heard the welcome sound. Opening the door, she smiled brightly. Luke stood on the porch and greeted her.

"Ready to go?"

"Yes. Where are we going?"

Luke proceeded to tell her about a small cafe just beyond the Kitty Hawk pier. It had been in his mother's family for the past twenty years and served delicious seafood. They drove the few miles up the beach road to the café and Luke turned in to the gravel parking lot. The lot was full, a good indication of the café's popularity.

"Do you think we'll be able to get a table?"

"I called my Uncle Bill. He's reserved a table for us."

They walked into the small building and Luke threw up his hand to wave at his uncle. Bill who was busy at the cash register pointed at a booth in the corner which bore a "Reserved" sign.

They slid into the booth and were approached by a waitress who handed them typed menus. Luke and Della took a cursory look at the paper sheets. But having already decided on steamed spiced shrimp, they waved them away.

"Just a couple of Cokes and the steamed shrimp plates for both of us," Luke said, smiling again at Della, who nodded in agreement.

The waitress soon brought back two trays of shrimp, a bowl of hush puppies and two bowls of lemon water. The duo dug into their lunch, peeling the shrimp, dragging them through cocktail sauce and popping them into their mouths. Soon the lunch was finished and Luke applauded himself for not spilling cocktail sauce on his shirt. They dipped their hands into the lemon water and wiped them with the warm, wet towels the waitress brought. Luke paid the bill, left a healthy tip, and they walked out to the car. They got in and drove over to Jockey's Ridge. Luke popped the trunk of his car and pulled out a box kite which he assembled handily. Taking off their shoes, they left them in the car, and then walked up Jockey's Ridge to the top.

Jockey's Ridge was the largest sand hill on the Atlantic Coast; it was so named because early settlers sat on its steep sides as in a grandstand to watch Banker ponies as they raced along the sand. Luke unrolled the kite's string and ran along the top of the ridge, pulling the kite behind him. A gust of wind captured the kite and it took flight almost immediately. Della shrieked with joy and the pair watched as the kite sailed higher and higher.

"You know, Della, some people say that Blackbeard buried his treasure chest full of gold under the sands of the dune. Nobody's ever found it, though. And many years ago, the land under these dunes was farmed. Early farmers actually grew vegetables and other crops right here."

"That's impossible to believe – there's just sand here now. Just great big mountains of sand. "

They took turns flying the kite and once Della nearly lost the kite's string. Luke reached over her shoulder to grasp the string, saving it from flying off into the blue sky. When the kite was captured again, Della laughed breathlessly.

"Good catch, Luke," she said, and put her hand over his on the string. Luke smiled down at her and hugged her to his chest. Della's insides churned with excitement as she felt the heat from Luke's body next to hers. Luke reached down and deposited a gentle kiss on the top of Della's head. Time stopped as Luke ran his fingers down her spine. He lifted Della's chin with his hand and pressed a kiss on her lips.

The two spent a happy hour watching the kite soar over the mountains of sand. When the hour was over, they half walked/half slid down the dunes, Della grabbing Luke's arm for support. At the bottom of the dune, Luke looked down into Della's eyes, which she was shading from the hot sun with her hand.

"This was so much fun, Della. Can we do it again sometime? I wish we could finish out the day but my shift at the fire station starts in a couple of hours."

"Of course," Della said. "I'd love to. Just give me a call. "

They walked back to the car and headed back to Della's apartment. Upon arriving at Louise's cottage, Luke stopped the car and put the gear shift into park.

"Thanks, Della. This has been a really nice day, the best day I've had in a long while."

He leaned over the bucket seat and gave her a quick kiss on her cheek, bringing a flush to her face.

She smiled and said, "Call me?"

"You bet."

He exited the car and opened Della's door, walking her up to her porch and holding her hand. He gave her a light kiss and then bid her goodbye.

Meanwhile, inside Louise's cottage, the phone was ringing. Though many people were beginning to use cell phones, Louise still had a house phone sitting atop the table by her chair. She leaned over to pick up the handset and answered. Her mind was still a little muddled from her long nap.

"Who did you say this is?" she repeated.

"I'm Astrid Olsen," came the refined voice over the phone. I work in graphic design and marketing for Colony Books. I've heard good things about your bookshop and I'd like to talk to you about how we could help each other. Could I stop by the shop tomorrow?"

Louise told her the shop was temporarily closed as she'd just gotten out of the hospital but if she'd like to come around to her cottage, they could chat. Astrid smiled and arranged to come by in the next half hour, "if that's convenient with you, Miss Louise," she inquired.

Louise got up from her chair and strolled slowly into the kitchen. She found the tea kettle and proceeded to make a pot of her favorite Earl Grey. She opened the breadbox and found a plate of peanut butter cookies that Della had brought her, setting them on the kitchen table.

I wonder what she could want with me, she pondered.

No sooner had the kettle begun to boil, than Louise heard a knock at the front door. She walked through the front hall, peered through the screen door and said hello to the visitor.

"Miss Louise?" said a petite blue-eyed woman dressed in a blue seersucker suit and heels. Her hair was light blonde and curled charmingly around her face. "My name is Astrid Olsen. I called you earlier about your shop?"

"Oh yes, come in, young lady," Louise answered, holding the screen door open. "Come right through here."

"I just love these old houses," Astrid said, looking around her. "There's so much history here. Has this place been in your family long?"

Louise shook her head and smiled at the opportunity to tell again the story of the house – how it had been built by a distant ancestor of hers, how it had been moved from the sound side of the road on logs to its location on the ocean, how it had weathered several terrible hurricanes and Nor'easters – all points of pride for the older woman.

Astrid followed as Louise directed her into the kitchen and pointed to one of the mismatched chairs around the oak table. She walked over to a cabinet to retrieve a tea cup and smiled as she saw a yellowed piece of paper tacked to the wall next to the pantry, at a child's eye level. Written there in pencil were the "House Rules for Children" –

1. No leaving the house without telling a grownup
2. Hang up your bathing suit and towel on the porch clothes-line after swimming
3. Remember your manners at the dinner table
4. Be kind and say thank you
5. Rest for one hour after lunch
6. Always tell the truth.

"We had to follow these rules or there'd be trouble for sure. I still think they are good rules to follow. "

She filled Astrid's cup with tea, then set it and her own empty cup on the table, and turned back to the stove to set the tea kettle down. She had spilled a bit of tea on the stovetop, so she grabbed a dish-cloth and began wiping it up. Then, filling her own cup of tea, she arranged it on the table and pulled out a chair for herself but looked out the window before sitting down.

"My daddy taught my cousins and me how to swim right out yonder," Louise said, pointing to the ocean. "He took me in so far that it was over my head and he showed me how to paddle around. Then this big roller came along, tons of water, and pushed me right out of his arms. I was scared to death, but I soon felt his big, strong arms coming up under me, protecting me, bringing me to shore. Law, listen to me runnin' on. Now, you wanted to talk to me about my shop?"

Louise sat down at the table and pulled her teacup to her. Astrid handed her a spoon from the cup of spoons on the table. She looked at the contents of her teacup and took a sip.

"Umm Umm! This is mighty good," Astrid said, taking a cookie from the plate in front of her. "Yes ma'am, I'm looking at several small towns and businesses along the East Coast as possible sites for new branches of Colony Books. Your shop seems to have the kind of charm that we think could be a real tourist attraction, and could bring new life to the town of Nags Head. I'll leave you with these brochures about the kind of thing our company is planning. And here's my contact information." Astrid handed her a thick, creamy business card with her contact numbers embossed on the front and the logo for Colony Books. She took one last swig of her tea and grabbed another cookie.

"One for the road! And hey, how about I take you out for dinner tomorrow night? We can go over to the Oasis for a fish dinner to thank you for seeing me on such short notice," she said with a smile.

Although initially Louise had been worried that Colony Books would shut her down, she had to admit to herself that she was flattered that a big business like Colony would consider her shop. So without thinking, she said yes, but only if she could bring along her niece. Astrid agreed that would be fine, shook her hand and turned to go. "I'll be back around 6:00 tomorrow night, Miss Louise," she said pulling the screen door behind her and walking down the steps. She jingled her keys and got in her rental car.

Louise began fanning herself, wiping perspiration from her forehead.

"Woo, it's a hot one today," she said to herself. "I better see if Della is free tomorrow."

Louise sat down heavily in her easy chair. She closed her eyes and fanned herself with the church fan on her table. It had been a busy morning, she thought. Too busy. Once again her mind strayed to thoughts of her officer of so long ago. Soon she was napping and her Coast Guardsman entered her dreams.

CHAPTER SIXTEEN

1942

In his office as Commander of Submarines for Berlin, Admiral Karl Dönitz paced back and forth with excitement. After the Japanese attack on Pearl Harbor, he had given orders to zero in on Atlantic shipping lanes on America's east coast. He'd just received word that some nine ships had been sunk in one battle near the Cape Hatteras Lighthouse. Reports had been radioed to him of fires night after night off the coast of the Outer Banks from ships the Nazis had sunk. Smoke from these fires had been so dense that the horizon was not visible for days from the shore.

Dönitz had been particularly pleased when told that a British tanker carrying over 10,000 gallons of gasoline exploded with a bang and a flash that could be seen almost all the way to Norfolk. His submarine fleet had been designed to stay at sea for quite a long time and orders had been given to rest a few miles offshore between attacks.

As the summer wore on, Dönitz ordered spies to go ashore in the dark of the night. They arrived in some of the rafts and lifeboats that residents found washed up on the sands in front of their cottages. These spies spoke perfect English and were given orders to pretend to be fishermen or vacationers. When on land, they'd climb the one hundred foot tall Jockey's Ridge and signal the Nazi subs offshore with any helpful information they'd learned. Later in the war, Jockey's Ridge became a bombing range and local children would pick up dud bombs or hand grenades with the firing pins still attached. Members of the Coast Guard were tasked with cleaning the dunes and beaches of this war debris and reminding cottage owners to install and use blackout curtains, something that Finn did constantly.

Occasionally, he was tasked with patrolling the beaches on horse-back after dark, but tonight he was to be in the air. Finn was piloting a spotter plane with Hawk on the Sunday evening after attending church with Louise Gates and her family. He felt a sense of calm in his gut, remembering the pastor's message about Jesus calming the storm. Finn and Hawk walked over the tarmac to their observation plane, and Finn bowed his head as he seated himself in the cockpit. He prayed silently, asking for wisdom and safety as he patrolled the shores that night. He'd warned the Gates family to tell all their neighbors along the coastline to pull their shades down before dark and close their blackout curtains. He'd noticed that the Gates family car's headlights had been painted half black as required by law.

Most of the night flights Finn carried out were flights of sheer boredom, but occasionally they were terrifying. On this particular night before sub-hunting, Finn was flying Search and Rescue north toward the little village of Duck. He'd received a radio message that another Coast Guardsman had landed his plane in the ocean to pick up a fisherman whose boat had sunk. But a sudden wave had caused the Coast Guard plane to capsize. Ten minutes into his flight he spotted what he thought was something floating in the water, but there was no plane to be seen. All of a sudden he saw that it was a man, his orange life vest lifting his head above the heaving waters of the Atlantic Ocean. Looking more closely, Finn saw another man in the water as well. Later, Finn learned that one of the men was the pilot who'd been attempting the rescue. The downed pilot's own Kingfisher had capsized while endeavoring to rescue the second man, a fisherman who'd been on the water past curfew. The fisherman's small craft had been upset when a huge breaker dumped gallons of water into the boat, causing it to sink. The downed pilot had been undertaking a rescue of that fisherman and had landed his plane on the water. But the surf's swell had caused the plane to take on water as well. And now the downed pilot and the fisherman he was attempting to rescue were clinging to the plane's wings which were awash. Carefully, Finn maneuvered his plane down onto the rolling surf next to the downed men. He stilled the engine and Hawk reached out to grab the pilot's vest, pulling him onto the plane's wing. He then picked up the fisherman and hauled him into the plane and onto his lap. A trail of blood followed the man's body and Hawk cried out to Finn.

"Hey, Finn, this guy's in a bad way. "

Hawk saw that the fisherman's leg had been nearly severed, the saw tooth marks indicating that he'd been attacked by a shark while waiting to be rescued. The fisherman's face took on a deathly pallor while the pilot who'd attempted his rescue lashed himself to the wing of the plane. Hawk radioed the Coast Guard station alerting them to the medical emergency they'd found and Finn flew them back to the station. There, two ambulances were waiting with emergency personnel to evacuate them to Manteo for medical attention.

After ascertaining that the fisherman was in stable condition, Finn checked the fuel level in the Kingfisher, then boarded his plane and went back in search of the U-Boats he'd originally been looking for. Hawk had been tasked with making the report to their commanding officer and as soon as he finished, the two men headed back out to the flight line for their plane. By this time it was dark, and the cloud cover was heavy, so it was practically impossible to see anything ahead of the plane. Finn had received notification that U-Boats were in the area, and it was with some trepidation that he flew along that same shipping lane. He'd have tough visuals, he knew.

A few minutes into his second flight of the night, Finn was flying over Jockey's Ridge when, out of the corner of his eye, he saw a flashing light, then another and another. He was certain it had to have been the German spies who'd been suspected of coming ashore incognito. So Finn radioed to the Coast Guard station about what he had seen. Only moments later, Coast Guardsmen raced to the area designated by Finn. There they found two men dressed in ordinary duck cloth trousers and denim shirts atop the highest part of Jockey's Ridge. They looked like ordinary Bankers, and told the Guardsmen that they were Kitty Hawk natives, waiting for their girlfriends. But when questioned, they failed to know the simplest things that most Bankers would know – how to harvest oysters and clams, how to net shrimp, what time the next low tide would be. The spies were picked up, flown to Norfolk and interrogated.

Later, flying out to sea, Finn spotted a gray hulk lying mostly below the surface off Cape Hatteras. He radioed his coordinates back to his commanding officer and began his bombing run. The U-Boat commander was just giving the order to go below when he spotted Finn's Kingfisher diving straight for him. "Alarm!" he cried out as he hurried down the conning tower ladder, just as Finn released one of his bombs.

The bomb was a direct hit just aft of the U-Boat's conning tower. Inside the U-Boat, the pressure hull was ruptured and more seawater began pouring in. The engine room was on fire and the commandant knew that his boat was doomed. So he ordered his men to abandon ship and to open the hatch to the conning tower. Twenty of the fifty men on board the boat were able to get out and hang onto wreckage from the explosion. The destroyer that had helped to locate the boat picked up the survivors several hours later. One of the survivors couldn't swim and, weakened from struggling to stay afloat, slowly slipped below the water. But the rest were brought on board the destroyer, given food and dry clothes and interrogated before transfer to Norfolk Naval Station. The crew of the destroyer went through the pockets of the men they'd rescued and found jewelry, watches, photographs and several Reichmarks. Two other spotter planes searched the area for floating bodies and flotsam and found only two bodies floating in an oil slick.

The Kingfisher flew back to the base and Finn reported to his commanding officer about the sinking. The officer commended Finn for his rescue; Finn saluted and turned to leave. He went immediately thereafter to take one more look at his plane and then headed to his barracks. It had been a long night. His rack looked mighty good.

CHAPTER SEVENTEEN

1994

The next morning after her lunch at the pier with Luke, Della dressed hurriedly in a pair of denim overalls over a short sleeved tee shirt. She tied a pair of work boots on her slim feet and walked over to the main cottage. Louise was waiting for her, a pad of paper in her hands.

"Aunt Louise, I'm free as a bird. I can help you in the bookshop for as long as you need me."

"That's wonderful, Della. I've written down some things you'll need to know. And here is the key to the front door. The back door key has been lost for a while but nobody goes back there anyway. Go on down and see what you think. And thank you, girl. This means a lot to me."

Della picked up the key and list of instructions from her aunt, gave her a quick kiss on her cheek and walked the two blocks to the bookshop. In the middle of four one-story shops on Virginia Dare Trail, known to all as the "Beach Road," sat L. Gates, Bookseller, her aunt's shop. In its previous lifetimes, it had once served as the town's bank, and then a post office and a small general store.

The shop was in a brick one-story building with two bow-fronted windows, one on either side of the front door. Each window was six feet wide and nearly as tall. Each window contained twelve panes with glass that was so dirty as to be almost opaque. Carved wooden pediments surmounted the door and windows, the white paint peeling and dirty. Above the faded door was a brass plaque, so tarnished that it was illegible. Della took a tissue from her backpack and rubbed the dust off the plaque. "L. Gates, Bookseller" it read. A sign on the door announced that the shop was "Closed." The flower boxes underneath the windows were empty of everything but weeds; One brick wall on the side of the shop contained a faded "Drink Grapette soda" sign that had been painted there many years before.

Della pulled the key from her overall pocket and inserted it into the lock on the front door. The door refused to budge at first. She pushed against it with her shoulder to no effect. After several attempts, she was about to give up when she heard a voice behind her.

"May I help?"

It was Luke and Della sighed with relief.

"Please, be my guest," she said, and handed him the key.

Luke had been walking the two or three blocks from the fire station when his legs took him unconsciously toward the bookshop. He inserted the key into the rusty box lock, turned it, and, using his shoulder, pushed open the door. Luke stepped aside to allow Della to enter and followed her in. The interior of the shop was not exactly what Della was expecting to see.

"Wow," she said. "I visited Aunt Lou's shop once about seven years ago when we were on vacation. It has really gone down since that last time I was in here. What happened?"

"Well, that trip to the hospital for Miss Louise wasn't the first time. She's been having heart spells for quite a while and I guess she just hasn't been able to handle the upkeep of the shop as well as she'd like."

That was a bit of an understatement. Della and Luke stepped onto the wide wooden floorboards, each step creaking beneath their feet and looked around in amazement. The shop was composed of two large rooms, one in front of the other. The back room, off a narrow hall to the side, contained Louise's office with a desk, a chair, two file cabinets and a heavy bookcase. A small restroom was off the hall as well. The front room was the book shop itself. It was dusty and cramped with tall shelves dividing tight passageways. Underneath the bow window on either side of the front door was a deep display shelf crammed with precarious stacks of books, new and old, waiting to be shelved. A musty aroma pervaded the shop indicative of either mold or a roof leak somewhere.

A wooden counter ran half the width of the rear of the shop, its surface covered in papers, books, rubbish and an old desk phone with a cloth-covered cord. A large, vintage brass cash register squatted at the end of the counter, its surface practically hidden by tarnish. Luke and Della laughed to see that the keys only went up to $5.00. Beside the cash register, a cast iron spike paperweight bore a large stack of receipts, each one pierced by the spike.

On the wall behind the counter, there hung a black and white photo of Louise Gates as a young woman. She was smiling broadly and standing with a handsome man dressed in a military uniform. Della ran her hands over the top of the dusty counter. Its chestnut hue needed polishing, but even under all the dust, Della could see the carved scrollwork at the corners.

"Just imagine what this counter would look like if I polished it," she whispered.

Just to the right of the counter, a sagging green velvet couch slumped, its upholstery worn on the arms. A glass-fronted locked cabinet beside the counter held several very old books, their crimson covers faded, and their pages brittle with age and disuse.

Della and Luke walked carefully around the shop, stepping over stacks and boxes of books, a mop and bucket and other cleaning supplies. There was hardly any space to walk through the cramped aisles. The crowded bookshelves were chaotic; it seemed that all categories of books had been shelved haphazardly – poetry, fiction, non-fiction, art, instructional manuals and a few children's' books. Layers of dust covered the shelves and piles of books on the floor.

On the wall by the front door, a framed newspaper article announced the projected opening of the building in its first form, the Nags Head Bank & Trust. Its yellowed page proclaimed:

"PLANS FOR OPENING OF NAGS HEAD
BANK & TRUST ANNOUNCED.

THE NAGS HEAD BANK & TRUST WILL BEGIN BUSINESS ON JANUARY 21, 1915. ALL PRELIMINARY STEPS HAVE BEEN TAKEN TO ORGANIZE THE COMPANY AND ARTICLES OF INCORPORATION HAVE BEEN DRAWN UP. INTERESTED CITIZENS OF OUR TOWN WILL BE DELIGHTED TO HEAR THAT THE BANK PRESIDENT WILL BE MR. THOMAS WILLIAMS OF ELIZABETH CITY. HE COMES TO THE BANK FROM HIS POSITION OF CASHIER AT THE HOBBSVILLE COMMUNITY BANK. THE BOARD OF DIRECTORS IS COM-POSED OF FOUR GENTLEMEN AS FOLLOWS: ARTHUR HUD-SON, R.T. HARRELL, L. M. MORRISON AND J.T. SMITH."

"Shew," Della cried, shaking her head. "It's a lot worse than I thought. Do people still come to the shop?"

"Well, before it was closed, a few did. Not many, though. Mostly the townspeople come to check up on Miss Louise. Everybody loves her around here."

"This place looks terrible. Do you think it's too far gone? Can it possibly be brought back to life?'

I don't know, Della, but I'm beginning to believe if it can be done, you can do it."

The mop had fallen down so Della picked it up and took it back to the closet in the office. She gave a swipe to the dust on the counter and stooped down to look under the counter. Finding nothing of importance down there, she shook her head.

Looking at Luke, she said, "Let's go. There's too much to confront right now. I've got to talk to Aunt Louise, see what she wants me to do first, before I tackle all this."

Luke reached a hand to her to help her up and they walked out the door. Della handed the key to Luke, asking him to lock the tricky front door. She thanked him for his help and headed toward her apartment. Luke started walking with her toward her home, but was stopped by a phone call on his cellphone. The firehouse alerted him to a commercial fire in town, so he apologized for having to leave so quickly. Then he took off at a run toward the firehouse.

CHAPTER EIGHTEEN

1994

At three minutes to six the next evening, Astrid Olsen turned her rental sedan into the driveway of Louise Gates' cottage. She turned the car around to make it easier to get back out on the road, and then shut off the engine. Taking a look in the mirror, she reached into the glove box and picked up a small canister of Binaca. Giving her mouth a quick spray, she returned it to the glove box, smiled into the mirror once more to check her teeth, and exited the car. Whistling a little tune, she walked up the steps and gave a cheery knock on Louise's door.

Louise opened the door and greeted her caller with a smile. She looked much refreshed from her regular afternoon nap and had changed into a green striped cotton shirtwaist dress. On her feet she wore beige Grasshopper shoes that matched her straw pocketbook.

"Well, don't you look a picture, Miss Louise?" Astrid said. "I declare, you're gonna have to fight off half the men on the Outer Banks tonight."

Oh, get on with you, Miss Olsen."

She walked across the porch and knocked on Della's door. Della opened it immediately, a tiny look of concern on her face.

"Hey, Aunt Louise. You look nice. You ready to go?"

"Yes, child, I've got a business dinner with a client. This is Miss Astrid Olsen from Raleigh. I told you about her last night. Astrid, this is my niece, Della. Astrid's wanting to talk to me about upgrading my bookshop and we're going over to the Oasis for a bite to eat. I'll be back in an hour or two. You can still join us, can't you? I meant to remind you earlier but I sat down in my chair and fell plumb asleep."

"Pleased to meet you, Della. "

Della shook Astrid's hand, said of course she'd go and took a few minutes to powder her nose and grab her purse. Then she locked her apartment door behind her as Louise and Astrid waited on the porch.

Astrid walked Louise to the passenger side of the car and helped her in. Then settling herself in the driver's seat, and waiting for Della to get settled, Astrid started the engine and they left for the restaurant. Della couldn't help looking out of the window which overlooked the parking pad. She wondered why Astrid wanted to take them out to dinner. Louise had told her earlier that Astrid worked for Colony Books but that she was a new hire and didn't realize Della's connection with her boss, Dylan Metcalfe. But Della's concerns were soon put aside, as she realized what a friendly girl Astrid was. On the way to the restaurant Astrid mentioned that her boss was interested in acquiring Louise's bookshop to make it part of his chain, but nothing more was said about that during the evening.

Supper at the Oasis was delicious as always. The restaurant, positioned on the causeway between Manteo and Nags Head, had a delightful screened dining porch where the three women were seated. The Oasis Restaurant was famous for its barefoot college coeds who worked there in the summers as waitresses. They wore white shorts and white sleeveless sailor tops with a navy tie under the collar. One of these waitresses approached the table with a smile and asked to take their order. After looking over the menu, they all agreed to start their meals with shrimp cocktails followed by crab cakes and lace cornbread. They finished off their meal with big slices of Key Lime pie.

An hour and a half later, Louise was walking up the steps to her cottage, on the arm of Astrid. The porch light was on and moths were beginning to be bothersome, so Louise didn't want to prolong the evening.

"Thank you for dinner, Astrid. I'll be back in touch."

I'd appreciate it, Miss Louise. I enjoyed your company tonight."

Della followed her aunt into the cottage and turned on the lights ahead of her aunt. She asked if there was anything she could get for her but her aunt waved her away.

"I'm just tired tonight," she said. "Too much activity for one day!"

Sitting down in her easy chair, and reaching for the remote control, Louise punched a couple of buttons. She found her favorite sitcom, but was asleep by the end of the second commercial. Waking up an hour later, she took herself to bed.

After dropping off the Gates women, Astrid Olsen drove back slowly to her room at the Wilbur Wright Motel in Kill Devil Hills. She'd originally planned to woo Miss Gates with compliments about her shop, but she'd driven by the shop on the way to the motel and saw its condition. There's no way she could pretend that it could become the latest branch of Colony Books.

Inserting the key in her room door, she opened the door, turned on the light, and locked the door behind her. She threw her purse on the bed, kicked off her shoes and pulled her cellphone out of her suit coat pocket. Punching in the numbers for her boss, she waited impatiently for him to pick up.

"Astrid? How are things there in Mayberry?"

"Well, it's pretty quiet here. I took Miss Gates out to supper. Dylan, she's awful nice. Are you sure you want to take away her business? She surely can't last much longer. She's in her seventies, I believe."

"All the more reason for us to move in. There's business for us in Nags Head, I feel certain. By the way, did you happen to see her niece Della?"

"Yes," Astrid replied. "She went out for a meal with us. Nice girl. She lives in an apartment attached to Miss Gates' house. I'm not sure what your plans are for a bookshop here in Nags Head, but I don't think taking over Louise Gates' old shop is worth pursuing. It's just too run-down."

"Yes, well, let me think about that," Dylan Metcalfe replied. "I may have to come down and do a little research into that."

The conversation closed and Astrid set her phone on the table by her bed, shaking her head. She was uncertain how to proceed but she knew one thing – she did not want to do anything to cause pain or problems for Miss Louise Gates.

CHAPTER NINETEEN

1942

I t was Finn's morning to patrol the beaches on horseback. It was a
seemingly ineffective tool against the German U-Boat, but sometimes it proved useful. Occasionally he had to walk the beach and
stand watch. Some nights, he and Hawk would climb a high dune
and dig out a trench to hide in and watch for German saboteurs.
But this morning, Finn went to the small stable behind the station
and grabbed a blanket, saddle and bridle from the tack room. He
dropped the saddle and blanket on the ground and grabbed a peppermint from a bucket hanging on a peg. Carrying the peppermint in his
hand, he approached the young horse in the first stall, talking softly
and reaching out his hand. The Coast Guard Station maintained two
horses for beach patrol. Scout, a young gelding with a gentle nature,
was Finn's favorite. He was a descendant of shipwrecked Spanish
mustangs and had been captured on the northern Outer Banks from
a wild herd living there. These horses were used to riding in the
sand and along the ocean's edge, making them perfect for the Coast
Guard's use. Finn picked up the bridle and put the peppermint over
the bit, making it easy to slip it into Scout's mouth. Scout chomped
loudly while Finn fastened the bridle buckles and pulled the reins

over his ears. Leading Scout to the fence rail, he tied the horse and grabbed a brush, giving the horse's back a good scrub.

"You like that, don't you, buddy? I'll bet that feels good to you. We've got to take a ride this morning."

Finn threw the saddle blanket over Scout's back, then hefted the saddle on top of the blanket and fastened the straps. He adjusted the stirrups to the proper length, and then untied the horse. He stepped into the stirrup and hoisted himself onto Scout's back and clucked to him to get started. Horse patrol meant looking for potential landing spots for the enemy, recovering lifeboats, rafts, bodies and sometimes parts of bodies from the sunken ships. It meant apprehending anyone who might signal to offshore ships. Finn wore a .45 pistol and a walkie-talkie strapped to his saddle whenever he rode Scout. His patrol area that morning was near the Coast Guard Station. The beach in that location was littered with debris. He spotted a white silk parachute washing ashore and waded out into the shallow water to grab it. He rolled it up and packed it into his saddlebag. Finn reckoned that the parachute might be worth something since silk was hard to come by these days.

Thirty minutes later, an empty life raft loaded with K rations in various compartments floated ashore. It was large enough to carry fifteen or twenty sailors, but sadly, no one apparently had used it. Finn pulled it up to higher ground and left it until he could return and bring it to the station.

But the life raft and parachute were soon forgotten. As Finn rode down the beach, he spotted something in the sand. When he approached, Finn was horrified to see that it was an unexploded torpedo. Though the beach was relatively deserted, Finn didn't want anyone around the torpedo which he believed had come from a Nazi U-Boat. So he got down from Scout and roped off the area of the torpedo, then raced back to the station to alert the bomb squad, who soon defused the weapon.

The rest of the morning's patrol was fairly uneventful except for swatting away the mosquitoes or flies that invariably pestered Scout. Finn rode up and down the beach, stopping at cottages along the way to remind people to use their blackout curtains before dusk. He went back to the station where one of the Guardsmen had made chili for lunch. After lunch and a briefing with his commander, Finn went back to the beach to recover the life raft. He was not surprised to find that all of the K rations from the raft had been taken. Times were hard for some people, he knew, and many food items and other supplies were rationed due to the war. Frequently the food and tobacco stored in the rafts were taken by beachcombers. He carried the raft back to the station and manned the radio for the remainder of his shift. He was eager for the day to end, as he had a date with Louise Gates that afternoon.

Meanwhile half a world away, Admiral Karl Dönitz was in a meeting with the Fuhrer. Dönitz reported to his commander that at this point in the war, Nazi U-Boats had sunk nearly 200 merchant marine and civilian ships and several US Navy ships off the Outer Banks. The month of May had brought fewer ships sunk but with the beginning of June, the Operation Drumbeat campaign was strengthening. According to Dönitz, this strengthening was due in no small part to the efforts of Captain Horst van Degen, one of the few commanders Dönitz felt he could trust. He opened the door to the outer office and called for van Degen to enter.

"Captain van Degen, our Fuhrer is entrusting us with a great mission which I am handing to you. It is a great honor for *das Vaterland* to trust in you. The Fatherland is well represented by you and the Fuhrer expects great success from you in this mission I am handing to you today. I want you to take six undercover saboteurs to the area that Americans call "Torpedo Alley." It will be the great American turkey shoot! These men will send back intelligence, and then will be responsible for the bombing of Hampton Roads, Virginia."

"*Jawohl, Herr Kommandant,* my boat should be ready soon. I shall be honored to carry out this mission," said van Degen when he was informed of the order. Within two weeks, van Degen's U-Boat 87 was ready to go with torpedo tubes loaded. The Fuhrer was pleased at the prospect.

CHAPTER TWENTY

1994

Della stood on the porch watching the sun come up. It looked to be a pretty nice day ahead. Since moving to the Outer Banks from Raleigh, Della had tried to take a brief run every morning before her shower and breakfast. She had pulled on a pair of khaki shorts and an old college tee shirt for her morning run. She had pulled her long hair into a high ponytail on top of her head to get it off her neck. She'd checked in on her Aunt Louise moments earlier and found her peeling a banana for her morning bowl of Cheerios.

It was 6:30 and Della had a good feeling about the day. After brushing her teeth, she took her towel and terrycloth robe with her and hung them over the door to the outdoor shower under her aunt's porch. Then she headed over the dune to the soft sand of the beach below the cottage, pausing to admire the sea oats. Stretching for a few minutes before starting her run, she looked back up at the cottage and saw that Aunt Louise was standing on the porch, her cereal bowl in her hand. It was a longstanding habit for Louise to eat as many of her meals as possible on the porch facing the ocean. There she watched the tides ebb and flow, the storms rage and the glorious sunrises warm her cottage.

Della waved her hand at Louise, and then took off at a run. Her destination was the pier about a mile away. Then she'd run back and get ready to start her work at the bookshop. Her job at Louise's bookshop was a prospect she was genuinely looking forward to, an optimism which she hadn't felt in quite a while – since she'd been let go at Colony Books. Della relished the feel of the wind in her hair and the sand under her toes. She kicked at the foam which the surf deposited at her feet, uncovering a perfect piece of blue sea glass. She pocketed the treasure in the pocket of her shorts and looked up at the sky with gratitude.

Thank you, God, for this beautiful day and this eternal ocean, she whispered, and then took off running again.

She stopped every so often to watch fiddler crabs as they scurried down into holes in the sand. Sea gulls and terns padded along the water's edge looking for something to eat. There was so much to see on the beach, Della thought. Then she stood up and headed toward the cottage again. Her skin glistened with perspiration at the end of her run and she hurried up to the outdoor shower under the deck of the cottage. Entering and locking the wooden shower door, Della slipped on the shower shoes she kept there and grasped the bottle of shampoo on the shelf. She turned the slightly rusty shower handle sending warm water coursing over her sweaty body. An unplanned *ahhh* came unbidden from her as she soaped her hair and body. After a quick wash, she pulled the towel from the hook on the wall and dried off. Then she pulled her robe down, wrapped it around her and tied it closed, walking back up to her apartment, her clothes from the run in her hand.

Pushing the door open, she walked inside to her dresser and pulled out her clothes for the day, dropping her sweaty clothes in the hamper. She slipped on a pair of khakis and a tee shirt. Pulling on a pair of socks and some heavy boots, Della grabbed up her brush and fashioned her hair into a messy bun atop her head. She looked in the mirror, applied a little lip gloss and headed out the door. It was a quick walk to the bookshop. She was just inserting the key into the front door lock when she heard the siren from the fire station. She turned and saw one of the town's fire trucks headed north to Kitty Hawk. Della followed it with her eyes as far as she could, and then hurried into the shop.

She was momentarily stunned again at the condition of the shop, then squared her shoulders and prepared to go to work. First, though, she went to the old heavy metal desk phone on the counter, ran her palm over the mouthpiece to get rid of the dust and dialed her mother's telephone number. She smiled to herself about the old fashioned finger wheel as she dialed. She ran her fingers up and down the cloth-covered cord, waiting impatiently for her mother's voice. When finally Maxine answered, Della breathed a sigh of relief.

"Oh Mom, thank goodness. I just saw a fire truck heading up the road in your direction and I guess I was worried."

"We're fine, honey. Don't you worry. What are you up to today?"

"I'm at the bookshop. I'm going to start cleaning up."

"Whew! You've got a job ahead of you. Well, call if you need any help. I'll be here all day."

"Thanks, Mom!"

Della cradled the heavy handset and breathed a sigh of relief. Then she walked back to the office to the closet she'd seen on her first visit. In the closet she found the mop, bucket and cleaning supplies she'd placed there earlier. She pulled them out and filled the bucket with water and soap in the restroom, then took them to the front room of the shop. She set them down, but realized that there were boxes of books everywhere that had to be moved. So she spent the next thirty minutes moving boxes before she was able to mop the floor. Then after mopping the floor, she got down on her hands and knees and rubbed each of the wide pine floorboards with lemon oil. With all the dust gone, the wide planks of the floor fairly glowed. Della stood after finishing the job and looked around.

This place is going to be beautiful, she thought.

She looked at her wristwatch and realized that she had worked right through the noon hour. So she took another look around and locked the door behind her. Walking across the road to the Ocean Tide Café, Della looked at the menu card taped to the window outside. She pushed the door open and was greeted by Eunice Howard.

"Well, hey, Della, it's been a while since you've been in here."

"Hey, Miss Eunice. I've been busy with one thing and another. I'm cleaning up Aunt Louise's shop across the road to try to help her get it open again."

"Well, I know Louise appreciates that. What can I get you today?"

"How about a burger and fries? Diet Coke all to go?"

"Sounds good, sugar. It'll be right out."

Della sat at one of the tables and waited for her lunch when she heard the diner's phone ring. Eunice picked it up and began making notes about the order the caller was making. She finished the call, told the caller that the order would be ready in about twenty minutes and tore off the order sheet from her notepad. She hung it over the cook's window where he could see it and picked up a cloth to wipe down the long counter. While Della sat at the table, she was mentally renovating the bookshop. Before long, Eunice emerged from the kitchen with a bag and a paper cup, calling for Della.

"OK Della, your order's up."

Della pulled a credit card from the back pocket of her jeans and paid. She smiled and thanked Eunice for her lunch, then picked it up and walked across the road to the shop. She set the bag and Diet Coke on the ground to free up her hands for unlocking the door. It still stuck a bit but was getting easier every time it was opened. She walked into the shop, and looked around for a place to eat. Grabbing a rag from the shelf in the cleaning closet, she wiped off the dust on the counter, making a place for her lunch. As she ate, she looked around the shop making a mental list of things to do.

After she finished her lunch, Della collected her paper trash and put it in the trash can, which she noticed was overflowing. She carried the trash can through the back hall, stopping to collect and empty the cans from the bathroom and office and took it all to the trash bin behind the store. As she came back in, she was reminded that the key to the store's back door was missing.

I've got to remember to get a locksmith here to change all the locks, she told herself.

After emptying the trash, Della came back inside and stopped for a minute to admire the floors, and then tried to decide what to do next. She decided to tackle the flower boxes outside the front windows. So, pulling on a pair of gloves she'd found in the cleaning closet, she went out the front door and began pulling the weeds out of the boxes and from the brick front and sides of the shop. Realizing that she needed fresh planting soil for anything she'd plant, she scooped the dirt from within the boxes into a bucket. She emptied the bucket into the trash bin and filled the bucket with warm soapy water. A few minutes of scrubbing with a rag and a brush got most of the soil off the flower boxes, but Della realized she'd need to repaint them. Her "To Do" list was growing longer.

Her final task for the day was to scrub the front door. So she emptied the bucket and refilled it with fresh water and soap, grabbing a clean rag from the shelf in the cleaning closet, and took it out to the front of the shop. Then, retrieving a small step stool out of the closet to reach the wooden pediment above the windows and door, she took a deep breath and went out to tackle the last job of the day. Three hours later, the door and pediments were clean again, but clearly needed to be refreshed with paint. So she went back in to the shop and emptied the bucket, wiping it down to be clean for the next day's use. She found a piece of paper and a stubby pencil on the cluttered counter to make her "To Do" list for the next day and began to write.

1. Call a locksmith – new keys and locks for both doors.

2. Get paint, steel wool and brushes for front door and window surrounds.

3. Get potting soil and flowers for flowerboxes.

4. Bring dust cloths and Endust to the shop.

She looked around the shop once more, grabbed all the cleaning cloths to be washed and walked out, locking the door behind her. As she headed toward her apartment, her brain was swimming with ideas for the shop.

CHAPTER TWENTY-ONE

1994

Della had borrowed her father's pickup and had done some shopping at the local hardware store. There she'd picked up the supplies she needed to continue her restoration of the bookshop. She'd gotten two gallons of paint (one semi-gloss black, one semi-gloss red) and some steel wool, more cleaning supplies, and potting soil. Then she'd bought several flats of colorful zinnias to transplant into the window boxes. She was feeling positive about the work she was setting out to do.

Two days later, Della was meeting a locksmith at the bookshop at 9:00 AM, so she hurried to get there by 8:00 AM to begin her work. She opened the front door upon her arrival and smiled to herself at the evidence of her work from two days ago. The floors were gleaming from their washing. Then she took a look at the shelves and her bubble burst – so many books! And all out of order! And so much dust!

She'd planned the layout of the various sections on a piece of notebook paper this morning at breakfast after discussing her ideas with Louise, and stuck it in the pocket of the overalls she wore. She extracted the list from her pocket and unfolded it, pressing the creases flat on the counter. She'd decided to make a children's book section in the right rear corner of the shop where the shelves were lower. She'd found a couple of wooden children's Sunday School chairs in the office and gave them a wipe down with lemon oil.

They look perfect as is, she thought. *No need to refinish or paint them.*

At 9:00, the locksmith showed up on time and proceeded to change the front and back door locks, giving her two shiny brass keys for each. Both doors stuck a bit from the humidity but the locksmith was able to shave a bit of wood from each door to make them easier to open. He pulled a rag from his back pocket and wiped down the shop bell over the front door. It was an old bell, made of brass in the shape of a dolphin with the bell hanging from his mouth.

"You know, Della, if you polish up this bell, it'd be right pretty," he said. So Della added that to her list of things to do.

Just after the locksmith left, Della began wiping down the lower shelves of the children's section. She'd removed all the juvenile books from the shelves and stacked them on the counter or in boxes. It was a small selection, she knew, and vowed to improve it as soon as possible. But she soon had the shelves dust-free and the books re-shelved, fiction separated from non-fiction. She sat back on her boots to admire her work when she heard the shop bell ring.

"I'm sorry, we're not open yet," she called, mentally kicking herself for not putting the closed sign in the window.

"I'm looking for work. You got any jobs?" a voice called out, and Della smiled, recognizing Luke's voice. She got up and went to the door to greet him.

"Hey," he said, "the door works great. And the shop bell is ring-ing again."

"Yep! New locks front and back! And check out these floors. Aren't they gorgeous? They've got to be heart pine. And the boards are so wide."

"Yes, I must say, Della, you're beginning to make a real difference in here. Now, I've got the day off today. I called your Aunt Louise and she told me you'd be working here today. So I wondered if you needed any help."

Della crossed her hands over her heart and shrieked. "Oh yes, indeed I do. How do you feel about moving some books and shelves?"

Luke gave her a thumbs up and began rolling up his sleeves. Della directed him to her layout plan on the counter and suggested they start by moving the books around so they could begin to rearrange the shelving units. They worked together to do that for the next two hours. When the shelves were arranged to Della's satisfaction, she took up a dust cloth and can of Endust and went to work cleaning them. Outside, Luke got a step ladder from the cleaning closet and began sanding the woodwork around the windows and doors. When he was about finished with the job, Della came outside and sug-gested they walk over to the Ocean Tide Café for a bite of lunch.

"My treat, Luke. I always take good care of my hired help," she said with a grin.

"Sounds like a plan, Della. Hey, when are you gonna take all this paper down from inside the windows – you know, to let people see what's going on in here?"

Della had taped brown butcher paper over the windows when she began cleaning up the shop. She hadn't been sure at first whether she'd be able to complete the job, and she didn't want anyone walking by to see the disarray inside.

"Well, I thought I'd wait for a bit to build up excitement. "

They locked up the shop and walked across the road to the Ocean Tide Café where Luke's grandmother seated them at a table in front of the window, the very same table where she and Luke sat on the day they met. They were soon digging into Eunice's famous "Meat and Three" special and laughing as they remembered Biscuit's welcoming Della to her new home!

"How is Biscuit these days, by the way?" Della asked.

"He's mighty lonely for you. He asked me if you wouldn't come over for dinner one night this week. He wants to introduce you to my folks."

"I'd love to," Della laughed. "Just name the date."

Luke promised to get a date from his parents and get back to her. After their lunch, Della paid for the meal over Luke's protestations and they walked back to the shop. Luke washed off the dust on the wooden door and window surrounds in back of the store, and then washed the shop windows while Della began shelving a few books. She'd bought a second hand table at a used furniture store and set it up near the entrance. Then she got the can of black paint she'd bought and two paint brushes and joined Luke out front. Della painted the lower parts of the woodwork while Luke painted the top. Then they tackled the window boxes for the flowers. Soon the job was finished and the two stood back to examine their work. After finishing the door and window surrounds, Luke hammered the lid closed on the black paint and proceeded to open the red paint can. They spent another half hour painting the door, which fairly gleamed when they'd finished.

"I think we make a good team, Della."

"I think you're right."

They gathered all their supplies and took them back inside to clean up. They washed the paint brushes in the bathroom sink and gathered all the cleaning supplies to carry them to the office. After washing their hands, they went back into the shop and looked around. It was beginning to take shape, they agreed.

"I can't thank you enough, Luke, for all the help you gave me today. I never would have gotten this far without you."

Luke reached down and moved a piece of hair that had escaped Della's bun, then moved his hand down to hold her chin gently. He leaned into her, looking deeply into her eyes, and kissed her gently. For a moment, Della forgot how to breathe.

"Umm Umm! That's a good payment for a day's work," Luke said, licking his lips. "You let me know when you need more hired help."

Della put her head on Luke's broad shoulder and smiled. "That's a deal, buddy. I just might call you again."

CHAPTER TWENTY - TWO

1942

At the end of his morning shift, Finn had given Scout a good brushing and an extra cup of oats. He scratched the blaze on Scout's nose and whispered to him.

"I've got a date with an angel this afternoon," he said playfully, pulling his fingers through the horse's forelock. He removed the silk parachute from his saddlebag and hung it on the clothesline to finish drying. Then he went into the office to make his report.

Once he'd finished reporting on his morning's patrol, Finn went to his quarters and grabbed a towel. He walked to the shower room and turned the water on, adjusting it so that the water hit squarely at the knot of nervous tension he felt in his neck. It was exciting to think about seeing Louise Gates that afternoon so he let the water run on his neck for a bit, and then showered quickly, toweling off afterwards. Wrapping the towel around himself, he walked back to his quarters, nearly slipping on a wet floor. He pulled a uniform shirt from his closet and a nicely pressed pair of pants, sharply creased, to wear for his date with Louise. He took some good natured ribbing from his roommate about his mysterious new girlfriend. Then he grabbed the keys to the Jeep from his desk, pushed his cap down over his eyes a bit in a cocky manner and walked outside.

He drove the few miles to Louise's grandparents' cottage and parked carefully by the maid's apartment attached to the house on the road side. Hopping out of the Jeep, he strolled up to the porch and knocked three times. Louise opened the door and welcomed him shyly.

"Hey Finn," she smiled. "Come in and say hello to the family."

Finn removed his cap and entered the hall, leading to the den. Seated at a card table were Louise's grandparents. They each had a deck of cards and were playing a form of Solitaire.

"Nana and Grandpa, Finn is here. Finn, you remember my grandparents, Arthur and Emily Hudson."

Finn extended his hands shaking the hands of both Arthur and Emily.

"Pleased to see you folks again. I enjoyed visiting with you all at church."

About that time, Louise's parents came in the door, their arms full of paper grocery sacks. Finn moved to help Louise's mother, taking her sacks from her arms. They sat the groceries down on the kitchen counter and began putting them away. A potato rolled off the table toward Finn who scooped it up and handed it to Louise's father. After putting away the groceries, Miles and Rhonda Gates came in to say hello to everyone.

"Hey, Finn. Miles and I have just been trying to find some groceries down at the R & R. Things seem to be in such short supply now. I guess you've got plenty down at the Coast Guard Station."

"Yes, ma'am. Uncle Sam takes pretty good care of us. I've even picked up a pound or two since I've been here on the Outer Banks.

Say, I was wondering if it would be ok to take Louise out for some ice cream. A fellow down at the pier is selling cups of chocolate and vanilla and I thought Louise might like some."

"Yes, of course, you children go on now so you can get Louise back before curfew," Rhonda said.

The air outside was hot and heavy with the promise of rain overnight. On the beach, the waves crashed with a fury against the shore. But to Louise, the late afternoon was perfect. Finn grabbed her hand and they hurried to his Jeep. Driving the short distance to the pier, they both hopped out simultaneously and Finn ran around to her side. He caught her around the waist and swung her around, settling her at last on the sand.

"I'm so happy to have a couple of hours with you, Louise. You don't know what these last few weeks have meant to me.

"I do know, Finn, because the times we've spent together have been so very special to me too. I pray every day for your safety."

The breeze from the ocean blew Louise's hair across her face and Finn carefully pulled it back, revealing her smile. She pulled a scarf from her pocket and tied it around her hair.

"There now, that's better," she said.

They walked onto the pier and saw the old man with the ice cream cart just outside the café. From the pier cafe nearby, the sounds of Benny Goodman's recording of "Stompin' at the Savoy" invited barefoot dancers onto the pier. A young man was there, taking up tickets from the dancers. Louise told Finn she wasn't much of a dancer but she would like some ice cream. The old man with the cart offered only the two flavors, but they looked delicious. So Finn bought one of each and they took the cups and wooden spoons and sat on a bench on the pier, watching the dancers. They each tried their own flavors and then dipped their spoons into the other's cup. Louise spilled a bit of her ice cream on her skirt and Finn pulled a handkerchief from his back pocket. He handed it to her to wipe up the mess and she told him she'd keep it and launder it for him. They finished their ice cream, deposited their cups and spoons in the waste barrel and began strolling along the sand. All around them all afternoon, fishermen were hauling in their lines and seine nets. Little children were following their mothers, headed for their summer cottages, dragging their shovels and pails behind them.

A young man with a camera was walking around the pier offering to take photographs of strolling passersby. Finn took Louise by the hand and hailed the photographer. He pulled a dollar from his pocket and pulled Louise next to him, the rolling surf behind them. The photographer posed them as he wanted them, and took a couple of photos. He wrote down Finn's and Louise's addresses, promising to send copies of each pose to them. But the light was fading and Finn knew he'd have to take Louise back home soon.

Their footsteps led them under the pier, where Louise leaned against one of the pilings. Finn was nearly six inches taller than Louise, and when he turned to face her, he bent his head down to her level. All of a sudden, the rest of the world melted away. Louise heard the crashing of the waves nearby, but all she saw and felt was Finn with his arms around her. Her heart began to flutter and she looked into his blue eyes, now half closed with desire. The kiss that followed was deep and tender. Finn wrapped her in his arms, his emotions soaring.

"Louise, I know we haven't known each other long – just a couple of months, but somehow I feel like I've met my soulmate in you. I wonder if you can possibly feel anything for me?"

"Finn, from the first moment I saw you in the café, I knew there was something special about you. Somehow every day is better when I see you."

"I have something for you which I want to give you the next time I see you."

"But Finn, I have nothing for you."

"Doesn't matter. I just have something that I want you to have. So now you have to see me tomorrow after my shift. You see, I've fallen in love with you."

Once again, Finn wrapped his long arms around Louise's small frame and he reached down for one more kiss. Pressing his lips to hers, Finn's heart raced in his chest. Louise returned his kiss with warmth, passion and tenderness. Beyond the pilings, the waves were crashing as the tide was beginning to come in. The water came perilously close to their feet and as they looked down, they began to laugh. They held hands and ran to Finn's Jeep. The Jeep's top was down so he drove hurriedly to get Louise back to her home before the rain fell. Arriving there, he looked over at her once more and smiled.

"I love you, Louise Gates."

"And I love you, Finn Ingram."

He walked her up to the porch, gave her a little wink and squeezed her hand. A feeling of warmth ran through Louise as she returned his squeeze.

"See you soon," he said, jumping off the porch.

Louise pressed her hand to her heart and watched him drive off. She began humming one of the tunes she'd heard that day at the pier. A smile on her face just wouldn't go away for the remainder of the day.

CHAPTER TWENTY-THREE

1994

The sun on this late spring day was already hot and a gentle breeze from across the ocean stirred the sea grass on the dunes. The tourist season had just begun but so far, the crowds (and shoppers) were few and far between. Della was headed once again to the bookshop for another day of cleaning. She knew she'd be by herself for the day as Luke had told her he was on call all day. But she was looking forward to dinner at his parents' house that evening.

She inserted the key into the lock, marveling once again at how easily the door opened now. She'd brought a sandwich and thermos of sweet tea for her lunch and set them on the counter, promising herself to look into buying a small refrigerator for the office. She looked around the shop, pleased at what had been accomplished so far. Deciding to work on the display shelves under the front windows, she pulled three boxes of new books which she had yet to enter into her account book.

I've got to get Aunt Louise computerized, she thought.

She at first figured she'd remove the brown paper covering the windows from inside, but then decided against it. It might be more

118

dramatic to have a big reveal when she'd finished the clean-up. So today, she got her cleaning supplies and washed and dusted the display areas under the windows. She briefly took down the brown paper from the windows to clean behind them. But she quickly taped it back up when she finished. She began thinking about how she'd display the books she'd ordered. On one side, she thought she'd display children's books with a few toys she'd ordered to sell. On the other side, her plan was to display beach reads. Then the table inside the entrance would be for a changing display of themes, perhaps starting with history books.

After cleaning the window wells inside, she took her Windex and cloths outside to tackle the windows. When one of the exterior windows was cleaned, she stood back and surveyed her work. She couldn't wait to fill the window well with books. She moved over to the other window and began Windexing the panes. She was glad the brown paper still covered the windows inside, since she knew she looked a fright after all the dusting and cleaning. With twelve panes in each of the two windows and then panes in the door, the job of cleaning them took quite a while. But it was satisfying work for Della and when she finished the exterior windows and door, she moved on to the display space at the base of the windows. She gathered cloths from her cleaning closet and a bottle of lemon oil. She rubbed the oil into the display floors until the grain of the wood showed through beautifully. Her mind was whirling with ideas for future displays.

After storing the lemon oil and cloths, Della picked up the flat of red, orange, yellow and pink zinnias and carried them through the front door. She had brought a small hand shovel and a watering can and set to work on the window boxes. First she checked to make sure they were cleaned of all the old dirt and plant materials. Then she brought out the bag of potting soil and filled both boxes. She divided the zinnia plants and planted them in the window boxes. Then she watered them carefully and straightened one of the seedlings that had fallen over in the watering. She stepped back to admire her work and began to see how lovely the shop was going to be.

Next, Della's eye settled on the brass plaque above the door. Luke had removed it when he was painting the door surround and then screwed it back in place, but Della could see that it was in desperate need of polishing. So she went inside and called Louis at the R & R to see if he had any brass polish. When she heard that the R & R carried Brasso, Della hung up, locked the shop and walked down to the grocery store.

"Hey, Louis. How are things?" she said upon seeing her former boss.

Drawing himself up to his full height, Louis replied, "Well, as good as can be expected since I'm still short of help."

"Yeah, I'm sorry about that, Louis. But my Aunt Louise really needed my help. She wants to reopen her shop. So, you said you've got some brass polish?"

Louis directed her to the display of Brasso and she selected a bottle. Then she took it to the cash register and pulled a five dollar bill out of her overall pocket.

"Here you go, Louis. Nice to see you again."

Louis rang up the sale and handed her the change. Della walked the short distance back to the shop and got a clean cotton cloth from the cleaning closet. She carried the stepstool out to the front of the shop and polished the plaque until it shimmered in the afternoon sunlight. Della stepped down onto the sidewalk and carried the stepstool back into the shop. Then she went back outside to the curb to examine her work.

The shop door with its ten window panes was painted a deep semi-gloss red. The door and window surrounds and window boxes were painted a semi-gloss black and the newly attached brass plaque above the door bore the words "L. Gates, Bookseller." The glossy painted wood next to the old red brick of the shop and the shine of the name plaque made for a perfect exterior. Della could feel the excitement in her heart as she saw the work she'd done. She couldn't wait to show her Aunt Louise.

At last, she told herself. *I'm doing something meaningful that I enjoy.*

CHAPTER TWENTY-FOUR

1942

Admiral Dönitz was in his new headquarters in Paris with the seven members of his staff. Each man had a specific job to do – receiving shortwave radio messages from the U-Boats, checking convoy movements, or reporting on U-Boat losses. It was difficult for Dönitz to hear of any losses and he dealt with them by taking walks in the Tuileries. So when he was given the go ahead to attack American shipping, Dönitz had chosen the Outer Banks as the most likely location for attacks. Apparently the American military had not foreseen the possibility of attacks on commercial and Merchant Marine shipping along the coastline. It was going to be too easy, Dönitz had thought to himself then.

But Dönitz soon recognized that his U-Boat attacks had brought more American military to the Outer Banks. One result was the presence of more Coast Guard stations positioned every seven miles along the coastline. Coast guardsmen patrolled the coastline on foot, on horseback, in Jeeps, in cutters, and in floatplanes. Nevertheless, Admiral Dönitz hoped that he could still harass large numbers of merchant vessels and influence the course of the war in Germany's favor by mining the waters of the Chesapeake Bay coastline and emplacement of saboteurs in towns and villages along the East

Coast. Unfortunately Herr Hitler didn't see things the same way, to the detriment of the cause of Nazi ideals. Hitler refused to give Dönitz the number of U-Boats he needed.

In Nags Head, Finn Ingram had just finished his morning horseback patrol of the beach along Kitty Hawk and was in the Coast Guard stable, giving Scout a good brush down. He scooped a cup of oats from the feed bin and put them in Scout's feed trough. He unhooked the hose from the wall, turned on the spigot and filled the water bucket, whistling as he worked.

Giving Scout a scratch on his nose, Finn walked back in to the station and sat at his desk, putting his feet up on his desk. He called Louise at the café and asked what time she'd be off work. She was mopping the floor after the lunch rush and had asked off for the afternoon as her grandmother needed help at the cottage. She told Finn that her shift would be over by one o'clock.

"That's perfect," he told her. "OK if I stop by to see you around 2:00 PM? I've got the afternoon off as well before my evening shift."

"Sure, but be forewarned. You may just be shanghaied into doing some heavy lifting for Nana."

"Be happy to. See you later."

Louise's heart sang as she finished mopping and cleaned the griddle. She hung up her apron and threw the dirty linen into the basket for the laundry truck. She called out to Marge, the café owner, that she was leaving and made her way down the gray boards of the pier to her bicycle parked near the road. She rode back to the cottage, parked by the porch and skipped up the steps.

"Yoo hoo, Mama, Nana, I'm here."

Emily came out of the kitchen, wiping her hands on her apron. She'd been making strawberry jam and her apron showed evidence of her work.

"I'm glad you're here, Louise. Your mother has gone to the store to get some potatoes for supper. I need you to wash some jars for me. I brought them up from the storage closet under the porch and they're really dusty."

"Sure! Let me put my things down and I'll be right there."

Thirty minutes later, Louise heard a knock at the door. She went to answer it and was delighted to find Finn standing there. She invited him in and brought him to the kitchen.

"See here, Nana. I've brought reinforcements. Finn tells me he's mighty good at drying jars."

So, Louise stood at the sink, her hands elbow deep in soapy water. Beside her, Finn was making good use of a long linen dish towel, drying the jars Louise washed. Louise's grandmother Emily took the jars to the counter next to the stove. Then she dipped a cup into the strawberry jam mixture on the stove and ladled it carefully into the freshly washed jars. Finn then capped the jars and Louise gave the jars one last good wipe with a damp cloth. Emily set the jars in the window and wiped her hands. The jars gleamed ruby red with the sun's beams shining through them. Emily pulled one of them down and pressed it into Finn's hand.

"You take this, honey. It's real good on biscuits with butter."

Finn thanked her and set it on the table to take with him later. Emily handed him a small plate with a buttered biscuit slathered with the warm strawberry jam from one of the jars she'd just processed. Louise handed him a glass of milk and got one for herself and her grandmother. Then all three sat at the kitchen table enjoying biscuits and jam. When they'd eaten the last crumb, Emily shooed them into the living room while she cleaned up the plates and glasses.

"You all get on out of here," Emily told the pair. "I've got to collect all the scrap metal and rubber I can find for the drive this weekend. "

Louise and Finn went into the living room, sitting down on the green velvet sofa. The sun was still high in the sky and the breeze outside blew the bathing costumes hanging on the clothesline strung across the porch posts. Finn and Louise talked quietly about the weather, the jams sitting on the windowsill, and anything else to avoid mentioning the war. Finn reached to hold her hand and smiled at her. The moment was magical for Louise as she remembered the kisses they'd shared underneath the pier. Louise pulled him up and walked with him to the radio stand to open it. It was a handsome Philco in a walnut cabinet that stood about three feet tall. Arthur had bought it for his wife for the cottage and it was the delight of the family. Seated nightly around the floor or on the green velvet couch, the family heard Fibber McGee and Molly, or The Great Gildersleeve, or performances by Jack Benny or Bob Hope. Sadly, they also had heard the reports of the invasion of Poland, bringing news of the war into their own home. But today, Louise was looking for music. She turned the knob, waiting for the radio to warm up, then pushed one of the buttons and found Glenn Miller performing "In the Mood." She grabbed Finn by the hand and twirling around with him, said, "May I have this dance?"

"Now how in the world am I going to dance without stepping on those pretty little toes with my big size 12 feet?"

Nevertheless, Finn put his arm around Louise's tiny waist, held her small hand in his large one and began to do a simple fox trot around the living room. Emily came to the door from the kitchen and leaned

125

against the door frame, smiling. Finn saw her, winked at Louise and led Louise to the sofa. Then he held out his hand to Louise's grandmother, saying, "May I have this dance, Miss Emily?"

Emily accepted with joy and stepped lightly into the center of the room, still wearing her apron. Finn danced with her until the end of the song, holding her lightly as though she were his date at a ball. The song ended and Finn bowed a bit to Emily and then to Louise.

"You ladies are wonderful dancers," he said, looking at his wristwatch, but I'm afraid my commanding officer has the next dance. So I guess I better go."

"Thanks for the help today, Finn. I know who to call the next time I need some help drying dishes."

"Yes, ma'am, Miss Emily. I'll be glad to help. Louise, can you walk me out to my Jeep?"

Louise nodded and reminded him to get his jam jar from the kitchen. Finn picked up the jam jar, took her hand and together they walked out to the gravel parking area in front of the cottage. The sun was beginning to go down in the west and Louise knew reluctantly that it was time to say goodbye.

"Be sure to go in now and close your blackout curtains. I've got to do some spotting tonight and I don't want to see any light coming from this cottage."

This made Louise sad and she put her head on Finn's shoulder. A tear fell from her eye as she looked up at him. She worried every time she knew he was flying spotter planes.

"You be careful now, you hear?"

"Yes, ma'am. I will. Talk to you soon."

"I'll be waiting to hear from you. You'll call tomorrow? I'll worry if I don't hear from you," Louise said wistfully.

"Don't worry, honey. Wild horses or Adolph Hitler himself couldn't keep me from calling you. Now don't worry. Just remember about those blackout curtains."

He looked up at the cottage to make sure he had a little privacy, and then put his hands on Louise's shoulders, pulling her to his chest. He looked into her eyes and leaned down, turning his head slightly to meet her lips with his. Her arms went around Finn's shoulders as she yielded to his kiss. He brushed her lips once more with his and then sighed as he lifted his head. Pulling away from her reluctantly, he wrapped his arms around her and held her tenderly for a moment.

"Tomorrow," he said.

CHAPTER TWENTY - FIVE

1994

Della dressed carefully for her date with Luke. He'd called her that afternoon and told her that he'd pick her up at 5:30. The Howard's home was in Southern Shores in one of the flat top houses. Luke had asked his mother to prepare a meal for the four of them and she gladly agreed.

When 5:30 arrived, Luke pulled into the parking pad in front of Della's apartment, climbed the stairs and knocked on the door. Della had waited impatiently for his arrival, so she opened the door before he finished the second knock. Luke burst out laughing in surprise and then stopped himself, giving a long low whistle.

"Wow, you look gorgeous!" he said with a wink.

Della smoothed the skirt of her poplin dress. The blue flowers in the fabric matched perfectly the French blue of her flats. Her chestnut hair was tied back with a black grosgrain ribbon and she wore a simple silver bangle bracelet. She looked up at him coyly as he reached for her hand and drew her to him. He looked tenderly down at Della for a long moment.

"I know we haven't known each other long, but Della, I just can't help it. I'm falling in love with you."

Della was speechless for a minute, and then nodded her head up and down as a tear came to her eye. Luke wrapped his arms around Della's shoulders in a warm embrace. They stayed connected for a moment. Luke drew a stray hair from Della's eyes, and cupped her chin in his hand. Then Della, trying not to weep, drew back and looked up into his gray eyes.

"I know, Luke. I feel the same way."

"Hey, I didn't mean to make you cry. We've got to go meet my parents."

"I know. They're happy tears. Would it be ok if I just popped in to see Aunt Louise for a sec?"

"Of course, let's go."

"Let me just check myself one last time. Come on in for a minute."

Della looked in the mirror over her dresser to check her appearance. She wouldn't want to meet Luke's parents after an ugly cry. Then Luke reached for her hand, Della grabbed her straw clutch purse and they walked out the door together. Della turned to lock the door. Then they walked over the porch to Louise's cottage.

"Yoo hoo. It's me, Aunt Louise, and I've got Luke with me."

"Come on back here a minute, you two."

They walked back to Louise's den to find her sitting in her favorite chair with the television turned to ESPN. She reached up her hand to shake the hand of Luke, who leaned down to give her a peck on the cheek.

"How are you tonight, Miss Louise? Have you had your supper?"

"No, child, Roy and Maxine insisted on bringing over some chicken from that new place on the bypass road. Probably won't be fit to eat, but you know your parents, Della. They think I can't do a thing for myself. They should be here in a few minutes."

"Well, I'm glad you'll have some company, Aunt Louise. Luke here is taking me to meet his parents tonight. We're eating at their house."

"Well, y'all run along now. If I know May Howard, she's got a good meal planned for you. I'll see you later."

With that, Luke and Della kissed Louise, one on each side of her face, and said goodbye. Luke walked Della over to the passenger side of his car and settled her in. The weather was fair, with a light breeze and Della felt so good that she rolled the window down, not caring if her hair got a little mussed. Luke got in and started the engine. In a few minutes, he was pulling into the driveway of his parents' home on Ocean Boulevard. The house was one of several known as "flat tops" built north of Kitty Hawk in a subdivision called Southern Shores. The house was in a group of the original Frank Stick-designed houses constructed of cement blocks made from local beach sand. A cluster of similar flat-tops, as they came to be called were built with the first phase opening in 1946. Luke's parents had bought one of these original houses early in the 1990s as a vacation home for their family. When Luke's dad Sam bought and began managing the local movie house in 1985, they moved to Southern Shores fulltime.

As soon as Luke pulled into the narrow driveway of his parents' house, his mother May came out of the front door, wiping her hands on the faded calico apron she wore. She went immediately to Della and was followed by her husband Sam, and Matt and Gideon, Luke's brothers. Luke's dog Biscuit came bounding out, his tongue hanging from his mouth.

"Whoa, Mom, I thought you said it would be just the four of us. Why'd you invite these two clowns?"

"Now, Luke, they just showed up and I couldn't just turn them away, now could I? And look who else they brought," May said, as a petite redhead, Matt's wife, came out of the front door, her arms cradling an infant.

"Well, if Ann and the little butterbean are here, then I guess that's all right," Luke said, chuckling.

Matt and Gideon began punching Luke, one on each arm, laughter coming from all sides. Biscuit romped over to Della and gave her a big, sloppy kiss of welcome.

"Well, hey, Biscuit. I've missed you!"

Gideon whistled when he saw Della. "Wow, is this Della? You said she was gorgeous, Luke, but you undersold her by a lot. Look, Della, you are just slumming by hanging out with this loser," he said, pointing to Luke. "I can show you a much better time."

"Now, now, enough of that," May said. "Dinner's almost ready. You boys come in and set the table while Ann and Della and I get acquainted.

They entered the neat whitewashed house crossing under the extended overhang. The cerulean blue door and window shutters added a pop of color to the tan of the sands surrounding the house. Entering directly into the living room, a large room with ten-foot ceilings, Della was drawn to the window wall, facing the Atlantic Ocean and the brick fireplace on the western wall. A large kitchen which Sam and May had recently upgraded with the addition of a

Wolf Stove and Sub Zero refrigerator was on the north side of the living room. They'd replaced the Formica countertops with white quartz. Four bedrooms and two bathrooms were south of the living room.

May sat on the sofa which sat perpendicular to the fireplace and patted a spot next to her.

"Come sit here, Della. I want to hear all about what you're doing with Miss Louise's bookshop. Luke tells me it's gonna be beautiful."

"Yes, ma'am, I hope we'll be able to open soon. I haven't even shown Aunt Louise yet. She's been a little frail. But Luke has been a tremendous help to me."

Ann emerged from one of the bedrooms where she'd been changing her daughter Grace and feeding her. But the noise level from the kitchen was keeping the baby awake. The three brothers and their father were setting the table haphazardly while popping each other with dish towels. May rolled her eyes heavenward in a look of surrender.

"There, you see, Della, what I have to put up with? And Sam Howard, you're no better!"

"I think it's wonderful, Mrs. Howard. I grew up as an only child so I love all this commotion."

"Luke said you were a keeper."

Finally the three sons appeared in the living room, white towels draped over their arms. They announced in an absurdly formal manner that 'Dinner was served!' Each of the men took their "dates" to the kitchen table on their arms. Gideon, not having a date, took his niece from Ann's arms and claimed her as his plus one for the evening!

As they stood around the table, Sam offered the blessing, and then told everyone to find a seat. The dinner, an informal meal of a Southern low country boil consisting of smoked pork sausage, corn on the cob, shrimp and boiled potatoes, was loud and raucous and, in Della's opinion, perfectly delightful. After the meal everyone, except Ann, who'd gone into a bedroom to nurse little Grace, went outside to watch the moon come out over the ocean. The tide was particularly calm that night and the air was still. Luke put his arm around Della's shoulders and hugged her. He kissed the top of her head softly whispering 'I'm glad you came.' Della looked up at him, her eyes gleaming, and whispered a silent 'me too.' At the end of the evening, Sam and May gave Della a big hug and told her to "come back real soon."

Luke took Della's hand and walked her out to his car, for the trip back to Della's apartment. When Luke drove into the packed gravel of the parking pad of the cottage, he stilled the engine of his car and drew Della to him.

"You're wonderful, Della. I hope you're planning to become a permanent beach girl. I don't think I could take it if you went back to Raleigh."

"I don't think there's a chance of that now. I've fallen in love with your family."

He kissed her, his lips warm and soft and fitting perfectly with hers. Then he opened the car door and went around to Della's side, helping her out of his car.

"Tonight was wonderful, Luke. I hope I can see your family again real soon. Call me?"

"I will and I know the family wants to see you again. They loved you. I could tell. I might even drop by the shop tomorrow during lunch to make sure you're not slacking off."

"I'd love that," Della said as she walked up the stairs. Luke ran up the steps after her, gave her another quick peck on her cheek, turned and jumped off the porch, pumping his fist in the air.

CHAPTER TWENTY - SIX

1994

Della listened to the morning weather report on the radio and realized it was going to be a hot one. She looked out of the window in her bedroom and saw the sun trying to come out. She knew that meant rain was possible later in the day. Stepping out onto her porch to confirm what she'd heard on the radio, Della quickly went back inside. It was going to be warm and humid, so Della reached in her dresser for a pair of cotton shorts and a sleeveless tee shirt. She showered and dressed, and then fixed a boiled egg and coffee for her breakfast. After washing up her few dishes, she kicked off her flip flops and walked barefoot across the porch to check on her Aunt Louise.

She knocked on the door and walked into the front hall, calling "Hey Aunt Louise! It's your boarder!"

There was no answer and a little twinge of worry made its way into Della's heart. She walked through the cottage and onto the back porch. There was no sign of Aunt Louise anywhere and the worry spot grew in the back of her brain. So Della walked down the back steps and through the sea oats scattered on the dune separating

Louise's cottage from the ocean. When she topped the dune, a smile came to her face.

"There you are!" Della said, spotting her aunt. It was low tide and Louise was walking barefoot in the shallow water. "Have you had your breakfast?"

"Child, I've been up since dawn. Had some bacon and grits about an hour ago. I've just been enjoying getting my toes in the water."

"That's good. I should have come over to eat with you! All I had was a boiled egg and coffee. Hey, I'm getting ready to head over to the shop and wondered if you wanted to come along. You haven't seen what I've done so far and I thought you might have some ideas for changes."

"Just let me get some shoes on and I'll be ready."

"OK. I've got to get my shoes on too. When you're ready, come on out to the car and I'll drive you."

"Now listen, Della, the shop is just a couple of blocks away. Don't treat me like an old woman. I could use the exercise. Let's walk."

So that's what they did. After both women got on walking shoes, they strolled to the shop. Louise carried a walking stick just in case, but only used it when she stepped off a curb. When they first saw the bookshop's exterior, Louise gasped. Della's first thought was that her great aunt didn't like what she'd done.

"Oh, Aunt Louise, if you don't like it, I can change the paint colors. I can change anything you don't like."

"Honey, I just can't believe how beautiful it looks. It's the way it used to be when I opened the shop back in the forties. And those flowers – my mother always planted zinnias. They are the perfect flowers for the flower boxes. Now I just can't wait to see the inside."

Della told her that though the front exterior was finished, the inside was still a work in progress. She said she wanted to keep the Grapette sign on the side of the building so she had just cleaned the bricks there with a power washer she'd rented. Then she handed a key to her aunt. The key hung from a brass fob with "L. Gates Bookseller" engraved on it.

"Where on earth did you get this?"

"I had them make it at the hardware store, Aunt Louise. I had the locks changed on the front and back doors so that it's really easy to open now. The wood was so swollen from the humidity that the door was always sticking. The locksmith shaved the door a bit. By the way, I made a copy of the key for me, too since I'm hoping my job is permanent," Della said, winking at her aunt. "Well, try your key. Let's go inside where it's cool. I've got the air conditioning turned down to the "frosty" setting!"

So Louise took another look at her shiny key and fob and, inserting it into the new Baldwin lock, she opened the door with ease. She marveled at its smooth operation, and then fell silent as she looked around the inside of the bookshop. It was her first visit inside in a few years and there had been quite a few changes. She walked around looking at the new table, the newly arranged bookshelves, and the floors. The wood beneath their feet had been polished and buffed so that it glowed.

"Well, I declare, Della. I declare," Louise repeated over and over as she walked around the shop.

"I hope that means you like what I've done so far."

"Child, I couldn't imagine this old place could ever look this good again. I'm not sure it ever looked this good."

Satisfied that her aunt was pleased with the progress so far, Della found a chair for her aunt and proceeded to tell her what her other ideas were for the shop. She pointed to the green velvet sofa, its tufted back missing a button and the arms a little frayed.

"I was thinking we could get this recovered if…"

But Della saw her aunt's smile fade and knew that was not a change that would happen.

"Della, honey, this sofa was in my cottage when I was a child. When I opened the bookshop, my parents told me I could have the sofa for the shop and my daddy helped me carry it down here and place it right there. I'd like to keep it just as it is, if that's ok with you."

"Aunt Louise, of course. This is your shop after all. In fact, it adds a little shabby chic to the place. I don't know what I was thinking."

Della moved over behind the counter and rested her hand on the top of the brass cash register. She hadn't gotten around to cleaning it yet so it was still quite tarnished and dusty.

"Now that old thing has got to go," Louise declared, pointing with her index finger at the cash register.

"Wait a minute, Aunt Louise. Luke's daddy told me about a local man, a Mr. Lester, who restores old equipment like this brass cash register. I think it would be beautiful and a real drawing card for the shop if we kept it. He's restoring the old telephone too. He's picking up the cash register when he brings back the telephone. It's going to be beautiful. "

"But the keys on the cash register only go up to $5.00!"

"I know, so we could just use it as a cash drawer and do all the computing on my laptop. By the way, we need to get you online here. We can really start to improve your sales if we get a website for your shop and do online sales. I can handle that for you, too."

Louise put her hand to her head and shook it. "You're in over my head now, girl. But if you think you can do that, go ahead."

Della was relieved to hear that as she'd already begun designing a webpage for the shop. And she'd begun accounting for all the books in the shop's inventory. It was going to make the shop so much more profitable – she was sure of it.

"Have you got some rags and Endust around here somewhere?" Louise asked. "This counter could use some work."

"Yes, I've been meaning to get around to that. Hang on. There's some back in the cleaning closet."

Della hurried back to the office and got the cleaning cloths and Endust. She gave them to Louise and cleared off the countertop. She stacked all of the papers, bills, and other things that were on top of the counter, then moved them to the stool behind the counter. Louise took the cleaning supplies and set to work on the counter. Soon the grain of the chestnut wood began to appear. Della got down on her knees and worked on polishing the scrollwork on the corners of the counter. When the two women finished, they stood back to look at their work.

"Just beautiful, Aunt Louise. This place is such a jewel box. I can't wait to open the shop again."

"It's really more beautiful than I remember. I have so many memories here. Having this place open and polished like this again is a dream come true."

Louise and Della then decided to work on straightening the desk in the office. Louise brought the Endust and cloths back to the office, and dusted the desk while Della went through the papers and cleaned the little brass lamp on the desk. Della looked around the office and noted once again the heavy bookcase against the wall. She'd tried since the first time she saw it to move the bookcase to dust behind it, but it was just too weighty.

Soon, Louise was tiring and ready to go back to her cottage. Luckily, Luke showed up at just that moment, calling Della on her cell phone to unlock the front door. He gave her a hug as he entered the shop looking around.

"You ladies have been busy this morning. That counter looks beautiful!"

"Thanks, we think it does too. We worked hard and I think Aunt Louise is exhausted. She was just leaving."

Luke had his car and insisted on driving Louise home. Walking her up to her porch door, he handed her the walking stick she'd almost left behind.

"Great to see you again, Miss Louise. You're looking good."

"Oh, go on with you. Thank you for the ride but I know you'd rather be down at the shop with Della. And I know for certain that she's hoping you'll come right back."

"OK, can I do anything for you before I go?"

"No, just get on back to the shop. That girl needs some help. "

Luke went down the steps, tossing a goodbye wave to Louise. He drove the few blocks back to the shop, and went inside. Della walked over to him reaching out for his hand.

"Does this mean you're back to help me?" Della asked. "You know those two window display areas need to be dusted."

Luke drew Della into an embrace and they sank down onto the green velvet couch. "Well, I can be persuaded, if the pay is right."

Della's face was creased in a huge smile as she handed Luke a can of Endust and a clean dust cloth.

"Dust first. Pay later," she said with a wink and a smile.

CHAPTER TWENTY - SEVEN

1942

The gray skies overhead cleared the beaches of any sunbathers. The dark clouds above threatened a summer rainstorm, but Louise still had to work. So she dressed in her uniform, a blue striped cotton shift with white collar and banding around the short sleeves. She tucked a white handkerchief in the breast pocket and tied her white apron around her trim waist, skipping downstairs and humming a little tune.

Outside the wind whipped the sand into little whirlpools and a few drops of rain began to fall. The telephone in the living room began to jangle, its clatter disturbing the peace of the morning. Louise called to her grandparents that she'd answer it and she ran to pick up the receiver.

"Hello?"

"May I speak to Miss Louise Gates?"

"This is she."

"Hey, Louise, this is Finn. How are you this morning?"

"Good! I'm just about to go to work. Are you on duty today?"

Finn told her he was working up by the pier this morning and asked if she needed a ride to work. Yes, indeed, she told him, looking out the screen door. The rain was already beginning to fall. That would be great, she thought, and would give her a little more time for breakfast. Agreeing on a time for pick-up, Louise thanked Finn again and hung up the phone. Sitting at the kitchen table, she poured herself a bowl of Rice Krispies and poured a little milk in the bowl. Her grandmother, who was at the kitchen sink, picked up the percolator, pouring Louise a cup of coffee. She added some sugar and cream and stirred the cup. Emily Hudson poured a cup of coffee for herself and sat down beside her granddaughter.

"Thanks, Nana. Yum! That's good coffee. Oh, by the way, Finn is picking me up for work this morning since it's raining."

"Well, this sounds like it's getting serious. You've been seeing quite a lot of him, haven't you?" As Louise blushed and nodded, Emily said, "Don't worry, honey. I like him too," her grandmother said, reaching her hand over to give Louise's arm a squeeze.

"How long are you working today, child?"

"Just the morning shift, Nana. I hope Finn will have some time off this afternoon. I'll let you know."

Louise picked up her dishes to take them to the sink, but Emily put her hands on her granddaughter's arm. Louise thanked her and handed the dishes to her grandmother, rushing up to brush her teeth. A few moments later, she came down the stairs, her sweater on her arm. Just then Louise heard a knock at the door and jumped to answer it. Finn stood there on the porch, his cap in both hands and a big smile on his face. Louise had to stop herself from swooning at his blonde hair and dimpled cheeks.

"You ready to go?"

143

"Yes, just let me grab my pocketbook and say goodbye to my grandmother."

Emily had taken her coffee on to the porch where she was sitting next to her husband. Louise kissed them both hurriedly and told them that she was off for work. Then she rushed to the porch and Finn took her by the hand.

"You know, I'm off duty after 1:00. Would you like to play some duck pins at the Casino? It's pretty tame there during the day."

"That sounds like fun. I get off after the lunch rush – about 2:00 so I'll come home and change, unless you want to bowl with a girl in a blue waitress uniform!"

"Louise, I'd bowl with you, no matter what you wore," Finn said waggling his eyebrows like Groucho Marx.

"I keep forgetting to return your handkerchief that you loaned me," Louise told him. "I've washed and pressed it. The linen is so beautiful with your initials and anchor worked in blue thread."

"You keep it to remember me by," Finn told her with a smile.

Louise knew that she could never forget him and told him so. Finn helped her into his Jeep, holding an umbrella over her head as they walked from the porch. Fortunately, Finn had pulled the canvas top up on the Jeep so they stayed dry. Too soon, they reached the pier and Louise stepped down from the Jeep. Finn reached for her hand and gave it a tiny squeeze which he held for a minute. Telling her he'd pick her up at the cottage around 3:00, he backed out of the parking lot and drove off to his work site, throwing his hand up in a goodbye. Louise scurried into the café, not even feeling the rain on her face or the smile that appeared there.

The morning sped along for Louise as the café was quite busy. Her tables were always popular because Louise was such a friendly girl. She collected a few tips from each of her diners which she pocketed, earmarking them for a special project which she had in mind.

Finn, meanwhile, was checking some empty houses along the shoreline. Dirty lace curtains billowed out from broken glass window panes in each of them. A front window in one of the houses had a silk banner with a gold star displayed prominently. It had been partially destroyed in a hurricane the previous year, and the Coast Guard was checking the empty houses periodically to make sure there was nothing out of the ordinary there. He noted that one of the houses contained some empty sardine cans and Coke bottles, but he chalked that up to vagrants. Nevertheless, he planned to continue his surveillance of the houses to make sure they were not being used for spying. Finishing his survey, Finn returned to the pier, eager to see Louise again. He pulled his Jeep into the pier's parking area and stilled the motor. Hopping out, he went into the café, but found that Louise had already left for home. Her father had come home early from his work in Norfolk and picked her up. So, he returned to the Coast Guard station to get ready for his date at the Nags Head Casino.

The Casino was a two-story white wooden building that had been built on the road along the ocean in the 1930s in front of Jockey's Ridge. A large sign attached to the front advertised "Casino" and 24 windows with shutters that propped open were on each side of the building. Parked all over the sandy parking lot were cars of every description – Fords, Packards, and Hudsons as well as lots of Jeeps. The building had started out its life as a dormitory for the stone workers who built the Wright Brothers Memorial. Later it became housing for the transient labor camp known during the Depression as Camp Kitty Hawk. In 1937, the building was purchased and turned into an entertainment center that drew thousands of beach-goers. The family-friendly downstairs had duckpin bowling, pinball machines and pool tables. A small snack bar served up hot dogs, burgers and soft drinks. Upstairs the music and dancing (in bare feet) to big names like Artie Shaw and Tommy Dorsey attracted more of an adult crowd, especially the military men who were stationed nearby.

Finn picked up Louise at her home and drove the short distance to the casino, parking the Jeep on the sandy concrete parking pad. The rain had ceased and the sun was still high in the sky making it warm and humid. Inside, Vera Lynn was singing "We'll Meet Again" on the brightly colored jukebox. Finn paid fifty cents to enter (girls got in free) and twenty cents for two Duck Pins games at the front counter. He asked Louise if she wanted to rent shoes. Since she wore bobby socks with her saddle oxford shoes, she told Finn to save his dime. So both Finn and Louise took off their shoes and bowled a game in their socks. Finn won the game, but Louise scored the only strike in the game in the last frame. When all ten pins fell down at once, she shrieked and jumped into Finn's arms.

"I've never done that before," she cried. Finn spun her around and the teens in the next lane clapped loudly for her. Finn impulsively kissed her full on the lips and Louise blushed bright red.

After the game, they put on their shoes, walked over to the snack bar and ordered two limeades, perching on the revolving blue leather stools at the counter. Finn reached over and put his big hand over her smaller one. On the jukebox, Vera Lynn was singing "The White Cliffs of Dover."

"My shift starts in a little over an hour, so I need to get back to the Coast Guard Station. I am beginning to hate every minute I'm away from you. I've never been in love before, but I am falling hard for you."

"Finn, I thought this summer was going to be so boring, living with my grandparents and parents. But meeting you in the café has brightened my life so much. I'm beginning to fall in love with you, too.

Finn fished a dollar bill out of his back pocket and threw it on the counter, saying thanks to the waitress. He put his arm around Louise's shoulder and suggested they go for a walk on the beach before he had to drop her back at the cottage. Louise felt a stirring within as the warmth of Finn's arm surrounded her. They crossed the road, took off their shoes and socks and stepped into the sand. It was still warm from the bright sun, and felt good on their feet. They walked slowly down to the water's edge and dipped their toes in the cool surf, rushing backwards when the water threatened to drench their clothes. A few clouds sailed across the lavender sky and the moon appeared low on the horizon. They stood looking up at the first stars beginning to appear.

"We better go," Finn said. "It's almost time to close the blackout curtains. But I want to see you tomorrow. I want to give you that gift I've promised you."

Louise shaded her eyes from the sun and looked into Finn's eyes. "I can't wait, "she said.

Finn pulled her into his arms, looking deep into her eyes. He encircled her shoulders with his arms and held her in a warm embrace. No words were spoken. None were needed. They looked once more at the sky. Louise pointed upward – a shooting star! Then lots of shooting stars!

"It's the Perseid Meteor Shower," Luke told her. It puts on quite a show every year about this time. I like to think it's a little gift from God, just for us."

Louise savored the slightly salty taste of Finn's skin as she reached up to kiss his cheek. She ran her fingers through his blonde hair and felt protected by his broad shoulders as they wrapped around her. He put his hand gently on Louise's face, as though she were made of tissue paper.

"You're so beautiful," he said as the gathering wind caught a lock of her hair setting it free. He pushed it behind her ear after kissing it. Louise looked up into Finn's sunburned face and wanted to disagree, but his lips on hers stopped her words. He pulled away from her and pointed up at the shooting stars again.

"You see? It's a sign. We were meant to be together. Every time I see a shooting star from now on, I'll think of this moment and of you, Louise."

Catching her hand up in his, they ran back to the Jeep, trying to beat the dusk.

CHAPTER TWENTY - EIGHT

1994

The work on the display area under the front windows of the bookshop was continuing apace, but was interrupted by a knock at the door. Luke said he'd get it and walked to answer the door.

"Is Miss Della Gates here?" said a familiar voice.

No, it can't be, Della thought. *What is he doing here?*

In fact, it was Dylan Metcalfe, Della's former fiancé, the one she'd left behind in Raleigh in the job she had at Colony Books. He was accompanied by his new assistant Astrid Olsen who'd taken Della and Louise out for a meal earlier. Dylan rushed to Della's side and took her into his arms. He planted a warm kiss on Della's cheek, and then held her at arm's length to admire her. Luke and Astrid looked on in surprise as Della scrambled to find words.

"Della, honey, this coastal life agrees with you. You're radiant! You've had a great vacation but I have missed you so much. You're not actually going to stay here, are you? I've talked to the company president and gotten a job for you, a promotion really, from your previous job."

Della was stunned into silence, as the last time she'd seen Dylan, he was cuddling up to a stunning redhead in a restaurant. She didn't know what to say, so she turned to Luke and said, "Luke, this is Dylan Metcalfe, my fia…my former fiancé. And this is his new assistant Astrid Olsen."

"Nice to make your acquaintance," Luke stammered, clearly ill at ease. "I've got to be going. My shift at the firehouse starts soon."

"Oh Luke, do you really have to go?" Della said to the back of his hurriedly retreating form. Without looking, Luke waved his hand goodbye, closing the door behind him.

Dylan looked around the shop with delight. Astrid had told him about the condition of the shop from her previous visit to the Outer Banks, so Dylan was not expecting to see much. But this renovation was clearly going to be a success. He walked around the shop, looking intently at the shelves, the table, the counter with the antique cash register and finally the sofa.

"Della, you're amazing! This shop has so much charm. You've made it both homey and welcoming. I can easily see it becoming a part of our Colony Books chain. I wouldn't change a thing, except maybe recover the couch."

"Well, you see, my aunt…"

"Oh yes, your Aunt Louise. Astrid told me all about her. She's what – about 95 now? I'd love to meet her and talk about my thoughts for the shop."

"That's probably not going to be possible just now, Dylan. She's recovering from a heart spell and doesn't see many visitors."

"Dylan," Astrid interrupted, "Why don't we take Della out for some dinner as you planned?"

"That's an excellent idea, Astrid. How about Owens' Restaurant? I'm in the mood for some seafood."

Della was hesitant to go out with Dylan even with Astrid along. He'd hurt her so much but some small part of her was curious about why he was here. So she reluctantly agreed to go out for dinner with Dylan and Astrid.

The two visitors told Della they'd see her in one hour and said they'd pick her up at her apartment at 5:30 to beat the tourist crowds. Della said that a ride was unnecessary but they insisted and left her alone in the bookshop.

She sat down on the green sofa remembering the look in Luke's eyes when he realized that Dylan was here to see her. The thing between them was so new that she wasn't sure if he was angry or sad or confused. She wasn't even sure about her own feelings.

Thirty minutes after leaving the bookshop, Luke went back to the fire station. Though he was not due to be on duty until the next day, he decided to pick up an extra shift, relieving the woman who was to have been on duty. He went to the kitchen to get a bowl of chili which the station's cook had made earlier. He sat at the table, poured himself a glass of sweet tea and took a few bites of chili, but his taste for it was gone. Somehow, he'd lost his appetite. Thinking of Dylan Metcalfe and how he had just waltzed back into Della's life with no apology whatsoever made him furious. He drained the glass of tea and took the remains of the chili back to the sink.

At that moment, the alarm went off in the station indicating an emergency nearby. Luke and two other firefighters suited up and jumped on the back of the truck. Spring winds had stirred up a small fire which had been reported in one of the storage sheds behind one of the old oceanfront cottages. The breeze off the ocean threatened to send the fire over to the cottage and the owner was frantic.

Luke and the other firefighters rushed to the scene, parked, and unrolled the hose from their tanker truck. The other two firemen trained the hose nozzle on the shed while Luke ran around the building looking to see if there were any people inside. Suddenly, the old woman who owned the cottage ran out from her house grabbing Luke by the arm.

"My grandmother's sewing machine is in there. It's all I have left from her and I was restoring it. Can you save it?" the woman screamed, tears flowing down her cheeks.

"Get back!" Luke yelled. "Get back! I'll see what I can find."

Luke began looking for the source of the fire while the men on the hose kept the water trained on the building's doorway. He checked the stability of the shed and, finding it still viable, Luke reached out his hands in their fireproof gloves, pulling the door open and looking around. Spotting a gas can near some rags, he directed the firemen to train their hoses in that area. In the back of the small shed, he spotted the treadle sewing machine, partly covered by a tarp. Looking overhead for signs of burning timbers, Luke hurried into the shed and picked up the sewing machine, its bulk difficult to handle with his heavy jacket and gloves. He was nearly to the door when he heard one of the firemen yell.

"Look out, Luke. Get out of there."

One of the ceiling beams which had been smoldering, had burst into flame and cracked in two, sending sparks onto Luke's back. Fortunately his self-contained breathing apparatus allowed him to breathe clear oxygen, and he was able to escape the falling beam and deposit the sewing machine safely outside the shed. He went back into the shed to check for further hot spots and was turning around when all of a sudden, the right wall of the shed collapsed, knocking Luke to the ground.

"Luke, Luke, you all right, man? Luke! " the other firemen called out but there was no response. Luke lay on the shed floor, the burning wall of the shed on top of him.

CHAPTER TWENTY - NINE

1994

Della walked back to the cottage to change for her dinner with Dylan and Astrid. The sun was bearing down on her shoulders and the humidity was rising. She would like to have worn the shorts and sleeveless tee shirt she had on, but supposed that wouldn't be right. So, looking into her closet, she selected an olive khaki skirt, a white blouse and tan sandals. She laid them carefully on her bed, then took off her clothes and stepped into her shower stall, drawing the curtain. The lukewarm water felt soothing on her tired body and she lathered her hair and body. Ten minutes later, she stepped out refreshed and toweled off. She debated drying her hair, but thought better of it when she saw the time. So she dressed hurriedly, and pulled her hair into a high ponytail. She dabbed a little lip gloss on but decided against any other make-up. She didn't want to make Dylan think she was trying to interest him.

Fastening her wristwatch on her arm, Della looked outside and saw Dylan's car pull into the parking pad outside her apartment. It was an SUV, obviously rented, quite different from the flashy sports cars Dylan preferred. She grabbed her cross body bag and put it over her head, then moved to open the door before Dylan or Astrid could knock.

Best to get this over with, she thought.

Dylan was standing on her porch admiring the view of the ocean that he spied between the cottages. Astrid was on her phone, checking the reservation at the restaurant.

"Hey, girl," Dylan said, his broad smile not quite reaching his eyes. "Are you sure your aunt can't join us. I'd love to meet her. Astrid told me what a nice lady she is."

"No, Dylan, she's not up for visitors. But if you don't mind, I'll just pop in to her house to let her know I'm leaving."

"Sure, sure!"

Della walked across the porch and let herself in, calling her usual "Yoo hoo, Aunt Louise." Louise was sitting in her living room, and paging sleepily through one of the magazines Della had brought her the day before. Outside, the breeze was beginning to kick up, predicting the rain that was to come. Della went over to her aunt's chair to say hello.

"Aunt Louise, I'm going out for dinner and I'm going to bring you back something. I should be back in an hour or so. "

"That's nice, sugar. You going out with Luke?"

A blush came to Della's face as she admitted that she was going out with Dylan and Astrid.

"Dylan came to the shop unexpectedly this afternoon and asked me to go out to dinner. Astrid is with him. Remember her? She took us out to the Oasis the other day."

Louise shook her head and closed her eyes. "The girl seemed OK but why in the world do you want to hang around with that rascal? After what he did to you?"

"It's just dinner, Aunt Louise. Don't worry. Now what can I bring you? We're going to Owens' Restaurant."

"Hmmmph! That's mighty fancy dining for a middle of the week meal. "

Nevertheless, Louise ordered the seafood platter and Della kissed her on her cheek. She went out to the car, telling Dylan and Astrid that she needed to be back soon to bring her aunt her supper. They drove the short distance to the restaurant in Nags Head and got out. The restaurant's gray-shingled exterior was bathed in sunlight and a delicious fragrance was emanating from the kitchen. They walked in, waiting for their eyes to adjust to the dark wood interior. Dylan directed them to a table in front of a huge ship model of the *Cutty Sark*.

Della hated to admit it, but it was an elegant place to eat. She was looking forward to the chic dining experience. The restaurant was sheathed inside with large heart pine walls now playing host to well-dressed diners from up and down the Outer Banks. All around the restaurant's interior, memorabilia from the Outer Banks was scattered or hung. Documents, maps, spyglasses and other items from the North Carolina Life Saving Stations, the precursor of the Coast Guard, filled display cases all around the entrance to the restaurant.

Dylan pulled out Della's chair offering her the view of other diners. The tables were covered with white linen tablecloths and polished silver. A waiter came to the table bringing a glass bottle of water so cold that condensation had formed on the outside. The waiter wrapped the bottle in a white linen napkin and poured water for each of them into cobalt blue glasses. He took their drink orders and went to the kitchen, promising to return soon.

"This place is kind of expensive, Dylan. I've never been here."

"Don't worry, Della. It's all going on the expense account. I read a review of it last night and it looks fabulous. And it's great to get the gang back together again."

Della sipped from her glass, set it down and said," Well, if you recall, Dylan, you kind of broke up that gang a few months ago."

"Oh, let's not talk about that now. I just want to enjoy a good seafood dinner with you and Astrid. She saw this place when she was here before and told me about it."

So the trio ordered from the elaborate menu. Dylan and Astrid opted for the pan-seared sea scallops with vegetable risotto while Della selected the sautéed shrimp and fried green tomatoes. The conversation was light and meaningless as they ate the delicious meal. Afterwards, Dylan insisted that they order a slice each of chocolate chess pie and coffee while they waited for Della's to-go order.

After dessert, Dylan paid the bill with his platinum American Express card. Della noted that Dylan had not left a tip, but saw Astrid go back to the table and place a fifty dollar bill under her plate. Della accepted the bagged dinner for her aunt and thanked Dylan and Astrid for the meal.

On the car ride back, Dylan insisted that Astrid drive so that he could talk to Della in the back seat. "You know, I've really missed being with you, Della. I was such an idiot to have dinner with Sharon. It was just dinner. And I can't believe what you've done with your aunt's shop. It's a treasure and so unique. I'd love to make it a part of the Colony Books chain."

Astrid pulled the car into the parking pad and Dylan got out opening Della's door. He walked her up the steps to her apartment while Astrid waited in the car.

"I hope you'll consider talking with your aunt about selling her shop to Colony Books. And I hope you'll consider giving me another chance. I mean it, Della. I've really missed you. I was an idiot."

He took Della in his arms and held her close to his chest. In a kind of muscle memory, Della remembered what it had felt like to be in Dylan's arms, and her resistance was lowered. Dylan looked into her eyes, the long lashes over his green eyes reminding her of kisses past. He leaned in and pressed a kiss gently on her lips.

"I've got to go in, Dylan. Aunt Louise will want her supper. I'll talk to her and get back to you."

Dylan put his hand tenderly on her chin and pulled her to him for one last, soft kiss. "I'll count on that," he said.

CHAPTER THIRTY

1942

The morning seemed to drag on forever at the Pier Café. Louise had gotten a ride to her job with her dad who had to be in Norfolk early. She practically sleepwalked through her shift as she daydreamed of seeing Finn that afternoon. Once, while cleaning off a table, she dropped a water glass which shattered into pieces. She looked up sheepishly at her boss and cleaned it up, apologizing and offering to pay. Marge said that wasn't necessary and Louise tried to focus more on her job for the rest of the shift.

Finally, the end of her morning shift arrived and she checked to make sure all her tables were clean. She refilled the salt and pepper shakers and cleaned the tops of the mustard and ketchup bottles. She wrapped enough utensils in napkins for the next day's rush and then told her boss good afternoon.

Her father Miles Gates had just driven down from his job in Norfolk and picked up Louise for the drive back to the cottage. Once there, Louise gave her parents and grandparents a quick hello, and then dashed to the shower for a hasty shampoo.

Someday, she thought, *we'll have an indoor shower and I won't have to take my showers under the porch.*

Nevertheless, it felt good to be clean and wash off the smells of the grill. She dabbed herself with dusting powder and threw on her robe for the walk upstairs.

In her bedroom, Louise selected a black and white polka dot day dress with a white collar. She liked this dress because the buttons down the front were bright red and the skirt was cut on the bias, making it swirl as she walked. She decided not to try to ink a seam along the back of her legs but wore a pair of spectator pumps. She called to her mother to ask to borrow a splash of her "Evening in Paris," and then rolled her glossy brown hair into a tight roll across the nape of her neck. She pinched her cheeks, looked in the mirror, and then skipped downstairs to await her caller.

She sat on the green velvet sofa and chatted for a few minutes with her parents and grandparents. She told them Finn was taking her out for an early dinner at a restaurant called Sammy's and then she'd be back before curfew, of course.

A moment later a knock was heard on the door and Louise flitted through the hallway to answer it. She opened the door and saw Finn there on the porch, looking more handsome than ever. She invited him in to speak to her parents and grandparents before they were to leave. They went into the family room where everyone greeted Finn, shaking his hand and smiling. Finn seemed at home with Louise's family, and it showed in his demeanor. Then it was time to go. Louise smiled up at Finn and took the arm he offered, calling goodbye to her family. They walked down the steps to Finn's Jeep and got in for the brief ride to the restaurant, which was situated across the road from the ocean. But no houses were in front of the restaurant so there was a perfect view of the Atlantic Ocean from most of the tables in the restaurant. Finn had called ahead to ask for a table with a view. He wanted the evening to be perfect.

Once inside the restaurant, Finn and Louise were seated by the hostess at the table he requested and given menus. A waitress soon took their orders and they decided on fried flounder, French fries and slaw, passing the menus back to the waitress. Finn reached over and put his large hand over Louise's smaller one. He smiled at her and brought her hand up to his lips. They made small talk as the waitress set small glasses of ice water on the table along with napkin-wrapped utensils.

"Louise, I know we haven't known each other all that long. But it seems that things have speeded up since the war began. And I've never felt about anyone the way I feel about you. I've wanted to..."

But just at that moment, the waitress returned bringing a tray with their meals and glasses of Coca Cola. Finn cleared his throat and thanked the waitress. He looked at Louise and grinned in a self-conscious way.

"Let's eat," he said. "We can finish what we started after..."

The meal was delicious and the two ate heartily, laughing and talking practically non-stop. Soon the waitress brought the check and set it down on the table. Louise felt she'd never been happier and Finn looked at her with love in his eyes. He picked up the check and stood up. Moving behind Louise's chair, he pulled it out and helped her up. After paying the bill and adding a tip for the wait staff, Finn put his wallet in his back pocket and put his arm around Louise's shoulder, guiding her through the door to the Jeep. But instead of getting in the vehicle, they walked across the road to the sand above the beach.

The sun was setting behind the restaurant and "lights out after dark" was the rule on the beach, so Finn knew their time together was brief. Finn and Louise stopped at the edge of the road and quickly took off their shoes. They walked carefully across the still-warm road and onto the beach, Finn pointing out the moon appearing low in the sky. The stars that were just beginning to appear in the sky overhead cast a faint glow on the sands below.

Stopping near the water's edge, he put his arm around Louise's shoulder and drew her to him in a warm embrace. Reaching his hand to her face, he stroked her velvety skin with his thumb. He moved his hand from around her shoulder to caress the back of her neck. Louise's pulse quickened as Finn enfolded her in his strong arms. A sigh of contentment escaped his lips and he reached his hand up to caress her hair.

"I'll have to get you back to your folks in just a minute, Louise. But I had to tell you how much our time together has meant to me these last few weeks. I don't know what the future holds for me, and I know you could do a lot better than me. But I've fallen in love with you and I have to ask you, will you marry me? Would you wait for me in case I am sent to another base?"

Louise's mouth dropped open and a smile came to her face. She reached her palm up to Finn's jaw, his five o'clock shadow beginning to appear. She closed her eyes and put her head on Finn's shoulder, then looked up at him again.

"Oh yes, Finn. I'll marry you. And I'll wait for you forever if it takes it. I love you too."

"And can I kiss you," he asked, smiling, "to seal the deal?"

Wordlessly, Louise reached up to meet Finn's lips with hers. Finn grasped her shoulders with his hands, and then wrapped his arms around her.

"I'd better get you back – it's almost dusk. But you've made me the happiest man on earth. I guess I better talk to your father soon."

They walked back to the Jeep and put their shoes back on. Finn reached behind the seat telling Louise he had something for her. Pulling out a package wrapped in brown paper and tied with string, he handed it to Louise. She unwrapped it carefully to find a box of Cracker Jacks atop billowing folds of white silk fabric. Pinned to the silk was a note which read, "Will you marry me?"

"I know silk is hard to come by these days. Maybe you can make a wedding dress out of this parachute," Finn told her tenderly. "And check the inside of the Cracker Jacks."

Louise opened the Cracker Jacks box and pulled out the prize wrapped in paper. She ripped the paper open to find a toy ring with a fake diamond. Finn took it from her and slipped it on her finger, promising to replace it with the real thing as soon as he got his next paycheck. As she hugged the fabric to her breast, Louise pulled Finn to her for another kiss. He stroked her hair tenderly and gave her a deep kiss.

"Oh yes, Finn," Louise told him. "This will make a beautiful dress."

The Jeep motor roared to a start and the two were on the road, racing to beat the moon, their hearts light and happy.

CHAPTER THIRTY ONE

1994

It was the day after her dinner with Dylan and Astrid. Della had decided to work at the shop to take her mind off the decisions facing her. So she walked to the shop, looking between the houses she passed at the ocean beyond. She was glad the bookshop was on the opposite side of Beach Road from the ocean side. The Outer Banks occasionally was host to hurricanes, and nor'easters that wreaked havoc with buildings built oceanfront. But, thoughts of storms and worry over Dylan flew right out of her head as she came in view of the bookshop.

The store was perfectly charming with its fresh paint and flowers in the flower boxes. Della had brought some brass polish with her and planned to work on the door handle. She hadn't gotten around to it after polishing the name plaque above the door. She unlocked the door and tossed her backpack behind the counter, then picked up a rag and a tub of brass polish. She went back out the door and then came in for a stool from the storage closet. She set the stool up in front of the door and began rubbing the polish on the door handle. Soon it bore a shine as bright as the plaque above which caught the rays of the sun rising in the east.

But the work of her hands did nothing to dispel the worry in her mind. Della was confused. She hadn't heard from Luke since he'd left the shop when Dylan came in. She wondered if he was angry because he'd seen Dylan giving her a kiss. She had to admit to herself that Dylan's kiss was nice. It reminded her of happier times with him before the breakup. And the mention of a promotion at Colony Books would mean quite a lot more in her paycheck. The Colony Books office in downtown Raleigh was in the finest, newest office tower in the capital city. Dylan had promised her a corner office and a territory to supervise that would include the states of Georgia, South Carolina, North Carolina and Virginia with the promise of more if the bottom line was good at the end of the fiscal year. That was a lot to consider.

But weighing the other side of the scales, she looked at the bookshop she'd begun updating. She'd gotten such a sense of accomplishment from each change she'd made. Already the people in the town of Nags Head were beginning to talk about the bookshop with excitement. Della was sure she could feel a buzz whenever people talked to her about her progress. And she'd gotten so comfortable living in Aunt Louise's cottage. The apartment was small but it had everything she needed. The nearness of the ocean to her door brought comfort and peace. It was hard to think about giving all this up. Della shook her head as though to clear it of cobwebs, picked up the stool and tub of polish and went back inside.

Soon the bell over the door jangled and Della went to answer the door, hoping it was Luke. But at the door stood Mr. Lester, the local Mr. Fix-it. Della had taken him the old telephone that had been in the shop for ages to see if it could be restored. Mr. Lester had been excited to try his hand at it and Della had hoped it would add a touch of nostalgia to the shop. He came in at her invitation and set a box down on the counter, pausing to look around.

"You've got this place looking really nice, Della. When you fixin' to open?"

"Soon, I hope, Mr. Lester. Were you able to fix the telephone?" she said eagerly.

He pulled the old black desk telephone with its cloth-covered cord out of the box. He patted it gently and smiled, handing Della his bill.

"What I love most about this phone is the great RRRING It will make. It's called a Model 302 desk telephone and was first introduced in 1937. Once the war started, they weren't able to make these in the metal housing, so this is a rarity."

"Oh, Mr. Lester, It's wonderful. Let's plug it in and see if it works."

OK, now hold your horses, girl. Let me tell you what I did. I took the dial off, cleaned, lubed and timed it. The outer edge of the dial has been stripped and repainted with a gloss black. Unless the dial is removed, this is something you will rarely ever even see, but this is how it would have come from the factory. The number plate has been cleaned. Louise Gates will think she's got a brand new phone!"

"Oh, and look at the cord. It looks brand new, Mr. Lester."

"That's because it is, Della. I put a brown cloth cord on it, because that was what was on it originally. The old one was just too frayed. You can get a black cord if you want. I took the handset and base apart and cleaned everything thoroughly."

"Well, Mr. Lester, you are truly a wonder. I can't wait to show Aunt Louise. Now I was wondering if you wanted to try your hand at cleaning up this old cash register."

"Sure, I can give it a try."

"OK, why don't you take it out to your truck while I write you a check?"

The old gentleman picked up the cash register, which was actually lighter than it looked and took it out to his truck. Della handed him a check when he returned.

"When you bring that back, I'll pay you whatever it costs and you can pick out a few books on the house as my thank you."

"Now, I'll just take you up on that, Della. See you soon."

Della called her mother as soon as Mr. Lester left, to give the phone a test run. The handset was quite a bit heavier than she was used to, but oh, what style it had. After talking with Maxine for a bit, Della hung up the phone and gave it a swipe with the dusting cloth. Then she remembered what Dylan had offered and the kiss he'd given her. She wanted to see Luke – why hadn't he called? But she decided that she'd put all these thoughts aside for another time and set to work on the inside of the bookshop.

Della began opening a box of books she'd received in a UPS delivery. Della had bought a selection of classic books from a bookshop in New Jersey that was going out of business. She was eager to see what was inside the box.

She took a box cutter from behind the counter and slashed open the box, feeling a bit like it was Christmas morning. The first book she withdrew was *Moll Flanders*, followed by *Robinson Crusoe*, *Rebecca*, *Frankenstein* and *The Complete Works of Shakespeare*. A second box she opened contained a selection of children's books: *The Secret Garden*, *Peter Pan*, several *Nancy Drew* titles, *Anne of Green Gables* and the fairy tales of Hans Christian Andersen and the Brothers Grimm. Just what the children's section needed! That had always been her favorite section when she worked for Colony

Books. A warm feeling grew in Della's heart as she imagined sharing these books with her customers. She began to realize that having a personal touch with locals and tourists who entered her shop was more appealing than supervising sales over four states. It seemed to her that this morning alone in the shop had gone a long way toward helping her make up her mind.

But that still didn't answer the question of why Luke hadn't called. Assuming he was busy at the firehouse, Della put the worry to the back of her mind. *He'll call soon*, she thought.

CHAPTER THIRTY - TWO

1994

Almost immediately after Luke's accident, an ambulance sped down the street toward the burning shed. Driving the van quickly onto the sandy driveway, the EMT team jumped out as soon as it was parked and headed toward the blaze. Two firemen had pulled Luke out from under the burning wall and he was lying unconscious on the sand. The emergency medical technicians brought a stretcher and checked Luke's pulse, heart rate and breathing. Noting that he was stable but critical, they loaded Luke carefully onto the stretcher, and then rushed him into the back of the ambulance. A fast drive with siren blaring brought them to the hospital where Luke was admitted into the emergency room and then wheeled to the Intensive Care Unit.

With great care the nursing staff undressed him, taking extreme caution in case he had suffered burns under his heavy firefighting suit. They were relieved to see that he had only suffered first degree burns on his right shoulder. The skin was red, and swollen but the more serious issue Luke faced was a broken rib, a direct result of the heavy wall falling on him. He was quickly connected to intravenous medications and the burn on his shoulder addressed. He was unconscious for twenty-four hours after his admittance, finally awaking as a nurse tidied up his room.

"Well, good morning, sleepyhead," the nurse said, pouring a small amount of water into a cup with a straw and holding it to Luke's mouth. Luke swallowed painfully and tried to speak but his throat was incredibly dry. The nurse gave him a little more water and told him she was going to change his dressing on the burn. Cautiously, the nurse helped Luke to a sitting position and gently removed the old dressing. He moaned a bit as he changed positions. The nurse cleaned the burn, and applied silver sulfadiazine cream and covered it with fine mesh gauze. She administered a pain medication for the broken rib and put her hand gently on his back. She adjusted the chest wrap which had been placed to correct the broken rib, loosening it a bit to make it easier for him to breathe.

"You're going to need to wear this chest wrap for the next few weeks," the nurse told him. She helped him back onto the bed and covered him with a sheet. Realizing that he was tired, he closed his eyes. Briefly, Della's face appeared in his memory, but soon the pain medication did its work and Luke fell into a deep and dreamless sleep.

On Beach Road, Della walked to the R & R to get a few groceries for her Aunt Louise and herself. Her former boss, Louis Murdock, looked up from the cash register, as she entered the store.

"If you've come back for your old job, don't bother," he said. I've got a new clerk who's a lot faster than you were."

"Thanks, Louis, but I'm not here for my old job. I've got my hands full at Aunt Louise's bookshop. We'll be reopening soon. You'll have to come see me there."

"Maybe," he said, "How's your boyfriend doing after the accident?"

Della was speechless, clearly unaware that Luke had been hurt. She anxiously asked Louis what he knew and Louis told her, with a more gentle tone, that Luke had been fighting a fire at a shed at an ocean-front cottage. He'd gone back in to retrieve some of the owner's property when a wall had fallen in on him.

At this news, Della grabbed Louis's arm and shouted, "Is he in the hospital? Is he OK?"

Louis told her that he had no idea. Luke's mother had come into the store that morning on the way to the hospital. She wanted to pick up some Nutter Butters for Luke. (Apparently, they were his favorite cookies.)

Della immediately left the store without buying any groceries. She stopped outside the storefront, pulled her cellphone from her jeans pocket and dialed Luke's parents' home phone. Ann Howard, Luke's sister-in-law, picked up on the second ring.

"Hello, Howard residence, Ann Howard speaking."

"Ann, this is Della Gates. I've just now heard that Luke was hurt. Is he still in the hospital? Is he ok?"

"Yes, Della, we wondered why we hadn't heard from you. Luke is in the hospital. He has a broken rib and some burns."

"Do you think I could go to see him?"

"I think that would make him very happy."

Della bid Luke's sister-in-law a hurried farewell and rushed back to her apartment. She changed clothes quickly and painted on a little lip gloss. Then, checking her final appearance in the mirror, she left her apartment and locked the door. She hurried over to her aunt's cottage, knocked quickly and let herself in.

"Yoo hoo, Aunt Louise? It's me."

She walked through the hall to the family room at the back where she found her aunt watching TV in her easy chair. The back door was open and the morning breeze off the ocean came easily through the screen door and open windows along the back wall.

"Hey, girl, I thought you had gone to the grocery store. I still need…"

"Aunt Louise," Della interrupted. "I can't stay. I'll get your groceries later. I've just learned that Luke was injured in an accident yesterday. He was fighting a fire at a cottage up the road and the wall of a shed fell in on him. He's in the hospital and I must go to him."

"Oh, Lord, child, go and tell him I'll be praying for him.

Della turned and rushed out to her car, heading toward the hospital. She entered by the emergency room door and was greeted by Rita Johnson, the hospital receptionist. Della asked to be directed to Luke Howard's room.

"Why, sure, honey. He's up on the third floor. Room 304."

"Thanks, Miss Rita."

Della hurried past the reception desk and made her way to the elevator. She was assaulted by the antiseptic smell as she always was in the hospital. She wondered what she'd find and if Luke would even see her. He must have thought she didn't care that he'd been hurt.

The elevator climbed slowly and finally a bell dinged to let her know she'd arrived at the third floor. A sign on the wall outside the elevator door directed her to the right and she walked to room 304. Her sandals clicked too loudly on the tile floor. Timidly knocking on the door, Della heard Luke's weakened voice telling her to come in.

"Oh, Luke, I just heard. Are you all right?"

"Della, you came."

Luke was lying on his side facing the door. His legs were covered by a white cotton sheet. His bare chest was wrapped in gauze and the burn on his back was protected with a large bandage. Luke's color was pasty and he looked as weak as a newborn kitten. His eyes were half closed, the effect of the pain medication he'd been given an hour before.

"You'll excuse me if I don't get up."

"Oh, Luke, I am so sorry. Do you feel up to talking a bit? I could just sit with you if you'd prefer or if you want me to go, I will.

Luke motioned to her to pull the chair next to the bed. Della touched his arm and smiled. A tear came to her eyes as she realized how close he came to losing his life. Luke's eyes were clear but sad. He told her about entering the shed to look for anything or anyone remaining inside. Wearing his heavy fire protection suit kept him from more serious injury, he recalled, but when the wall of the shed had burned to the point that it was no longer stable, it fell inward bringing the roof down and knocking him to the ground, unconscious. Fortunately, the other firemen there rushed to his assistance immediately, pulling him out from under the smoldering wood. The ambulance's arrival a few moments later ensured that Luke received the emergency medical assistance he needed. Telling the story to Della seemed to exhaust him and he closed his eyes, turning his head on his pillow. A silence of a moment ensued and Della wiped tears from her cheek.

"I thought you'd be packing up to move back to Raleigh," Luke whispered.

"Oh, Luke, you misunderstood. Dylan means nothing to me anymore. I hadn't invited him to come to Nags Head. He just showed up with that offer. I don't have any interest in returning to my old job in Raleigh and I have even less interest in Dylan Metcalfe."

"You know you'd be crazy not to return to Raleigh," he responded. "You'd probably make five times what you'll make at Miss Louise's bookshop, maybe more."

"I'm learning that there are more important things in life than money and position."

Della sat with Luke for an hour, occasionally fetching him water or wiping his forehead with a cool, damp cloth. Then, sensing that Luke was tiring again, Della got up to leave. As she did, Luke reached for her hand and looked up into her eyes.

"Come back, soon, Della."

"I will, Luke. I will."

She bent to give him a soft kiss on his forehead and left the room, closing the door quietly behind her. Realizing what a close call he'd had, Della leaned for a minute against the wall outside Luke's room and offered a prayer of thanks to God for preserving him.

CHAPTER THIRTY - THREE

1942

Finn exited his commanding officer's quarters with a look of determination on his face. He'd been tasked this day with heading out above the Atlantic to search for U-Boats. Convoys of commercial vessels were traveling daily between the US Navy bases in Charleston, South Carolina and Norfolk, Virginia. These vessels carrying fuel and goods necessary for the war effort were prime targets for Admiral Dönitz's Operation Drumbeat.

Just the day before, one of the other Coast Guard pilots at the base had intercepted a U-Boat which had torpedoed a 6,800 ton ship sinking it near Oregon Inlet. The torpedo had detonated in the engine room, exploding a hole fifty feet wide in the hull. Luckily, all thirty-one crew members of the ship were able to be rescued as they had gotten the lifeboats in the ocean in time. Finn prayed a quick prayer for guidance and safety as he walked to the hangar.

There in its slot, Finn's OS2U Kingfisher sat waiting for him. The plane was painted in its wartime blue camouflage with US Navy markings. The mechanics had given it a green light, refueling it and thoroughly checking every moving part. Finn felt confidence in his team and his buddy Hawk Hawkins, who regularly flew with him as observer. Hawk ran up to the hangar, apologizing for not being on time, but Finn held up his hand, telling him not to worry.

"I was just talking to the captain," Hawk said breathlessly. "He reminded me of the cutter that was lost off Cape Hatteras in the hurricane last month. He said U-Boats weren't the only things we had to worry about. The beach down there was covered with empty lifeboats, wreckage and fuel from the cutter. Not a pretty sight. He said the weather report for this morning's flight looked good but just to be careful."

Finn and Hawk checked the armament on the plane before climbing aboard. Both the forward-firing fixed Browning machine gun and the observer's flexible mounted Browning machine gun in the rear were oiled and loaded. For today's run, Finn had instructed his crew to load the two 100-lb. bombs rather than a single depth charge.

Hours before Finn boarded his plane, out in the Atlantic Ocean, an 8,000 ton vessel, the *Ciudad de Valencia,* was ferrying wool, hides, asbestos and numerous other goods to Norfolk. The captain of the ship was nervous as he plied his vessel through the notorious "Graveyard of the Atlantic." He knew that many ships had been wrecked upon the dangerous shifting sands and inlets of the area near Hatteras Island. But in a rush to get back to his home port, he wasn't thinking of U-Boat danger and had eschewed a naval escort. So on this night, the *Valencia* was on its own. The crew had extinguished all the ship's lights and at 2200 hours, felt that they had safely made it through the danger area.

Three miles east of the *Valencia, Kapitan* Horst Van Bergen, 27 years old, blonde and blue-eyed, aboard U- 32 had just taken his sub on top of the ocean to refresh the air inside. After fifteen minutes, Van Bergen spotted the *Valencia* and gave the order to begin tracking her. At his command the sub's crewmen lined up the ship in readiness for attack.

Suddenly, he shouted into the voice pipe, *"Los"* (Away!) At that point the torpedo with a 1,100 pound explosive-filled warhead was released from the sub and headed straight for the unsuspecting *Ciudad de Valencia* at more than 30 knots.

The crewmen on the deck of the *Valencia* had just finished their evening meal and were talking and looking up at the stars in the clear sky. The ocean that night was calm, deceptively calm. Suddenly, the crewmen were horrified to see a dreadful sight – a torpedo, just below the surface of the water just fifty feet from the *Valencia*. In an instant, the torpedo struck the *Valencia* amidships. A giant hole opened below the waterline tossing the ship in the ocean waves. Crewmen immediately began launching the lifeboats, putting on their lifejackets, and lowering men into the boats. The torpedo had disrupted all electronic communication on board, so the captain was unable to discern the seriousness of the hit. Meanwhile in the radio room, the telegraph man began sending out on the ship's shortwave radio first an SSSS signal (meaning a U-Boat had been spotted) and finally a desperate SOS (meaning the ship was under attack.) Over and over, he tapped out the message along with the most recent coordinates for the ship.

Finally as the ship began to be consumed by flames from the torpedo's strike, one crewman, his clothes on fire, jumped into the ocean and was not seen again. Seeing that, the *Valencia's* Captain and remaining crew lowered themselves into the last lifeboat, hoping and praying that the vortex of the ocean as the ship began going under would not pull them under as well.

Onboard the U-32, *Kommandant* Horst Van Bergen smiled to himself, and ordered the radioman to notify Admiral Dönitz of another successful sinking. That made two in one week, Van Bergen thought. He ordered the sub to submerge, and then headed to his cabin to take a rest and record the hit in his logbook.

In the sky over Kitty Hawk, Finn and Hawk were flying low, spotting for U-Boat action when they heard the distress call from the *Valencia*. Hawk entered the coordinates and relayed the location to Finn who guided the Kingfisher in the direction of the sinking ship, his heart in his throat.

The crewmen in the lifeboats had managed to row away from the burning hulk and watched with a mixture of fear and awe as their ship stood on end and slowly sank under the waters of the Atlantic. Somehow the men in the lifeboats were managing to keep near each other, calling out from time to time to make sure all were still alive. They tried valiantly to keep away from burning debris on the surface of the ocean. Occasionally a piece of furniture from the ship would come bouncing up onto the surface of the waters, threatening to overturn a lifeboat, so surveillance was of paramount importance. The black smoke made it difficult to see, so they began a system of calling out their lifeboat number and the words "all safe."

The crew were waiting as patiently as possible for the rescue they hoped would come when suddenly, the crew in lifeboat number three felt a bump underneath their boat. A few minutes later a second bump was felt and suddenly the lifeboat was surrounded by five shark fins sticking out of the water. The crew began hitting the noses of the sharks, some with oars and some with their fists. Most of the sharks fled at that, but one kept circling the lifeboat. The crew aboard called to the other lifeboats for help. One of the men in lifeboat number two had brought his loaded sidearm aboard the lifeboat and took aim at the shark. It was a direct hit, killing the shark instantly.

Hawk could see the orange fire from the burning ship on the murky horizon long before they got to it. Clouds of black smoke rose from the fires making it difficult to see any survivors. Suddenly he spotted four lifeboats in the oily sea beyond the fire. He radioed the Coast Guard station to relay the information to a nearby destroyer which had attempted to escort the Valencia earlier. The destroyer headed to the location.

Soon the destroyer located the four lifeboats and was able to rescue the crewmen. One of the men fell into the water but was picked up almost immediately. It was just in time, though, as the blood from the dying shark had interested the other sharks who now began heading toward the lifeboats.

Finn and Hawk, meanwhile, were searching the Atlantic for signs of the U-Boat that had sunk the *Valencia.* Hawk spotted the U-32 and pointed it out to Finn. Van Bergen and a crewman on the bridge saw to their horror the approach of the plane.

Van Bergen screamed, "Alarm! Dive! Dive!"

The men on the bridge immediately scrambled down the ladder of the conning tower, and closed the hatch. The sub began its crash dive as Finn gradually dropped the Kingfisher's altitude and dove in. He dropped the two 100 pound bombs on the U-Boat to devastating effect. One hit directly aft of the conning tower and the other hit on the sub's bow. Almost immediately, smoke and flames erupted and the U-Boat seemed to lift right out of the water revealing the entire conning tower. Minutes later, pools of oil began coming to the surface.

Inside the U-Boat, the walls were breached and seawater began rushing in. Soon the water inside covered the men's thighs and was steadily rising. The lighting inside the U-Boat failed immediately, leaving only red emergency lights on. Fear and chaos reigned throughout the sub as the crewmen rushed to spin the wheel reopening the hatch. They climbed up to the conning tower and jumped from the sinking sub into the ocean. Finn counted seven men in the water, one of whom had been on fire, and dropped a lifeboat to them.

He radioed to a nearby destroyer to pick up the survivors from the U-Boat and transport them to Norfolk to be interrogated. Van Bergen was one of the survivors and tried valiantly to look out for his remaining crew, all of whom were covered in oil. One of them who was not a strong swimmer tired and slowly slipped below the waves before he could be rescued. Finn turned the Kingfisher back toward the Coast Guard Airfield where they soon landed. Both men went in to the office to type up their incident report and then headed for the showers, exhausted.

The next day Finn and Hawk went up at the same coordinates to search for any further survivors. But all they saw were nine dead bodies in life jackets, and many large sharks circling the area.

CHAPTER THIRTY - FOUR

1994

Luke had been kept in the burn unit of the Outer Banks Hospital for a week following his injury while fighting the fire at one of the old cottages along the beachfront. His family as well as Della had visited him as often as they were allowed. The burn on his shoulder was healing nicely and probably would leave only a small scar if any. However, the broken rib he suffered when the wall of the shed fell on him was still painful and he had to keep the chest wrap on for a bit longer.

Nevertheless, he'd been given the all-clear to be released from the hospital and Sam and May were there right at the exact time he'd been allowed to leave. May was solicitous of her son's well-being, asking for the written instructions for changing his dressing and chest wrap. Sam brought his car up to the hospital door while May waited with Luke for the orderly to bring the wheelchair. Once he brought it to Luke's room, his charge nurse helped him into the chair and bid him goodbye with a bag full of ointments and bandages and a prescription for painkillers if he should need them.

After the orderly wheeled Luke down to the entrance, he helped Sam load Luke in the front seat of the car while May sat in the back with

Luke's belongings. It was a trip of about forty minutes to Southern Shores and his parents' home, and Sam drove slowly, not wanting to do anything that would cause more pain to his son. When they rolled into the driveway, Luke began laughing, causing his broken rib to announce its presence. He reached for the area of the broken rib to check the pain and shook his head.

"Ow ow ow!" Luke cried holding his sides as he saw what his brothers were up to. They'd made a huge banner and hung it across the front of the house. Written in big black letters across the banner were the words "Luke Howard, Our Hero!" Matt and Gideon were posted on either side of the driveway tossing confetti at the car as it rolled to a stop.

Sam got out of the car and went around to help his son out and into the house. Matt helped his mother and Gideon picked up all of Luke's belongings, bringing them inside. May insisted that Luke go right to bed, warning his brothers to leave him alone. She brought him a tray with a bowl of chicken noodle soup and a sandwich with a glass of sweet tea. Though he wasn't particularly hungry, Luke ate a little bit to make his mother and father happy. Soon though, his brothers brought in little Grace with Matt's wife Ann to bid him good night.

Ann leaned over and whispered in Luke's ear. "I got a call from Della. She'd like to see you tomorrow if that's ok."

Luke was clearly still weak from his injuries, but when he heard these words from his sister-in-law, a broad smile broke across his face.

"Please tell her yes," Luke whispered, and fell back on his pillow. He was asleep in minutes.

In Raleigh that same evening, Astrid Olsen had a meeting with Dylan Metcalfe. They had returned to the capital city and had spent a long day going over accounts of stores across the state. Dylan had met with his father Alton Metcalfe earlier in the day; Alton was not pleased with the lack of progress his son had made so far in securing the Nags Head bookstore belonging to Miss Gates. Dylan was worried that his future in Colony Books was in danger so he called Astrid in to his office to discuss strategy.

Astrid was at her desk in her cubicle when she got the call from Dylan. She had become less attracted to working for Dylan after she met the Gates women and as she learned more and more of Dylan's shady dealings. Della had told her of how Dylan had cheated on her when they were engaged and from that point on, Astrid began to see the flaws in his character. Nevertheless, when he called her into his office, she grabbed her mini-tape recorder and went right in to see what he wanted.

"Sit down, Astrid. I want to brainstorm some ideas with you. Why don't you record our conversation and then type it up for me. Then I can put a presentation together for my dad."

So Astrid pressed the record button on her tiny recorder and set it on the desk in front of Dylan. He leaned back in his chair and looked out the plate glass window behind his desk.

"Just look at this view, Astrid. That Nags Head location just doesn't compare, does it? Now, I'm just spit balling here, but I really think that Nags Head bookshop is just a non-starter. It doesn't have the panache that I think our Colony bookstores should have. So what I'm thinking is we make an offer for the bookstore and the two or three little shops that are on either side of the shop. Then we raze all of them and erect a superstore or perhaps a resort hotel. We'd be the only game in town."

"But, Dylan," Astrid said, "You promised that sweet old lady that you just wanted to make her shop one of our chain. You told her how charming you thought the shop was and that you'd leave it as is… I don't understand."

Dylan took a long sip of the coffee he had on his desk. He didn't say anything for a minute and walked around his desk to peer out the plate glass window at the view below.

"Astrid, if you want to advance at Colony, you'll have to toughen up. It's just business. There's no room for a lot of sentimentality here."

The conversation went on for another fifteen minutes during which Dylan outlined his plans for what he was calling "Colony Nags Head." Astrid carefully recorded all of Dylan's thoughts and told him she'd have them typed along with her additions in two days. That was too long to wait for Dylan, but Astrid told him she had a doctor's appointment the next day, so he'd have to wait. At exactly 5:00 PM, Astrid left the Colony Tower in Raleigh and got in her car. She called the motel where she'd stayed on the Outer Banks previously and secured a room for the night with a late arrival. She then immediately called Louise Gates to schedule a meeting with Della and her, but Louise said they'd have to meet in the morning. Within an hour of leaving her office, she was on Highway 64 heading east toward the beach.

She arrived on the Outer Banks and drove straight to a general store on the beach called The Trading Post. It was a variety store where you could get most anything one would need for the beach – Tee shirts, night shirts, tooth brushes, soap, toothpaste, suntan lotion, bathing suits and floats. Since Astrid had driven straight from work, she had not taken time to pack a suitcase. So she bought a nightshirt and a pair of shorts, flip flops and a tee shirt to wear the next day. She called Della to inform her of the meeting in the morning, stressing the urgency of getting together. Receiving no answer, Astrid left no message, assuming that Louise would inform her niece.

At 5:00 PM in Nags Head, Della stopped working at the bookshop; she'd made so much progress and was really getting excited about reopening. But foremost on her mind on this day was going to visit with Luke. She called the Howard's house from the shop and inquired about Luke. Sam told her that he was already asleep and it would probably be a more successful visit if she'd come by in the morning around 10:00 or so. Della agreed and thanked him. She asked him to let Luke know she was thinking about him and would drop by in the morning to visit. Hanging up the phone (she still mar-veled at how solid the old phone felt compared to newer versions) she picked it up again to call her parents.

Roy and Maxine usually bowled in a bowling league on this particu-lar night of the week, but Roy had fallen off a ladder while hanging a shutter at their home and was temporarily out of commission with a sore back. So, Della suggested that she pick up some barbecue from Pigman's and bring it up to their house that night. She'd bring Aunt Louise along as well if she felt up to it. Maxine thought that was a terrific idea and went about setting the table in preparation for her company. Meanwhile Della called Louise to see if she felt like going (she did) and then placed an order to Pigman's for some barbecue and slaw.

In an hour, Della had picked up Louise, stopped to pick up the bar-becue order and had arrived at her parents' home in Kitty Hawk. On the way over, Louise told Della that she'd received a strange call from Astrid who said she needed to talk to them both as soon as pos-sible. Louise had told the girl they'd see her in the morning, plan-ning to meet for breakfast at the Nags Head Fishing Pier Restaurant. Louise had no more information to give Della about Astrid's call, and figured she'd explain it all in the morning. They had a delightful evening at the Gates home, polishing off a delicious barbecue dinner. Afterwards, they played a few hands of Rook, Roy's favorite card game. Della and her mother handily beat Roy and Louise but promised to give them a rematch soon. At 9:30, Louise said she was about to turn into a pumpkin, so she and Della headed back to Nags Head.

The next morning, Astrid called Della at 7:00 asking to meet as soon as possible to discuss a very important matter. Della had no idea what she meant, but was intrigued and walked over to rouse Louise. Louise was already dressed and ready to go. So Della went back to her apartment, threw on a pair of navy slacks and a red tee shirt and red sandals, pulled a brush through her hair and grabbed her keys. She picked up Louise and the two women drove to the fishing pier. The restaurant on the pier was legendary for its delicious breakfasts eaten on the screen porch with the sound of the ocean waves as background music.

The two women walked up the long wooden pier boardwalk and opened the screen door of the restaurant. Louise was the first to spot Astrid sitting at a table on the screened porch overlooking the surf. Astrid motioned them to come over and Louise told the hostess they were meeting someone, pointing in Astrid's direction.

Astrid stood as they approached the table. She was wearing the items she'd purchased the night before - a pair of denim shorts and navy blue flip flops and a tee shirt which bore the legend "I'd rather be fishing." She apologized for her apparel but explained she'd left directly from work and had to purchase clothing on the beach.

Louise said not to worry and they sat down. Astrid had already ordered and asked if the Gates women needed to see menus. Since they'd eaten there many times, both knew what they wanted and ordered quickly from the waitress who had approached their table.

"Now, child," Louise said to Astrid. "Tell us what's so important."

Astrid began revealing what she had learned about Dylan's "Colony Nags Head Project" from her meeting with him the day before. But their food arrived before Astrid could get into the details. The waitress refreshed their coffee and ice water, and then left. Diners continued to come into the screened porch dining area, so their conversation was hushed. Astrid proceeded to tell them of recording her conversation with Dylan the day before and its implications for L. Gates, Bookseller. Naturally, Della was intrigued and wanted to hear it immediately but Louise suggested they go to her house where they could have more privacy. So after quickly finishing their breakfast, they paid their checks and walked out onto the pier boardwalk. Astrid looked over her shoulder at the breakers crashing on the sandy shore below and sighed.

"This place is so beautiful" she sighed. I can see why you want to preserve the old ways. I grew up in Norfolk and only came here once as a child. My family always went to Nantucket for our vacations, but this place still has a bit of wildness and emptiness to it. There are fewer and fewer places left like this now."

Della agreed and suggested they go immediately to her aunt's cottage. They drove the short distance, parked and went inside. Louise recommended that they sit outside on the back porch. The sun was not at its hottest yet and there was a cool breeze blowing off the ocean beyond. Astrid parked herself on one of the lean-out benches, while Della and Louise sat in the two rocking chairs facing her.

Without a word, Astrid extracted her mini-recorder from her purse, set it on the bench beside her and pressed "Play." Louise and Della leaned forward and listened carefully as they heard Dylan outline his plans to demolish the bookshop they'd worked so hard to refurbish. A tear came to Louise's eyes as she remembered her Finn.

"Back in 1943," Louise recalled, "I needed something to take my mind off the anguish and fear I felt because of the war. So my grandfather Arthur Hudson and my father Miles Gates loaned me the money to buy the shop on Virginia Dare Trail for my bookstore. I opened the shop in December of 1943 and it was in constant operation until 1989 when my health was challenged. I'm determined that Dylan Metcalfe, with his sleazy plans, will not destroy my shop!"

Astrid told them of Alton and Dylan's previous successes at takeovers in other towns. She told them of feeling uncomfortable as she watched other small businesses fail and be destroyed by Colony Books' desire for monopoly in the book trade. Della shook her head and put her hand on Louise's arm.

"Don't worry, Aunt Louise. We won't let that happen, right, Astrid?"

"That's exactly right. And you've got someone on the inside now."

CHAPTER THIRTY - FIVE

1942

Three days after sinking the U-Boat, Finn was again scheduled to fly spotter plane with Hawk. They decided to have lunch at the pier café, as Finn was hoping to see Louise on the job. Hawk, who'd just spoken to his parents in Roanoke, VA, drove one of the Coast Guard jeeps. The day before had been hot and humid but this morning the sky was clear and the temperature was mild. It felt good to the men to ride along the Beach Road, the wind blowing off the ocean waves.

Hawk parked the Jeep on the sands below the pier and the two men walked up the boardwalk to the café screen door. Hawk entered first and spotted Louise behind the counter. She was loading a tray of food to bring to a table and held up one finger, smiling when she saw them.

"Be right there, fellows," she said cheerily. "Sit anywhere."

Hawk led Finn to a table in the center of the café and the two men waited for Louise's arrival. Soon she brought two menus and two glasses of ice water, setting them in front of the men.

"Hey, what brings you all in here? I wasn't expecting to see you today," she declared brightly.

"Well, Hawk, here, came in for a burger. I came in to see my girl," Finn said winking at Louise.

"Well, Hawk, since you asked so nicely, your burger is coming right up with fries and a Coke, right?"

Hawk nodded and Finn indicated he'd have the same. The lunch soon arrived and it was as delicious as they expected it to be. Louise was an attentive waitress, bringing them refills of their drinks and the dessert menu when they finished. Hawk ordered a piece of chess pie and Finn ordered a piece of chocolate cake with coffee for both of them. Louise couldn't help cutting her eyes over to Finn's table every so often as she worked, her heart soaring when their eyes met. When the two Coast Guardsmen finished their meal, Louise put the check on the table. Finn put his hand over hers, looking into her eyes.

"Can you take a break?" he pleaded.

"I think so," she said, as she walked with the men toward the cash register. She rang up their meals, accepting their cash and Hawk walked over to the table to put down a tip.

"I'm going to walk over to the beach for a minute," Hawk said, giving the two lovers a moment alone. Finn walked back over to the table, placed a dollar bill on the table and turned to the chef.

"I'm borrowing your girl for a minute," he said and grasped Louise's hand. They walked out onto the boardwalk and Finn pulled her to him. Louise looked around, but seeing no one around, she gave in to his embrace. He leaned down, pressing his lips softly on hers, and stroking her hair.

"I'm spotting tonight again so I probably won't see you tomorrow. I'll have to write up a few reports that are overdue. It seems I've been too busy thinking about a certain girl."

"Okay, just be careful, Finn. You know I'll be praying for you."

"I love you, Louise Gates."

"I love you, Finn Ingram."

Hawk came walking up the sand hill toward the pier and started the engine in the Jeep. Finn gave Louise's hand one last squeeze, pressed his lips to hers one last time and turned to go. Louise's heart stood still for a minute as she sent up a prayer to God for Finn's safety that night.

Hours later just before dusk, far out to sea, the US Coast Guard Cutter *Cherokee* was zigzagging south on a course roughly parallel to the coastline of North Carolina. Named in honor of the Native American tribe, she was on her maiden voyage after being christened in the Newport News Shipyard. The cutter's radar antenna went around and around, searching for enemy subs atop the water. Inside a tiny room behind the bridge, a young radar operator had covered his ears with his headphones as he focused on the green radar screen in front of him. The radar had been installed at the shipyard and the young Coast Guardsman was learning how to use it. He was intently watching for any indication of a U-Boat. On the bridge, William Jameson, the young lieutenant commander, looked overhead at the clear sky, the calm sea and the million stars above. *Perfect night to go hunting,* he thought to himself.

In the air three miles away, Finn Ingram and his observer Hawk Hawkins were scanning the horizon in search of signs of U-Boats. Suddenly the young pilot saw the evidence of a solid object a mile or two ahead. Was it a fisherman's boat, a cutter, or could it possibly be a sub? Finn pointed it out to Hawk. Neither man was sure what they were seeing. Nevertheless, Finn reported his sighting over the radio. The young radioman aboard the *Cherokee* reported the news to the lieutenant commander. Overhead, Finn repeated his alert, listening for a response from any nearby cutters or destroyers. It was indeed a U-Boat and Hawk gave him the thumbs up signal to move in for the kill. The Kingfisher began banking toward the U-Boat whose deck crew had spotted Finn's plane.

Oberlieutenant Hans von Halper, who commanded U-Boat 33, screamed at his men to get to their stations. Unfortunately for the crew of U-Boat 33, von Halper had drawn near to the shore so that the seafloor was too shallow for a deep dive. He ordered the helmsman to steer toward deep water, hoping to evade the ever-advancing plane. In a last ditch attempt to save his sub, he ordered his gunners to their stations, hoping that they could ward off or bring down the plane with the machine guns on the wintergarden (a platform off the conning tower.) In the air, Finn pressed the switch to release the bombs onboard. He pulled up immediately and Hawk relayed that they'd made a direct hit. He'd seen the U-Boat's identifying number painted on the conning tower with the image of a wolf beneath it. So he was able to identify the sub he'd sunk. Instantly a huge hole had been torn open on the side of the U-Boat. Inside U-32, the hydrostatic shock waves caused by the bombs loosened all the sub's joints and caused catastrophic failure of all the instruments onboard. The U-Boat had been lying in water too shallow to evade the Kingfisher and thus its fate was sealed. However, U-Boat crewmen rushed to fire their machine guns.

"*Schnell! Schnell! (*Quickly! Quickly!) Von Halper cried. The gun crews began firing the machine guns toward the Kingfisher. Suddenly, Finn realized the plane had been hit. He began radioing frantically, "Mayday! Mayday! Mayday!" and gave the coordinates for his location, praying for a nearby destroyer or cutter to come to his rescue. He turned back to check that Hawk was okay, but saw to his horror that he'd been killed, a bullet from the U-Boat's machine gun having struck him in the heart. Without warning, ammunition from the sub's machine gun punctured the plane's fuel tank and the plane burst into flames. Immediately after this burst of shelling, the plane began a nose dive headed toward the ocean's waves.

Just before the plane crashed into the sea, Finn released his seat belt and safety harness and crawled out of the plane. Hawk's body was thrown from the plane in the crash. Landing in the water, Finn saw that the U-Boat had begun to sink, its two halves going down in a whirl to the ocean floor, two hundred feet below. But the waters surrounding the sinking sub were full of oil which had caught fire. Finn swam desperately away from the oily water but the waterspout kept pulling him toward the flames.

He was about to give up when the face of Louise Gates appeared before him and he made a desperate effort to swim away from the oily flames. Somehow, he was able to propel himself to safety, and he found a wooden tabletop floating nearby. It must have come off the U-Boat, he told himself, and he swam toward it. Clinging to the table, he was able to launch himself on top where he examined himself. Only then did he grasp that he'd been burned on the left side of his face. Finn knew that he had to stay alert, but went into shock. Because so many of his blood vessels had been burned, he didn't realize it, but he'd begun to experience inadequate blood flow throughout his body. His hands clung to the table edge while his feet dangled in the cold ocean water. The table dipped precariously in the pitching sea, but somehow Finn stayed on. Soon, he slipped into unconsciousness. Overhead, the night sky grew dark and a million stars shone. With his last conscious thought, Finn prayed that Louise would be safe.

CHAPTER THIRTY - SIX

1942

Louise Gates cleaned the last table from her afternoon shift at the pier café. She'd wrapped the utensils with napkins for the next day's service. She'd helped the boy who washed dishes by drying a stack of a dozen plates. Then she'd taken off her apron and signed out. It had been a very busy day at the café and she was exhausted. She told her boss good afternoon, and then headed to her bicycle which was parked under the pier. Walking under the pier, she remembered the day Finn had taken her there for ice cream and they'd kissed as they leaned against one of the pilings. She recalled the way he'd looked at her and the feel of his arms around her. She remembered the way the ocean water very nearly got their shoes wet as they stood in a warm embrace. She walked her bicycle up off the sand and onto the road, and then pedaled toward her grandparents' cottage.

Out in the ocean at 1900 hours, the Coast Guard cutter *Cherokee* had just heard a Mayday distress call from Finn's plane. Lieutenant Commander William Jameson heard the coordinates and gave the command for the ship to proceed at once to rescue any survivors. The sky overhead was darkening and stars were beginning to come out. But though Jameson's ship cruised to the coordinates they'd been given, there was no sign of a survivor.

Finally Lt. Commander Jameson ordered the cutter's 24 inch searchlight to be trained on the seas ahead. After a search of two hours, one of the Coast Guardsmen onboard the *Cherokee* spotted a tabletop floating to the starboard side of the cutter. Something was on the table, but it was unclear at first what it was. The cutter slowed its engines and the seemingly lifeless form of Finn Ingram took shape. Floating nearby was the body of Hawk Hawkins, his flight suit stained red with his blood. The ship's commander directed the radioman to send a message to the Outer Banks Coast Guard station with their find, and directed the station to be ready to assist in the rescue if necessary. The *Cherokee* lowered a lifeboat into the ocean waves and called to Finn, but it was easy to see that he was unconscious. So two divers jumped in after the lifeboat, corralling the lifeless body of Hawk Hawkins and that of Finn Ingram, very nearly dead. They pulled them into the lifeboat and awaited the Cherokee. The cutter soon pulled alongside the lifeboat and transferred the men's bodies to the vessel, rushing them ashore for hospitalization.

The US Navy, wanting to keep secret as much as possible any knowledge of U-Boat activity in the area, was tight-lipped about the incident. No news reports gave evidence that any member of the military in the Outer Banks area had been hurt or killed. Two Coast Guard officers and a chaplain drove to the home of Hawk's parents in Roanoke, VA to deliver the sad news of the loss of their son. Finn's parents received a telegram that Finn had been injured and had been taken to Norfolk Naval Hospital to be treated for severe burns.

After dinner that night, Louise ironed her uniform for the next day's work. She opened the package containing the parachute Finn had given her and began thinking of how she would design her wedding dress from its beautiful silk folds. She went to sleep after offering a prayer for Finn's safety.

Morning came, a hot and humid day, and Louise biked once again to her job at the café. She thought of Finn and wondered when he would be returning to her. But in Norfolk, Finn had been transferred to the burn unit at Norfolk Naval Hospital. His parents were on a train with Finn's sister headed to Norfolk and the hospital.

Finn had immediately been seen by several general surgeons and a plastic surgeon. The surgeons in the burn unit operating room carefully cleaned and debrided the burned area of Finn's face, a procedure which involved removing the dead skin. Intravenous fluids containing electrolytes were administered to him and an ocular specialist came to take a look at Finn's left eye, but said it was too early to tell if he would retain vision.

Finn was in such bad shape that the surgeons kept him in a drug-induced coma for a period of four weeks. During that time, Finn endured ten surgeries on his face to cut away the damaged and burned skin. The surgeon secured skin grafts from Finn's back and groin area and had to repeat the process several times when the grafts didn't adhere. Then the dressing had to be changed every few days, (and not sooner) to allow the graft to hold.

Occasionally, Finn would develop an infection and had to be given intravenous antibiotics to combat the infection. Nurses applied plenty of antibiotic creams and lotions and taught Finn's mother and sister how to apply them without hurting Finn. Finally after a month, he was brought out of a coma and given liquids and soft foods, but he found eating this way was difficult to take as his mouth on one side had been affected.

After five months, Finn was ready to be moved out of the burn unit and into the general population of the hospital. Unfortunately, Finn had completely lost the vision in his left eye which was disfigured from the burn. The burns on his face had begun to form keloids and had become a reddish brown in color. He had lost all sensation on the left side of his face.

His parents had continued to visit weekly from their home in North Carolina. They were hopeful that he'd soon be transferred to a hospital near them, but Finn was unwilling to go. He became severely depressed and after looking at himself in a hand mirror once, had not spoken again for months. He'd refused to look at his face after that. Finally, when his burns were somewhat healed, he was released to the care of his parents and began seeing a therapist. It took a year and a half for Finn to begin feeling somewhat normal again, though he refused to look at himself in a mirror. He had to learn to rely on the vision in the one eye he had left. Brushing his teeth was difficult as the skin on the left side of his mouth had drawn together a bit. Speaking at first was hard for Finn. His throat seemed constantly dry and the change in his mouth made words come out in an odd manner. Ultimately he stopped speaking altogether unless it was absolutely necessary.

The therapist Finn saw worked with him weekly for three years, and on the day Finn turned twenty-five, the therapist released him from his care. He'd helped Finn find a job in Norfolk doing office work for the Veteran's Administration. His parents secured a first floor apartment for him near the VA office. They had tried repeatedly to get him to make contact with Louise again, but Finn insisted that he never wanted her to see him as he was now. Though he led a fairly solitary life, he was ultimately able to get a driver's license again. He began to be a productive member of the VA office staff, advancing after some time to a position in management. But he never dated again and he never married. And for the next forty-five years, though he thought of her every day, Finn never spoke Louise's name.

CHAPTER THIRTY - SEVEN

1942-1945

By late in the summer of 1942, the U-Boats were gone from the coast of North Carolina. Life began to return to normal for most people, a sort of new normal – busier, and more watchful, certainly. Overhead, the skies were full of planes and in the waters offshore, long convoys continued their treks north or south. People now began to listen for news from the battlefronts in places they'd never heard of before. Walter Winchell's news reports could be heard from the radios in most homes, beginning with the familiar, "Good morning Mr. and Mrs. America, from border to border and coast to coast and all the ships at sea. Let's go to press."

But for Louise Gates, things would never return to normal. She'd waited for days and then weeks for word of what had happened to Finn. But since she was not Finn's next of kin, she was unable to learn of his fate. The military never issued any communiques about the U-Boats until 1945. They made no announcements on the radio or newspaper; nevertheless, the Outer Banks residents had seen the fires, smelled the smoke of burning oil and picked up debris and worse from their sandy shores. They had known about the U-Boats.

So, fearing the worst, but hoping for a positive outcome, she took out the brown paper package which Finn had given her so many weeks ago. Setting the Cracker Jacks box on her dresser, she took a look at the cheap toy ring she still wore. She held in her hand the Buffalo nickels he'd given her.

I'll wait forever, Finn, she thought.

Then she pulled out the length of white silk of the parachute Finn had given her. She'd washed and pressed it, and carefully put it away. But once every week or so, she'd taken it out to remember the night Finn had given it to her.

Finally she decided to make the wedding dress she'd promised Finn she'd make to wear on their wedding day.

If I'm never able to wear it, she thought, *I'll at least have the memory of what might have been.*

So, she walked down to the R & R to have a look at patterns. The small general store carried a very few patterns in-house and a large pattern book from which you could order the pattern in the size you were looking for. Since the beginning of the war, patterns, fabric and sewing notions had been hard to come by, since any metals (like those used in sewing needles) and many fabrics were pulled out of reach of the general public and saved for use by the military. Paper that could be used to make sewing patterns was also hard to find, as it was collected regularly in drives for metal, paper, rubber and rags.

Entering the R & R, Louise greeted the owner, Mrs. O'Quinn, and made her request to see the most recent pattern book. But Moira O'Quinn shook her head and confessed that the most recent book she had was from 1932, all others having been donated to a Boy Scouts paper drive. And she couldn't get patterns of any kind these days. Still, Mrs. O'Quinn said, Louise might get some idea of the kind of dress she could make from that old book. So the pattern book was brought out to the counter and Mrs. O'Quinn produced a stool for Louise to sit upon. Louise had brought a small tablet with her and proceeded to make a few drawings of the kind of dress she thought she could make.

Thanking Mrs. O'Quinn, she closed the pattern book and walked back to the cottage. Della's mother was an expert seamstress and, though she'd donated her used patterns for the war drive, she offered to help her daughter to construct a dress. Privately, Rhonda worried that her daughter was so heartbroken over Finn's absence, but she wanted to do whatever might make Louise happy. And right now, the only thing that seemed to cheer up Louise was the idea of making a wedding dress from the parachute silk.

On the day after looking at patterns at the R & R, Louise and Rhonda had put all the leaves in the big kitchen table and stretched out the parachute fabric across its length. Rhonda marveled at the fabric's elegant sheen and softness, but worried that her daughter was being unrealistic. Rhonda and Miles, Louise's parents, had called the Coast Guard station on the Outer Banks to see if there had been any word about Finn. They were told that his plane had been shot down after he'd sunk a U-Boat and he had been severely injured. When they told this news to Louise, she'd broken down in heart-rending sobs. She asked over and over where Finn had been taken, but her parents had no answer for her. Finally, Miles drove to see the Commander of the Coast Guard station and inquired if Finn had left behind any home address where his daughter might find news of her fiancé. The Commander, after some reluctance, gave Finn's home address in North Carolina to Miles, but cautioned him that Finn's parents might not want to speak to anyone. Nevertheless, Miles took down the address and drove back to the cottage with the information.

Louise had snatched the piece of paper bearing Finn's home address from her father's hands and clutched it to her breast as though it were Finn himself. She took the paper up to her room and closed the door. Sitting at her desk chair, she pulled a sheet of precious stationery from a box in the top drawer and began to write.

Dear Mr. and Mrs. Ingram,

My name is Louise Gates and I live in Nags Head, NC. I met your son at the café where I work when he came in for a meal. We began dating and formed a close relationship, so close that Finn asked me to marry him, to which I said an enthusiastic YES! Then I learned that Finn had been injured in his plane. I have tried every way I know how to go to see him and learn that he is ok, but to no avail. Finally my father was able to secure your address from Finn's commander at the Coast Guard Station. I am very much in love with Finn and want to see him. Would you let me know where he is and how I can reach him? It would mean so much to me.

Sincerely yours,
Louise Gates

Within two weeks' time, Louise received a reply from Finn's mother:

My dear girl,

My husband Henrik and I were pleased to hear from you. Finn had written to us several times about you and we had so hoped to meet you. But as you know, Finn was injured and has been hospitalized since that day. Henrik and I go weekly to visit him in Norfolk Naval Hospital and we have asked if he'd like us to contact you. So far he has said no. To be frank, Finn's face was terribly burned in the incident and he is refusing to see anyone except Henrik, our daughter Birgit and myself. If anything changes, I will be sure to let you know. But as you can imagine, communication during this time is very difficult. Please pray for our dear son and thank you for reaching out to us.

Sincerely,
Marte Ingram

As the month of August and then September and October came and passed, Louise heard nothing from Finn. She wrote a few more letters to his parents and once got her father to drive her to Norfolk to visit him. But she was told upon requesting a pass to his room, that Finn had requested no visitors except his parents and sister. So, telling herself that he would soon change his mind, she continued working nightly on her wedding dress, using one of her mother's sketches for a pattern. She'd had enough silk fabric to make a beautiful gown with a sheer mesh insert around the neckline. The mesh had originally been attached to the outer edge of the parachute to aid in steering. Rhonda suggested adding ruffles on the shoulder and hips, to balance the drop waist, long sleeves, and full skirt with train. Along the back Rhonda had covered and attached twenty rounded buttons which she'd removed from her own wedding gown. As a final grace note, Louise embellished her wedding gown with tiny, delicate embroidery around the hem. When finished, it was magnificent, a masterpiece in silk.

What a pity, thought Rhonda, *that there's no wedding for the dress.*

Fall on the Outer Banks seemed colder than usual. By the end of May, 43 U-boats had been lost. By August, Admiral Karl Dönitz had ordered most U-boats to withdraw from the Atlantic because of heavy losses to new Allied anti-submarine tactics. And the fires and explosions from freighters and tankers being sunk off shore had ceased. Still, though, there was a sense of unease everywhere. Local boys from small towns like Buxton and Elizabeth City, Sunbury and Salvo were being drafted and sent eventually to places with names like Guadalcanal, El Alamein, Naples, the Solomons, and Wake Island. It seemed the war would never end.

At the Pier Café, supplies had become so difficult to obtain that the owner reluctantly decided to close for the duration of the war. This left Louise with nothing but time on her hands. She came home on her last day of work, dejected and sad. She went to her hope chest at the foot of her bed, lifted the lid and carefully withdrew the paper parcel bearing the wedding dress she'd made. She'd saved every remnant of silk from the parachute that hadn't gone into the dress and used them to fashion a dresser scarf. She tried on the dress one more time, standing in front of the full length mirror in her parents' bedroom. A tear escaped her eye as she realized that she might never wear it and she took off the dress. Folding it carefully, and rewrapping it in Finn's paper wrapping, she put it back in the cedar chest, closed the lid and dried her eyes.

Meanwhile Louise's parents and grandparents were aware of the sadness that had overwhelmed Louise since Finn's loss and tried to think of how they could help. Her grandfather and father loaned her the money to buy a small shop building on the road by the beach. It had been empty since a couple of years before the war began, and he offered it to Louise. The shop was a brick building with two main rooms that had once been a branch of the Nags Head Bank & Trust. Arthur felt it might give her something to occupy her time and bring her out of the melancholy that her parents and grandparents witnessed in her. At first Louise said no. But finally, Louise realized that she had to find some happiness in life and as 1943 ended, she started to imagine what kind of shop she'd like to have.

She'd put several hundred dollars away in a small savings account, some of which she had earned while working in the café. Her grandfather gave her a collection of around a hundred books from his personal library, everything including westerns, mysteries, sports and classics. As no shelving was available at the time, Louise began the time-honored Nags Head practice of scavenging wood that washed up onshore from sunken ships. After a few weeks, she was able to secure enough lumber to fashion some crude shelves for her store.

Her mother Rhonda and her grandmother Emily wanted to help her so they began providing food for sale in her shop. The few baked goods they were able to make with ration cards for sugar and butter were big hits. As the Outer Banks entered the summer, Miles and Arthur planted a garden in some land that Arthur owned in the Nags Head woods. The dirt there was rich and fertile, and the crops grew profusely. Miles even had some beehives that provided the family with honey, which made an excellent substitute for the sugar that was heavily rationed. Rhonda and Emily used the produce from their husbands' garden to make delicious foods and baked goods and offered them for sale in Louise's shop. Louise spread linen placemats over her rough wooden shelves to make mouthwatering displays of the food.

In another corner of the little shop, she displayed the books that her grandfather had given her. She painted a small sign advertising "L.Gates, Bookseller" and put it in a window of the shop. Another sign mentioned the foods available for sale on any particular day. With the increased military population on the Outer Banks because of the war and the shortages that were everywhere, she soon had a flourishing business, enough that she was soon able to install a phone in the shop, one of the first ones on the beach.

In time, Louise was able to focus her thoughts on how to improve her little shop. She was surprised to find that she had lots of ideas for the future and her demeanor brightened considerably. And by war's end, though she never forgot him, she was able to think of Finn Ingram as a dream she once had.

CHAPTER THIRTY - EIGHT

1994

Della had visited Luke several times as he recuperated from his injuries. He was at his parents' home and Sam and May Howard were always delighted to welcome her when she came. Della was always a bit cautious around Luke, not wanting to hug him in case his injuries still bothered him. But he really seemed to enjoy having her there. Soon she got him walking a bit as his broken ribs began to knit together.

Luke's brothers, Matt and Gideon, gave him a hard time about how long he was on the disabled list, saying he was really milking it. Luke's sister-in-law Ann brought little Grace to see him occasionally and that always cheered him up. And so the month of August passed with very few unusual things happening around the beach town. Tourists came and went. The beaches were full of children and sunbathers as well as one beached whale and the occasional pods of dolphins arching in the ocean. Soon Luke was able to go back to the fire station and he began to handle light duty. This worried May, but Sam helped her realize that their son needed to get back to life as it had been before his accident.

On August 26th, Della was sleeping soundly in her bed in her apartment. She'd heard weather reports on the evening news a few days
before about a storm that had formed in the tropics of the Atlantic.
Just to be on the safe side, she'd lowered all the wood batten shutters
and taken in the wooden sticks which propped them open. Closing
the shutters created an oven in her apartment, so she had borrowed
a small rotating fan from her Aunt Louise. But all it did was stir
the hot air. She'd brought in everything from the porches surrounding her apartment and Louise's cottage hoping that the storm would
blow over.

Nevertheless, the tempest roared through the group of islands making up Puerto Rico causing massive amounts of destruction. Three
days later an odd pink sunset foretold of the storm to come on the
Outer Banks and at 2:30 AM on August 26th the storm, now named
Hurricane Arturo, a category 3 storm, barreled into the southeast
coast of North Carolina headed for Nags Head. The towns of Frisco,
Buxton, Avon and Salvo were the first to receive the full blunt of
the winds, which roared up to one hundred fifteen miles per hour
at its height. The Atlantic Ocean tides swelled over the land to
meet the waters of the sound, flooding Beach Road and many of
the lower-lying structures therein. Old shipwrecks from Civil War
days were brought to the surface of the ocean as the waves rolled
fiercely. Broken barrels from commercial vessels washed up on the
sands. Whitecaps crashed upon the walls of beachfront cottages,
tearing some of them to bits. Others were lifted off their founda-
tions. Because of the strength of the wind, sand was embedded in
the shingled walls of oceanfront cottages. Porches of these houses
were covered with sea foam. One of the local piers near Nags Head
was completely washed out to sea. The storm sank a Navy destroyer
off the coast of Cape Hatteras with 27 men lost.

Fortunately, Louise's cottage was well-built on tall pillars which stood sturdily amidst the onslaught of the rain and ocean water. Della woke from a sound sleep, hearing the gales and pounding rain outside. She threw on her rain slicker, went out onto the porch and closed her door behind her securely. Shielding her eyes against the driving rain, she ran to her Aunt Louise's door to check on the older woman. The wind from the southeast tossed her into the porch wall, but she righted herself and threw open the door to the cottage. Inside all was dark. Della tried the light switch by the door, knowing it was useless.

"Aunt Louise," she called frantically. "Are you okay? Where are you?"

"I'm back here, child. I'm fine."

Louise was sitting quietly in her easy chair, looking out the back windows of her cottage at the storm tossed ocean waves beyond. Two candles in hurricane globes sat atop the mantelpiece and a red oil lantern rested on the table by her chair. A crocheted afghan was thrown across Louise's legs and a serene look was in her eyes.

"Have you had anything to eat? The power's been out for a while."

"Yes, honey, I boiled some coffee right after supper. It's over there in that big thermos if you want some. I'm just enjoying the fury."

"Enjoying the fury? This could be really dangerous, Aunt Louise. Do you think we better evacuate?"

"No, honey. This house has stood for a hundred years and it'll stand for this storm too. Have you heard from your Mama and Daddy?"

"No, do you think I should call them while I've still got a charge on my phone?"

"It wouldn't hurt. They probably can't sleep through this anyway. Give them my love."

So Della called her parents who, indeed, were not sleeping. Their brick house in Kitty Hawk was standing firm, though it was surrounded by six inches of water. Della's father asked about the condition of the bookshop, and Della's face fell.

"Oh, Daddy, I just don't know if it is still standing or not. This storm down here in Nags Head is so fierce. Aunt Louise's cottage is in good shape, and my apartment hasn't sprung any leaks. But that beautiful old weathervane on top of the roof of Aunt Louise's cottage blew off in all that wind. I picked it up but one of the directionals is bent. I'm glad you told me to let down the shutters."

"Well, don't go out again in this storm for any reason. The weathervane can be repaired and the shop can be replaced. You can't. We love you, honey. We'll be down in the morning to help out."

"I love you too, Daddy. Kiss Mama for me. Aunt Louise is fine and she sends her love."

Louise got another afghan from her bedroom closet and pointed to the sofa.

"You just lie down right there, young lady. We're going to weather this storm together. You know I'm reminded a little of Hurricane Hazel back in 1954. That was some storm, I tell you, much worse than this one. The water covered Beach Road so bad that the asphalt broke up and the sand beneath it just heaved up every which way. The bookshop was just a few years old back then, and I had to replace all the windows. The wind just blew them right out. There were right many oceanfront houses that were just picked up and moved or smashed on the ground like firewood. "

The two women talked quietly as the hurricane raged outside. Occasionally a crash of thunder and a bolt of lightning out over the water would punctuate their conversation. As sleep began to overtake them, Louise whispered a prayer of thanks to God for protecting them and all those they loved. Della breathed an "Amen" and closed her eyes.

Around 6:00 AM, Della brought a couple of rolls and the rest of the coffee to her aunt for breakfast. The rain was beginning to lessen and the sky to the east over the Atlantic Ocean was beginning to show a little light. Both Della and Louise wept a little and thanked God again for bringing them through the terrible night's storm.

When the darkness finally lifted, Della peered outside to see that the sea oats on the sand dunes nearby were nearly covered with the sand which had been washed over them. On the beach, debris had been swept up on the sands below the cottage – broken barrels and boxes, a broken surfboard and a sand pail that rolled over and over in the wind. Bits of sea foam blew from the sands below and settled in Della's hair as she stood on the back steps.

She went back inside to see if her phone still had a charge. Luckily it did, so she called her parents who were eating breakfast. At just that moment, the lights popped back on!

"Hallelujah!" shouted Louise with a grin. "Now it seems to me you've got one more phone call you ought to make." She pointed Della to the kitchen table and left the room.

Della smiled to herself, knowing who Louise meant, and sat down to call the Howard house.

Luke answered on the first ring.

"Hey, Della, are you all okay?"

"Yes, I stayed over here with Aunt Louise all night. There's a lot of water around but no apparent damage so far. And the power just came back on. How are things up in Southern Shores?"

"Well, I don't think we got it as bad as you. And you know, Mom and Pop's house is as sturdy as they come. My brothers helped them get ready for the storm. How about your folks?"

Della told him she'd just talked to them and so far everything seemed just fine.

"How about the bookshop, Della?"

"I don't know, Luke. I've been afraid to think about that and I haven't mentioned it to Aunt Louise. I thought if it turns fair this afternoon, I'd walk over there to see how it looks."

"Okay," Luke replied, "but wait for me. There may be downed power lines or other problems. I'll finish helping Mom and Pop around here and come over after lunch. Then we can go together."

After boiling an egg and fixing a piece of toast for her aunt, Della dashed back to her apartment and showered quickly. She put on a pair of jeans and a Meredith College tee shirt along with a sturdy pair of short Hunter waterproof boots. (She wasn't sure what she'd find at the bookshop.) Then, after cleaning up the kitchen and seeing to it that Louise was settled with a cup of coffee and a book to read, Della perched on the sofa to wait for Luke. Her parents soon appeared on Louise's porch, with a thermos of coffee and baked goods to share. Maxine hugged her daughter while Roy went around the house, inside and out, checking for any problems. Two hours later, a knock at Louise's door told Della that Luke had arrived.

Della grabbed her rain slicker and scurried to the family room to tell her family where she was going. Luke came in behind her, greeting the ladies politely and shaking Roy's hand.

"You-all be careful, now, you hear?" Louise called out, as Roy and Maxine nodded their heads in agreement. "Look out for downed wires."

"Yes, Ma'am," Luke answered, "I'll take good care of your girl."

Della smiled at this and took Luke's hand as they stepped off the porch. The rain had stopped and they walked quickly in the direction of the shop. The two were talking happily, treading carefully over the flotsam and jetsam of the previous night's storm. Suddenly the bookshop appeared before their eyes and their conversation ceased. They simply stared in disbelief.

CHAPTER THIRTY - NINE

1994

The Beach Road in front of the bookshop was inundated with sand and salt water. Road signs were bent at odd angles and lawn chairs and beach umbrellas were splayed about the road, obviously far from their original location. The few wax myrtles or live oaks in the yards along the road had either been uprooted or bent to the ground.

Abandoned vehicles, partially buried axle deep in sand, dotted the road here and there. Already, Luke could hear the sound of heavy equipment being brought in to move the sand and restore the road. It wouldn't be long, he knew, before the beach was restored to its former order. But the shop was another matter entirely.

"Oh, Luke!" Della cried. "All our hard work."

L. Gates, Bookseller had suffered more than its share of damage in the overnight storm. The zinnias in the flowerboxes outside the windows were destroyed, the wind having blown out the soil after the hurricane. One of the bow windows in the front of the shop had been splintered by a small wooden chair sent sailing by the winds. Rainwater had entered the broken window and soaked the freshly polished display area underneath as well as the books Della had positioned there. An inch of water covered the front floor of the store and Della sighed as she recalled the hours she'd spent polishing those floorboards. Most of the books and shelving seemed to have survived intact and, luckily, Louise's green velvet couch was dry.

Luke led Della around the store carefully, looking for trouble spots and making sure that the power to the store was cut off. They walked down the back hall to the office and restroom area. Both seemed to have no water on the floor but in one corner of the office, a window had been blown out by a flying picnic bench. The bench had flown into the heavy bookcase, knocking it askew, its contents scattered everywhere.

Della put her hands to her mouth to prevent crying out, but Luke could see the pain she felt. He drew her to him and put his arms around her, cradling her head on his shoulder. For a minute, they stood together, Della sobbing quietly and Luke rubbing her back and whispering soft words of encouragement in her ear. Della was the first to pull away, rubbing the palm of her hand across her face to wipe away the tears that had fallen. She shook her head as she looked at the mess surrounding her.

"Well, where shall we start?" Luke said kindly. "I've looked around and I think it's ok to turn the power back on in the store so we can see what we've got here. I saw a shop vac in the storage closet. Want me to start getting rid of the water in the shop?"

"Yes, we probably better start there. I'll see if any books are salvageable in the display window area that got broken."

Della found that about half the books in the display area of the broken front window were a total loss. There were a few that could be sold for a dollar or two and a few that were still pristine. She gathered those up and put them in a box on the counter, then began to tally the losses around the shop. Meanwhile, Luke had completely vacuumed up all the water from the floor of the shop. Della wanted to put down more wax, but Luke suggested waiting a couple of days until it had a chance to dry completely.

Eunice Howard, doing clean-up at the Ocean Tide Café had seen her grandson and Della going into the bookshop and walked over to see how bad the damage was. The café had suffered very little damage and was open for business, though not many customers had come in as yet. Eunice carried a paper bag with two slices of chocolate pecan pie and two bottles of Coke which she set down on the counter as she came in.

"Oh, law, child, all your hard work! What do you think you'll have to do to get up and running?" Eunice asked.

"I don't know, Miss Eunice. I'm hoping it looks worse than it is. Luke has already vacuumed up all the water from the floor. Now we just have to wait for it to dry before I can polish it. I need to get the display window fixed right away."

The bell over the shop door tinkled as Roy and Maxine came in. Since their home was relatively undamaged by the storm, they had left Louise at her cottage and come to help their daughter at the store. Roy had become an accomplished woodworker since retiring and volunteered his services. Della and he examined the bow window in the front of the store; it would not be the easiest fix, but Roy felt that he could tackle it right away. In the meantime, he tacked up tarps over it and the window in the office.

Meanwhile, Maxine and Eunice walked to the back of the store with Luke to see the damage from the picnic bench to the office window. Maxine and Eunice immediately began picking up the books and papers that had landed on the floor. They tried to straighten the bookcase which had been knocked away from the wall, but found it was too heavy. Maxine looked behind it to see if anything was blocking its movement and suddenly called out to Eunice.

"Come look here, Eunice. What's that behind the bookcase?"

"Looks like a door to me. Lucas? Look over here a minute. See what this is."

Luke stepped over a chair which was turned over in his path and looked behind the bookcase. There he saw a small door, about four feet in height and about three feet in width. Luke crept behind the bookcase, being careful not to unsettle it further and felt for a handle.

"Nana, I think there's a flashlight in Della's desk over there. See if you can find it and bring it to me."

Eunice righted the chair which had fallen over and found the flashlight in the top desk drawer. She brought it to Luke who trained it on the door. There was no handle, only a keyhole. He tried opening it but without success. Della and Roy came in at that moment and peered behind the bookcase to see what was going on.

That's going to take a skeleton key to get that open, Della," her father said. "I don't have one, unfortunately. But I think there's a locksmith up in Southern Shores. We can get him to come open it."

My parents live up there, Mr. Gates," Luke said. "I know that locksmith. He lives next door to my parents. I'll call them and get them on the case."

Barely an hour later, Sam and May appeared at the bookshop with a ring of keys in hand. Their neighbor, the locksmith's wife, had fallen and sprained her ankle, and he was tending to her. So he loaned them his ring of keys to try to open the door.

After the Howards took a quick look around at the damage to the shop, Della directed them to the back office and the bookcase which had been knocked away from the wall. Sam handed the key ring to Della who squeezed behind the bookcase while Luke held the flashlight trained on the keyhole. Key after key was tried with no luck. Finally when there were only three keys left that had not been tried, Della inserted the first of the three and turned it away from the door jamb. The room was completely silent so that she heard the metallic, mechanical sound of the tumbler moving. The key turned and Della looked around at the six people in the room with her. What could possibly be in there, she wondered?

CHAPTER FORTY

1994

U sing the skeleton key as a door handle, Della pulled hard in an attempt to open the door. But it wouldn't budge. The rain and the steamy heat had caused the door to swell. She made several attempts, and then looked helplessly to Luke. He motioned her to come out from behind the bookcase, worried that it was unstable.

Luke, Sam and Roy cleared a path behind the bookcase and managed to move it further away from the wall. This gave Luke more room to work on the door and he was ultimately able to pull the door free from the door jamb. He picked up the flashlight and trained the light into the closet's interior. On the floor of the closet, there were stacks of papers and a small tin money box. On the floor at the back of the closet was a small Victorian cast iron parlor safe. It was painted black with brass fittings and had a small dial, its numbers covered in dust. Luke tried the door of the safe, but of course it was locked shut. He handed the small money box to Della and backed carefully out of the low closet. Sam gave his son a hand standing up. Luke dusted his hands and turned to face his dad.

"Pop, can you contact the locksmith to see how to open this old safe?"

"Of course, son. Your mother and I will drive back home in just a bit and see if he can come down here for a few minutes to help out."

When Della saw what Luke had uncovered in the interior of the small closet, she stopped and said, "This stuff belongs to Aunt Louise. Don't you all think she should be here when we look at it?"

Of course they all agreed and Roy left immediately to pick up his aunt. Upon arriving at her cottage, he assured her that it was safe to travel on the Beach Road and informed her of what they had found in the office. Roy also tried to prepare her for the hurricane's destruction to her beloved bookshop. Nothing daunted, Louise got up right away and slipped into a pair of rubber galoshes and a plastic raincoat. She tied a plastic rain hat over her curls and put her hands on her hips.

"Well, Roy Gates? What are you waiting for?" she said with a hint of a smile.

Roy put his arm through Louise's and helped her to his car. The trip to the bookshop was a little longer than usual because of the sand across the road and all the people who had driven out to see the destruction from the hurricane. Once a gust of wind blew a child's float toy across Roy's windshield, but soon enough, they arrived and parked on the street in front of the shop.

Upon entering, Louise gasped a bit and tears came unbidden to her eyes. "Oh, Della, child, all your hard work," she said, shaking her head.

"Now don't you worry, Aunt Louise. Everybody here has already told me they'd be able to help me put the shop back together. Daddy even thinks he can repair the bow window and the office window in back. We'll be in business before you know it. And look, your old telephone works like a charm."

Della picked up the phone and held the handle to Louise's ear so she could hear the dial tone. Louise held the handle and rubbed its smooth metal surface. She turned the dial once, listening for the distinctive sound it made, a sound that no cellphone could ever repeat. Replacing the handle on the phone, Louise smiled.

"You know, Della. I believe you can do anything. Now let's see about that old closet."

They walked back to the office where Sam and Luke were continuing to fiddle with the locked safe, but with no success. Della walked her aunt over to the area behind the bookcase, watching carefully to make sure they didn't trip. Luke placed a chair for Louise near the door of the closet so that Della could bring out the things within.

"You know, I had that bookcase temporarily moved there thirty years ago. Can't remember why. I guess I forgot to move it back," Louise chuckled.

"Here are the documents we found, Aunt Louise," Della said, handing her a stack of yellowing papers. Louise flipped through them briefly, noting that they were receipts for bills paid, the deed to the shop which Louise's grandfather had given to her, as well as lists of purchases and some personal letters and journals.

Della handed her the tin cash box, which seemed fairly heavy for its size and had an interesting clinking sound as though there were coins inside. The box, which measured about 10 x 12 inches, had no lock, just a push-button catch-and-release lid. Inside were divided trays to store paper currency. The cash in the box included ten $1.00 silver certificates, a USA transport mileage ration book, one Hawaiian emergency issue $1.00 bill, and twenty-three twenty dollar bills. Della lifted the tray of cash from the small box and saw underneath seven Buffalo nickels. Louise saw those and put her hands over her heart.

"Someone very special gave those to me a very long time ago," she said, her voice quivering. She picked them up and closed her fingers around them, holding them next to her breast.

After seeing what was in the cash box, Sam and May Howard turned to leave. Roy and Maxine Gates began picking up the detritus of the storm, filling trash bag after trash bag. Maxine got a dust cloth and furniture polish and began to buff the chestnut counter which Della had worked so hard to restore. Soon, it was gleaming again and she went to work on the shelves and display areas.

It was nearly 4:30 that afternoon before Sam and May returned with their next door neighbor. Gil Kessinger had opened his lock shop out of his garage in 1938 and he was frequently called upon by Outer Banks residents as well as the police and the military for his expertise in opening locks. When Kessinger entered the bookshop, he was more than a little surprised.

"Why, Miss Louise, you've really been working on this place, haven't you? You know, in the years after the war, we used to take our two little ones and look in the windows. You always had such interesting displays. 'Course we couldn't often afford to buy much, but we loved to look. Then the last few years, it's kinda sat empty."

"Yes, I've had some heart spells," Louise told him. "But I'm feeling like my old self again. And I've got some new blood in the enterprise – my great niece Della. She gets all the credit for the fix-up. And her dad tells me he can have the repairs done in a jiffy. Right, Roy?"

Roy rolled his eyes at his aunt and said, "Well, it may take two jiffies, but I'll get 'er done!"

Gil Kessinger pulled up a stool and sat in front of the parlor safe, examining it. What he saw was a Victorian period cast iron safe with a working combination lock. It was made in the early 1900's, he told them, admiring the worn pin striping and faded black paint. Painted in gold letters across the top of the door were the words "H. Harris Safe and Lock Company, Pittsburgh, PA." The safe sat on four wheels, so it would be easy to roll out of the closet.

"I'll need you all to be quiet," he told the gathered group, "so I can hear the clicking sound as I turn the dial. That will mean the bolt has disengaged. "

All was silent as Kessinger worked, turning the dial first one way and then another. Suddenly he turned to look at the assembled group triumphantly. He grasped the large handle and turned it to the right opening the heavy metal door. Inside were cubicles and a locking compartment with key in the lock. Kessinger pulled the heavy safe to the door of the closet and turned the key in the compartment door and stepped out of the way. Looking at Louise, he stretched out his hand, while Luke brought a chair to the closet entrance.

"Miss Louise, I think you should open this," Kessinger said.

Louise brought her palm to her mouth, her eyes wide. She got up and walked to the closet, seating herself in front of the safe. She drew a breath and then reached inside. In one of the cubicles, she withdrew a yellowed set of papers about 8 x 10 inches in size. Upon opening it, she read aloud, "This is a stock certificate for some of the earliest shares of Coca Cola Company stock. It was issued to Arthur Hudson, my grandfather. He met Asa Griggs Candler on a business trip to Atlanta and agreed to buy shares in his company. My grandfather left me these in his will and I'd completely forgotten about them. They must be worth a lot of money now."

Louise set the certificate aside and looked into the safe at the locked compartment. She turned the key and pulled open the door slowly.

Oh my, I haven't seen these in decades, Louise thought to herself.

Inside the now unlocked compartment, she withdrew a large paper parcel tied with cotton string. Holding it close to her heart, Louise cried softly. She set the parcel down upon the desk and pulled the cotton string to open it. Around her, Della, Luke, Sam and May, Roy and Maxine, Eunice, and Gill Kessinger waited with baited breath. Louise carefully unfolded the package to reveal white silk fabric, a monogrammed linen handkerchief and a folded piece of paper.

"I guess I better explain all this," Louise said, wiping at her eyes.

CHAPTER FORTY - ONE

1994

The group in the disheveled office looked at one another, not knowing what to expect. Louise Gates had been one of the most open people on the Outer Banks, a solid citizen with, seemingly, no secrets. What could these objects locked for decades in a hidden safe possibly mean?

Della suggested they move into the bookshop which had been cleaned up a bit more than the office. They all walked carefully into the bookshop where Louise settled herself in the middle of the green velvet couch. She motioned for Roy to sit on one side of her and Della on the other. The rest of the assemblage found chairs or stools and sat facing Louise in a semi-circle.

"Della, see that black and white photo hanging on the wall behind the counter. Go yonder and fetch it to me, please."

Della did as she was asked, handing it to her aunt. Louise looked at it sadly for a moment, and then turned it around so the others could see it.

"This young girl in the picture was me, back in 1942. That man beside me was my fiancé, Finn Ingram. Oh my, wasn't he handsome?"

At the mention of the word fiancé, all Louise's audience gasped slightly and looked from one to the other. No one had ever heard her speak of having been engaged. Roy and Della had always just thought of her as their beloved spinster aunt.

"Let me explain," Louise said, seeing the confusion on their faces. "I met Finn in 1942. I was a young girl of 18 working as a waitress at a café on a pier in Nags Head. A hurricane took down the pier many years ago, but in 1942, it was the place to go for breakfast or lunch. This, of course was during the war, and we had lots of restrictions – food and goods were rationed or unavailable, houses had to be blacked out by dusk; we weren't even really supposed to be on the roads after dark and if you had to be, you had to either tape over half of your headlights or turn them off completely.

"You see, in the first half of 1942, Hitler's Nazi government had been sinking commercial and tanker ships all over the Atlantic to prevent them from bringing supplies to Great Britain. The United States had just entered the war after Pearl Harbor in December of the previous year, so Hitler began sending U-Boats over to the Western Atlantic, specifically the shipping lanes between Norfolk and Charleston. (That's where there was a heavy concentration of US military, back then.) And it was thought that it would be especially easy to sink lots of this commercial and military traffic right along the coastline of North Carolina. Remember how the area down near Hatteras has always been known as the Graveyard of the Atlantic – those sandy shoals have foundered lots of ships for hundreds of years.

"Anyway, a Coast Guard station was established on the Outer Banks and a lot of the Coasties, as we called them, used to come to the Pier Café, (that's all we ever called it,) for breakfast or lunch. That's how I met Finn. He was eating at my table one day, struck up a conversation and a few days later asked me to go on a date. He took me for ice cream and I spilled a little on my dress, so he very gallantly offered me his pocket handkerchief to clean it up. Later when I was going to return it, he said to keep it so I would always remember him, as if I could ever forget him. That's the very handkerchief you see right there."

Louise wiped more tears from her eyes and took the length of silk fabric from the package. She stood and shook it out, revealing the beautiful wedding dress she'd made, now a little yellowed with age.

"We fell in love and Finn asked me to marry him," she continued. "He gave me a parachute that had washed up on the beach one day. Fabric was hard to come by during the war, and silk was nearly impossible, so it was a real treasure. After he asked me to marry him, he suggested I could make a wedding dress out of all this silk fabric. He didn't have a ring to give me, but he'd given me a box of Cracker Jacks and inside it was a toy ring which he put on my ring finger. He promised to buy me a better one with his next paycheck.

"When he gave me the fabric, it had a handwritten note pinned to it – this is it," she whispered, holding up the note. "Finn had written 'Will you marry me?' on it. So of course I said yes."

Her breath caught as she realized what would come next in her story. She sat for a minute hugging the photo to her breast with one hand and stroking the silk of the dress with her other. Della put her arm around her aunt's shoulder and gave her a hug.

"Aunt Louise, if this is too hard, you don't have to tell us," she said.

"No, I've carried this inside me for too long. Finn was a flight operations officer in the Coast Guard. He flew a Kingfisher seaplane along with his buddy Hawk Hawkins. I can't remember what Hawk's real name was. They just called him Hawk. Anyway, Finn piloted the plane and Hawk sat behind him as observer. They were looking for

U-Boats in the waters off the coastline. It was a dangerous job –
so many lives had been lost on ships that had been torpedoed by
the U-Boats. And the government didn't talk too much about the
dangers the U-Boats posed back then. I guess they didn't want to
scare us or something. But those of us who lived along the coast
– we knew they were there. Whenever a ship would be torpedoed,
you could feel the windows shaking in the house. You'd see black
plumes of smoke and great fires out on the ocean. A lot of the ships
that were sunk were tankers carrying fuel and when they were torpedoed, the ocean waves would be covered in oil. If there were any
survivors of the sunken ships, they'd sometimes float on pieces of
wreckage for days. And when they were found, they'd be covered
completely in black oil. Oh it was terrible, I tell you."

Louise stopped to wipe a tear from her eyes and blew her nose in a
tissue that Roy handed her. She sat up straight on the couch and ran
her finger along the velvet upholstery of the couch.

"Did I tell you that this couch once sat in my cottage when the cottage belonged to my grandparents? When Finn would come to see
me there, we'd sit on this couch and listen to the radio – Charlie
McCarthy, Bob Hope, Jack Benny. We had some swell times."

"So that's why you didn't want me to recover it," Della said, nod-
ding her head in understanding.

"The last time I saw Finn, he'd come into the café for lunch with
Hawk. They were flying spotter that night. After lunch, I walked
with him out of the café for a minute. He kissed me and said 'I love
you, Louise Gates.' Those were the last words he ever spoke to me.
That evening, he and Hawk were out over the Atlantic when they
spotted a U-Boat riding atop the waves. The U-Boat had come too
near the shoreline for a deep dive, so they were pretty much sitting
ducks. Finn dropped two bombs on the U-Boat and it began to go

under. But before it sank, the machine gunner on the bridge was able to fire off a hail of automatic fire right into the fuel tank of Finn's Kingfisher and of course that started a terrible fire. One of the bullets killed Hawk instantly. Of course, the plane went down and Finn was, from what I've been told, horribly burned on the left side of his face. He stayed in the water for a while until a Coast Guard cutter picked him up and carried him to Norfolk Naval Hospital.

"Communication was different back then, so I didn't hear that he'd been shot down for quite a while. Finally my daddy went to the Coast Guard commander at the Outer Banks station and learned that Finn had been shot down but that's all the information he was given. They did give Daddy his home address, so I wrote his parents to ask if I could see him, but they said he didn't want to see anyone. I tried several times over the years but each time I was told no. Finally, I gave up and packed away this wedding dress – I knew I'd never wear it with anyone else."

"Oh, Aunt Louise, that's such a sad story," Della cried.

"No, seems like I've always had him close to my heart all these years. I don't even know what ever happened to him. I hope he had a good life. I've never been lonely because I had all of you to love. Now, enough of this – let's see what we can do about getting this place back in shape."

Louise got slowly to her feet, clutching the wedding dress, handkerchief and note to her breast and walked over to Maxine.

"Maxine, honey, can I get you to take this down to my cottage and put it on my bed? I don't want it to get messed up."

Maxine said of course she would and Louise went in search of a broom and dust pan.

Time for tears will come later, she told herself.

CHAPTER FORTY - TWO

1994

The weather in late August on the Outer Banks could be hot, humid and changeable. The hurricane of the last week was a perfect example. But the days after Louise told her family of her past engagement to Finn were clear and perfect. The temperature stayed in the mid-seventies and the sky was an amazing cloudless blue. Roy had stapled tarps over the windows to protect against the weather. But the weather was so perfect that Roy was able to proceed immediately with the repair of the windows at the bookshop. The office window was an easy fix, but the bow window was a little more challenging. The muntins and many glass panes to be replaced were not a problem but the curved sill and rails would take a little more time. Nevertheless, Roy took on the challenge with gusto. He'd become a little bored since retiring from his grocery business and the prospect of fixing the windows and helping his aunt and daughter brought him joy. Within three weeks the office window was done and the bow window was in the works.

Della still had paint left over from her earlier work so she painted the windows as soon as her father fixed them, keeping them covered from the inside to allow for a grand reveal soon. A week after the hurricane, the wooden floors were dry, thanks to fans Della had placed in the shop to hasten the drying. After determining that the floors were dry, Della polished them again with a floor waxer she rented at the R & R. The shelves hadn't received too much water so Della was able to restock them and reorder the books that had been water damaged.

Roy and Luke had stabilized the taller shelves around the edge of the shop. Della found a second table and placed the two small tables in the center of the shop. On one, she placed the most popular new works of fiction, putting new non-fiction titles on the other one. She planned to change the displays weekly to keep things interesting. Then she went to work reorganizing the shelves. Louise suggested a special section just for local interest books and local authors, an idea that Della loved. Louise looked in the locked, glass-fronted cabinet beside the counter where several very old books could still be found, their crimson covers, and their pages unharmed by the ravages of the storm. *Wuthering Heights, Sense and Sensibility, A Tale of Two Cities, A Christmas Carol, Frankenstein, and The Hound of the Baskervilles* – all of these first editions in maroon leather bindings with gilt lettering – all were safe from the storm. Louise breathed a sigh of relief as she saw these treasures. Della set up sections for travel books, poetry collections, and small press novels that might not be distributed widely.

One afternoon, Della and Louise were working alone in the shop when the bell over the door tinkled, signaling a visitor. It was Mr. Lester who'd repaired the old shop telephone.

"Oh, Johnny Lester, I hope this means you've got my cash register all fixed up," Louise said cheerily.

"Yes, ma'am. I've got it right outside in my truck. Is this a good time to bring it in?"

"YES!" Both Della and Louise squealed at once and Mr. Lester grinned, going outside to fetch the cash register. He put it on a moving dolly and rolled it into the shop. Della gave the counter one more swipe with a dust cloth and then helped Mr. Lester lift the cash register onto the counter. They arranged it carefully and then stepped back to look at the machine.

Louise could barely believe her eyes. The cash register practically glowed. Its brass finish had been polished and sealed. She asked how it had been accomplished.

"Well," Lester replied, "First I had to get all the dirt and grime off the cash register, so I washed it with a little dish detergent. I used a toothbrush to get into the tight places. Then I used brass polish on it, again using a toothbrush in the tight places. Then I took a soft towel and buffed it all over. The marble pad above the cash drawer was broken, so I replaced it with a new piece of marble. Everything on the register works now (all the keys, signs, bells, drawer, keys/locks, and counters.) It's a real beauty and should catch the eye of anyone who comes in the shop."

"Yes," said Louise with a droll comeback, "Perfect so long as we don't charge more than $5.00 for anything in the store!"

"Now Aunt Louise, I told you we'd just use it for a cash drawer. We'll put everything else on a tablet!" Della told her aunt with a smile.

Louise chuckled and asked Lester how much they owed him. He presented a bill to Della and she wrote him a check. Johnny Lester pocketed the check in his billfold and wrote out a receipt.

"I 'preciate the business, Louise. I'm looking forward to coming back when you open and getting those two books I was promised!"

Lester left the shop, and Louise and Della ran their hands over the burnished surface of the cash register, unable to believe it was the same mechanism. Della adjusted it just a bit to square it up with the edge of the counter. Then they began looking around the rest of the shop. They cleaned and polished every wood surface in the shop. Roy had used his wood shop to build a small rolling ladder to reach the upper shelves. Dividers were created for titles of classic fiction, history, philosophy, mystery, and children's books (a section which was lacking, so more books had to be ordered.)

Della had Luke help her move the green velvet couch back to its original location. Louise came into the shop on the day they moved it and smiled. It was what she had hoped to see. That afternoon, Roy finished the bow window repair so Della took some paint that she'd had left over and touched up what needed to be covered on the window and door surrounds as well as the flower boxes. The flowers in the boxes were a total loss, so Della had had to buy more potting soil to fill them. As it was too late in the season for zinnias, she bought chrysanthemums to fill the boxes.

When the exterior was refreshed, Della set to work on the display area behind the bow windows. As she had planned, she devoted one window to beach reads and spread beach sand along the floor of the display area. Then, among all the beach novels she set there, she placed sand pails and shovels, lots of seashells and fishing netting. Louise declared it perfect. The other window was devoted to children's books and Louise wanted to arrange this one. She placed colorful volumes like the *Nancy Drew* series, *Winnie the Pooh, Peter Pan,* and other classics in the window well surrounded by toys that matched the books. Della thought it was delightful.

Della thought the shop needed some new signage. The shop was so iconic in Nags Head that it had never needed a sign other than the brass plaque. But now with so many tourists vacationing on the Outer Banks, Della wanted to have something painted to hang outside the shop. Louise felt that a new sign wasn't really necessary, but admitted that she might not be the best judge. So she and Della agreed to compromise and decided on a small sign hanging from two hooks on a post by the road. The sign was wooden and painted in black lettering on a white painted plaque. When Roy hung it for his aunt, Louise was delighted.

The last update Della insisted on was to computerize the entire shop. She made a tally of every book in the shop, and began tracking sales and comparing day-to-day sales. She even began creating a store website so they could sell books online.

When all of this was done, Della called Louise and Luke to the shop. When they were together, seated on the green velvet couch, Della told them she thought it was time.

"Time for what, child?" Louise asked.

"Time to uncover the windows and re-open your shop, Aunt Louise!"

CHAPTER FORTY - THREE

1994

The bookshop was an unqualified success. Its opening day brought in locals and tourists in a never-ending stream of customers. Maxine had offered to serve refreshments so she made coffee and tea as well as tea cakes and slices of Ocracoke Island fig cake. Her delicacies were so well received that Louise asked if she might be interested in catering food and drinks as an offering in the bookshop. Maxine asked Roy if he could construct a small counter and add plumbing and electricity in the rear of the shop. Roy, who was fast becoming a construction expert, agreed and soon made a little coffee bar with two small tables and chairs which became quite popular with shoppers. The shop and coffee bar became the kind of place where locals liked to hang out to laugh, to chat, do a cross-word, or to be alone with a book while in the company of others.

Luke frequently stopped by the bookshop with Biscuit in tow. Luke's brother Gideon had taken Biscuit for training and Biscuit was much calmer these days, but he still had a great preference for Della (and the dog biscuits she kept under the counter.) Customers loved it when they'd see that beautiful yellow Lab lying quietly on a rug in the children's section, with a small child reading aloud to him.

On one of these days near closing time, Luke came in to the shop, seeming a little nervous. He had called Della earlier in the day and asked to take her out for a drink after work. When he arrived, he entered the store unobtrusively, keeping his hand in his left pocket covering a small box. In fact, he'd bought a gold watch for Della and planned to ask her to marry him that day as soon as she locked the door. He walked in quietly, seeing that she was talking to a customer, a man who leaned confidently over the counter. Luke looked around the shelves to see if there were any new books that might interest him, and inadvertently overheard the conversation between Della and the customer. Luke was stunned to realize that it was Dylan Metcalfe and he was holding her hand. He was offering Della a position with Colony Books at a much higher salary with shares of the company in addition if she would only come back to Raleigh.

Della spoke softly in deference to Dylan's feelings but told him in no uncertain terms that she would not be leaving L. Gates, Bookseller. Furthermore, she told him that her aunt Louise Gates had told her that she would not be selling her shop to Colony under any circumstances. Unfortunately, Luke heard only the part where Dylan offered Della the advancement. He knew he had nothing comparable to offer her so he put the box back in his pocket and slipped quietly out of the store.

After receiving the final no from Della, Dylan turned on his heel, saying, "You're making a BIG mistake, Della. This store is going to fail and then where will you be? Don't come crying to me for a job when that happens!"

When Luke didn't show up at closing time, Della called him but got no answer. She figured he must have received a call from the fire station so she wasn't too worried. But when he didn't call the next day, she began to be concerned. When she had a few moments around lunch time when the shop was empty, Della called him again.

"Hey Luke," she said tentatively. "Is everything ok? I thought we were supposed to go out for a drink last night."

"Yeah, I looked in but it looked like you were busy."

"Wait, what's going on, Luke? Is this your lunch hour? Can I come down to the station? It looks like we need to talk."

"I've got about 15 minutes."

So Della put a hastily-written sign in the door announcing "Closed temporarily. Back in about 20 minutes." She walked hurriedly down to the fire station where Luke was waiting out front with a can of Diet Coke in his hand. Della looked at him but he seemed distant.

"Hey, Luke. What's going on?"

"I don't know, Della. You tell me."

"What do you mean?" Della said, scratching her head. Are you ok?"

"I'm fine. Congratulations on the new job."

"What job?"

Luke then proceeded to tell her what he'd overheard in the shop the night before. On hearing Luke's comments, she blew a breath out and sighed deeply.

"Oh, Luke, you didn't hear the rest of the conversation. Dylan did come to the store to offer me a position at Colony. He even offered me shares in the company, but I told him I wasn't interested and never would be. I told him Aunt Louise would feel the same way and would never sell him her shop. I think he finally got the message and, to the best of my knowledge, he left the Outer Banks last night and drove back to Raleigh."

Luke set down his soda can and reached for Della, grasping her shoulders and pulling her to him.

"Oh, Della, thank God. I'm so sorry I misread the situation. Can you forgive me?"

"There's nothing to forgive, Luke. I'm just glad we're ok. We are ok, aren't we?" Della said, looking up into his eyes.

"Oh yes, we are so ok. Come with me just a minute. Have you got time? Have you locked the shop?"

Della told him that she had and followed him to a bank of ten red lockers along the back wall of the fire station. Luke guided her to his locker with "Howard" written in permanent marker on the door. He unlocked the padlock and opened the door. Withdrawing a plastic bag marked "Dare Jewelers," he captured Della's hand and led her to a bench near a ladder truck. Della looked puzzled, yet followed as he led her. She sat down on the bench, a puzzled look in her eyes. All of a sudden, Luke kneeled before her, extracting a velvet box from the bag. She opened it to find a gold wristwatch with an inscription on the back which read, "Will you marry me?"

"Della, this isn't exactly how I'd planned this. I thought maybe you might want to pick out your own ring so I got the watch instead. But I guess the fire station is as good a place as any. I've fallen in love with you and can't imagine my life without you. Will you marry me? If you say yes, I promise I'll take care of you and love you and be faithful to you for the rest of my life."

Della reached for Luke, putting both hands on his cheeks and drawing his face to hers. She kissed him deeply again and again.

"Is that a yes?" Luke asked.

"Yes! Yes! A thousand times yes! And any ring you give me will be perfect!"

At Della's words, five firemen stepped out of the kitchen, yelling hurrah and applauding. They came up to Luke, slapping him on his back and offering congratulations.

"You know, a little privacy would have been nice," Luke told them, laughing.

Buck Harrison, one of the firemen, replied, "We hadn't expected to be witnesses to your big proposal, but since we were…well, we were just going to enjoy it."

Della threw her arms around Luke's neck and kissed him full on his lips. The firehouse erupted in applause and cheers.

CHAPTER FORTY - FOUR

1994

Dylan drove back to Raleigh that night, furious that he'd been snubbed. He worried about how he'd tell his father that he'd failed to secure the Nags Head shop. He planned to find another small town where he could move in Colony Books before telling his father of his failure. He was angry and a little embarrassed that he'd been unable to persuade Della and Louise Gates to sell their dinky little shop. Well, he told himself, no need to dwell on that. I'll just get Astrid to come up with another small town that needs a Colony Book store.

The next day, he was in his office before 9:00 AM waiting impatiently for Astrid Olsen to come in for the meeting he had arranged. She was late coming to the office and Dylan became more and more upset. Eventually, she did come into his office, carrying her briefcase and a grande skim latte.

"Morning, Dylan," she said.

"Sit down, Astrid. We need to talk. This Nags Head shop is not going to work out for us, so we've got to start looking elsewhere. I want you to start a search for small towns where we can place our bookstores. My dad has asked me to up our store count by at least twenty this year."

Astrid sat quietly for a minute, and seemed to think. She took a sip of her latte and looked squarely in Dylan's eyes.

"Frankly, Dylan. I'm not going to be able to help you. I'm offering you my two week notice this morning. I plan to resign from Colony Books effective two weeks from today."

"What?" Dylan exploded.

Before he could say anything else, Astrid explained, "I just can't work in a company where the main objective is to steal an old lady's life's work. Miss Louise doesn't deserve that. I've talked to her and she told me how much of her heart and soul has been put into those four walls. She just doesn't deserve it."

"Get out! Just get out of my office!" Dylan erupted. You'll get your severance pay, but I don't want to have to see your face anymore."

"I'm prepared to work my two weeks, Dylan." Astrid replied calmly. "You don't have to do this."

"Just get out of my sight."

Astrid gathered her things and left Dylan's office as quickly as she could. She went to her cubicle and cleared out her desk, planning to drive home to her parents in Norfolk that day. She went to her apartment, packing a bag for a few days' visit with her family.

After a visit in Norfolk of a couple of days, Astrid realized that she needed to see Della and Louise again. So she drove down one morning to the Outer Banks, eager to let them know that she had cut all her ties with the Metcalfes and Colony Books. It seemed important to her to do that.

Before leaving, Astrid had lunch with her parents, who told her that they were planning a family get together soon. Astrid thought that was a great idea and then got into her car heading south. The sun that afternoon was bright and the temperature was mild. Astrid rolled down all the windows of her car and opened the sun roof, reveling in the day. The traffic was light and she arrived at Nags Head, just at 5:00 PM. Parking her car on the street in front of the bookshop, she got out and was amazed at all the upgrades Della had made. As she entered the shop, she was greeted enthusiastically by Della. Astrid immediately told her about resigning from Colony Books. Della worried that Astrid was now out of work and asked if she could stay around for supper so they could talk more. Astrid indicated that she could and would be happy to see Louise as well. Della made a call to her mother and to her Aunt Louise to set up a dinner with Astrid.

Maxine then called Luke and Louise and told them to come over for dinner that night. She'd made a pot of spaghetti and had salad greens, tomatoes and a baguette. Luke offered to pick up Louise and Della and they followed Astrid to the Gates' home. The meal was delicious and Astrid admired Della's new engagement watch.

"I knew it," she said. "I just knew you two were going to get together! I'm so happy for you."

Louise told Astrid she was saddened by the fact that she had lost her job. Astrid responded by telling her not to worry.

"I'm going to spend a few weeks just enjoying being with my family in Norfolk. Then I'm going to start looking for a job maybe in Norfolk or even…maybe on the Outer Banks! I feel good about the future.

"In fact, day after tomorrow, our family is getting together to celebrate my great-Uncle Finn's birthday. He's turning…"

Astrid couldn't finish her statement because Louise had drawn a very visible and audible breath, putting her hand on her throat. Della looked around the room at her parents and at Luke. No one said a word.

"Are you OK, Miss Louise?" Astrid said, looking at her dinner companions.

"Did you say...Finn, Astrid?" Louise whispered.

"Yes, Miss Louise, my Uncle Finn is turning 72. And we are giving him a birthday party. He's such a dear man.

"You said Finn?" Louise repeated. "What is his last name?"

Astrid told the group that her Uncle Finn's last name was Ingram and everyone in the room gasped. Astrid, of course, had no idea what was going on and she asked why they had the reaction they did. Louise asked Astrid if her uncle had ever served in the military.

"Why, yes, Miss Louise, he was in the Coast Guard right here on the Outer Banks during World War II. He's my mother's older brother."

CHAPTER FORTY - FIVE

1994

C hill bumps popped out all over Louise's arms and she shivered as she realized what she'd just heard. She was astonished that Finn was alive and living so close to her. She explained to Astrid that she and Finn had dated during that terrible time when Nazi U-Boats had terrorized the Outer Banks coastline. They had become so close and had fallen in love. Louise told Astrid that Finn had asked her to marry him and to wait for him if he was ever transferred to another base. That's what she'd done – she'd waited for 50 years for Finn. Though she was saddened that so many years had passed and so many opportunities for happiness had gone by, she couldn't understand what had gone wrong. She asked Astrid to explain the intervening years.

"Why? Why? Why wouldn't he let me see him? We were engaged to be married. I loved him with all my heart," Louise cried. Her shoulders shook and tears rolled down her cheeks. Her heart was beating fast and her legs shook.

Astrid looked to Della for an explanation and Della told her a shortened version of what happened when the hurricane exposed the secret closet behind the bookcase. She told her about the wedding dress Louise had made from the silk parachute Finn had given her and about the Crackerjack ring. Della told her about the monogrammed handkerchief that had belonged to her uncle and about the note He'd pinned to the parachute silk.

Astrid had gone over to stand by Louise, worried that she might be having a heart attack. When she saw that it was not the case, she took a deep breath and went back to her seat. She looked at her dinner companions and said, "I'll tell you what I know or at least everything my mother has told me.

"Uncle Finn was stationed here on the Outer Banks during World War II, but of course you already know that. He was a flight operations officer for the Coast Guard...but you know that too. On the last night he was on the Outer Banks, he'd gone up in his plane to spot for U-Boats. He and his observer saw one and dropped two bombs on a U-Boat and it started to sink. But just before it went under, a machine gunner on the bridge of the U-Boat fired a volley of shots and hit Uncle Finn's plane. His observer...I can't remember his name..."

"Hawk. It was Hawk Hawkins," Louise inserted, between sobs.

"His observer was killed from the machine gunner. The machine gun fire hit the fuel tank of Uncle Finn's plane, and he crashed into the ocean. The fuel from the plane's fuel tank ignited and Uncle Finn was drawn into it. His face was horribly burned on the left side from the explosion. He was in the ocean floating on some wood until a Coast Guard cutter picked him up out of the water.

"After that, he was taken to a hospital in Norfolk where he stayed for a couple of years. He had to have a lot of surgeries and he's still pretty disfigured on that side of his face and he has no vision out of his left eye. From what my mom told me, I think he was pretty depressed and refused to see anyone except Mom and her parents for a long time."

"He…he didn't even want to see me?" Louise asked tentatively through her tears.

"As I said, Miss Louise, he was pretty depressed from what I've been told. My parents told me that he refused to see anyone. He said no girl would want to be seen with him anymore."

At this, Louise began crying again. Roy handed her a box of tissues and pulled his chair beside her, wrapping his arm around her. She pulled a couple of tissues out, wiped her eyes, gave her nose a big blow and then looked again at Astrid. Her throat tight with passion, she began to speak, her voice quivering with the emotion she felt.

"Oh but I would have. I've thought of Finn every day for the last 50 years. Tell me what his life has been like all these years. Did he ever get married? Did he have children? "

"No, Uncle Finn has stayed single all his life. No children. Let me call my mom and let her tell you the rest."

So Astrid called her mother in Norfolk and explained the incredible coincidence of finding her Uncle Finn's old fiancé. She put Louise on the phone and turned on the speaker feature so all in the room could hear.

"Hello," Louise said uncertainly, "This is Louise Gates speaking."

"Oh, Louise, this is Birgit, Finn's younger sister. I wanted to contact you so many times over the years, but Finn always said no. He lost a lot of his old self-confidence when the U-Boat gunner shot down his plane and he was burned."

When Louise asked what the intervening years had been like for Finn, Birgit hesitated. She wasn't sure how much Louise already knew and how much Finn would have wanted her to share. But finally, she decided it was time for the two lovers to meet again.

"Finn led pretty much a solitary life for a while after his plane went down. He had a hard time with his facial disfigurement (that's why he chose not to see you. He didn't want you to have to see it and deal with all of his hospitalizations.)"

"Oh, Birgit, I would have done it all. I wish I could have been there for him. I just never knew what became of him. But I held him in my heart and thought of him every day."

"He was eventually able to leave the hospital and he got some therapy for his depression," Birgit went on. "He got his driver's license renewed and got a job at the Veteran's Administration office in Norfolk and made it to management there. He retired a few years ago but now works part-time at the VA. He now lives in the Norfolk Naval Senior Center – He has an independent living apartment there."

Louise, who had stood up to talk to Birgit, sat down with a thud in her chair. She put her palm on her forehead and looked up at the ceiling, dropping the phone.

"You mean to tell me – all these years he's been just an hour and a half away from me and I never knew it? Oh, what a loss – we could have had all those years together."

Louise put her head in her hands and cried bitter tears. Her shoulders shook and Della went to her, surrounding her with her arms. Astrid picked up the phone, and told her mother to hold on for a minute. She helped Della get her aunt settled and then looked at Louise with a smile.

"Well, Miss Louise, what's wrong with going to see him now?" Astrid said to her holding out the phone. "It's not too late, you know."

Louise's head shot up as she was suddenly realizing that there was a possibility of seeing Finn again after all these years. She looked hard at Astrid, then picked up the phone from her, and addressed Finn's sister on the line.

"Birgit, do you think you could take me to see Finn? Do you think he'd even want to see me? After all these years, I'm not quite the young girl he remembers."

Birgit told her that she thought it was a fine idea and she thought it would be the perfect birthday gift for her brother. She told Louise to prepare herself for Finn's appearance – that he looked quite good for a 72 year old man except for the left side of his face which was quite disfigured.

"Pshaw!" Louise said. "Why I'm so old, he probably won't even recognize me. But I would give anything to see him again – to have him in my life. "

"Then let's do it," Birgit told her. "I've always wanted to meet you, Louise. Finn spoke so glowingly of you before his plane went down. You bring your family over to our house for the birthday party (Astrid can give you the address and details.) and we'll finally make all this turn out right."

Louise felt like a girl again. It seemed to her that all those decades of loss and loneliness when all she had for companions were her family and her books – all those years had vanished. It hardly seemed possible that she was going to be with Finn again. Della and Luke drove her home listening to her talk the whole way about her memories of those days during the war.

Before she went to bed that night, she picked up the mayonnaise jar full of Buffalo nickels on her dresser, holding it close for a moment. She straightened the white silk dresser scarf underneath it, made from remnants of a parachute. She remembered the day so many years ago when her Coastie had given her that white silk parachute. When she knelt beside her bed for her nightly prayers, she thanked God for saving Finn and for the privilege of getting to see him again. When she rested her head on her pillow that night, she looked up at the ceiling.

"Well, God, You answered my prayer. But You sure took Your time to do it!" she thought.

Then she closed her eyes, fell into a deep sleep and dreamed of Finn and those days of so long ago.

CHAPTER FORTY - SIX

1994

Two days later, Louise was looking through her closet, pushing hangers bearing her dresses over and over to find just the right thing to wear. She wanted to look as good as possible when she saw Finn again for the first time in so many years.

Oh, what am I worried about? I'm an old woman and he's an old man, blind in one eye. He'll just have to accept me as I am.

Truthfully, Louise was so excited about going to see Finn that she was more than a little nervous. So she called Della over from her apartment and asked for her help in selecting a dress. Della walked across the porch to her aunt's door and called out to let her know she was there.

"Come on back, child. I want you to help me pick out something to wear."

"That's easy," Della replied. "That cornflower blue dress with the white sprigs of flowers all over it. It's my favorite dress of yours and it will look perfect for today."

"Do you think so? I'm just so anxious I can't think straight."

"Well, don't worry. It will all turn out all right. Now I've got to finish getting dressed myself. Luke's coming to pick me up and we'll take you to Mama and Daddy's house. You can then ride with us or with Mama and Daddy over to Norfolk."

Della skipped back over to her apartment, excited for her aunt and hopeful that the day would bring her joy. In the back of her mind, though, she knew that it could bring Louise more heartache if Finn refused to see her. So she focused instead on getting dressed. She chose a navy cotton skirt with a white eyelet blouse and white flat sandals. She tied her hair back with a navy grosgrain ribbon and dabbed a little make-up on her face. Then she went over to the main cottage to wait for Louise and Luke.

Soon she heard a knock at the door and walked through the hall to open the door. It was Luke, dressed in khaki slacks, a blue plaid shirt with the sleeves rolled up and boat shoes with no socks. Della's heart went into overdrive as she saw her handsome date. He came into the house, closing the door behind him. The front hall was dark and Louise was still dressing, so he wrapped Della in his arms in a tender embrace, pushing her slightly against the wall. Finding her welcoming, Luke pressed his lips to hers, his body warm with desire. Hearing Louise approaching from her bedroom, he pulled away, wiped the lipstick off his lips and grinned at Della.

"When I kiss 'em, they stay kissed!" he said as Louise entered the family room.

"OK, you two lovebirds. It's about time to ride. Now let me see, have I got everything?"

"You look perfect, Miss Louise," Luke said and Della agreed.

She was wearing the dress Della suggested with white wedge-heeled sandals and a white straw purse. Along with her purse she was carrying a small shopping bag, about which she said nothing. They locked the cottage door, and got into Luke's small white sedan. Louise remarked that the first time she had ridden in it, Luke and Della were driving her to the hospital after a heart spell. Della remembered and said she was so glad her aunt's doctor had adjusted her medications so that she had been feeling much better since then.

"Della," Louise responded, smiling broadly, "What we're doing today is the very best heart medicine I could ever get."

The trio soon pulled into the sandy driveway of Della's parents' Kitty Hawk home. It was on Beach Road opposite the oceanfront, so they had been spared the worst of the recent hurricane. Nevertheless, with unobstructed views of the ocean across the street, they had breathtaking views of the Atlantic Ocean. The house itself was a classic Outer Banks box style home with three main level bedrooms, two baths and a captain's watch atop the house which they used as a sunroom. Wide decks full of rocking chairs surrounded the entire house.

Luke got out of the car and ran around to open Louise's and Della's doors for them. Louise pressed her hands down her dress front, checking for wrinkles. She was nervous and hoped she still looked OK. Inside the galley kitchen, Maxine was busy wrapping up some cookies she had made to carry to Finn. Roy was sitting on the deck drinking a cup of coffee and he hailed them as they climbed the stairs.

"Well, Aunt Louise," Roy said, standing as the three stepped onto the deck, "You think you're ready for this?"

"Honey, I've been waiting 50 years for this day. Let's get going!"

Roy went inside to get Maxine, who had packed a cooler with ham biscuits and deviled eggs along with the cookies "just in case they need a little something else," she said. Louise decided to ride with

Roy and Maxine "to give the lovebirds some privacy," she told them. When the cooler was packed inside Maxine's SUV, they pulled out of the driveway with Luke and Della following behind.

They had originally planned to go to the Norfolk Naval Senior Center where Finn had an apartment, but as they were driving to Norfolk, Della got a phone call from Astrid. They had decided to move the birthday party from Finn's apartment to Birgit's home where they would have more room. So Della texted her mother with the change of plans and sent the new address to her.

Arriving at Birgit's home, they were greeted by the mother and daughter on the large front porch which overlooked the Hague waterfront. It was a beautiful brick turn of the last century home with a porch with white ionic columns. Astrid introduced Louise and the rest of her group to her mother who invited them in. The entry hall featured an elegant winding staircase, 12 foot ceilings, and wooden pocket doors leading into the rooms on either side of the hall.

"Lars and I bought this house when we married," Birgit said in her charming Norwegian accent. My husband Lars was a physician and the house was located close to the hospital. In fact, Lars and I met because he was one of the young doctors who first treated Finn after he was burned. He passed away last year. Let's go right through here," she said indicating the door to the right. They walked through a parlor with rich molding and a marble fireplace atop oak floors. Birgit pointed them through to a sunroom where Finn was seated to their right in a large green rocking chair.

As they had approached on his blind side, Finn had no sight of them initially. Louise stepped back momentarily and Roy, concerned for his aunt, touched her arm and looked at her. She shook her head as though to tell him that she was ok.

"Finn, we've got company," Birgit said, touching him on his left shoulder.

"Now who in the world – is that my favorite niece, Astrid?" he said grinning in his lopsided fashion.

"Uncle Finn, I've brought some people you're going to want to see. Can you turn a bit in your chair?"

Finn, with the same erect stance of so many years ago, stood up, his physique still plainly recognizable to Louise. He looked vigorous and strong, belying his 72 years.

Louise looked at Finn with tenderness and hope mixed with sorrow at what he had suffered. Finn turned toward Astrid so that his niece was in his line of sight. For a moment, he smiled his crooked smile, misshapen because of the burn he had endured. Then his eye moved to Louise and his legs gave way beneath him.

"Is this…? No, it cannot be," he muttered.

He sat suddenly with his mouth open. He crossed his hands over his heart, and then put one of them over the left side of his face, ashamed of his deformity.

Seeing the passion on the faces of both Finn and Louise, Birgit looked at the others with eyebrows raised. "Why don't we cross the street and have a look at the waterfront?" she said, pointedly.

"Good idea. It looks beautiful," Maxine agreed and she followed Roy, Della, Luke, Astrid and Birgit out of the sunroom.

The silence that filled the room after they left was palpable. Louise reached out and touched Finn's shoulder. He tentatively put his hand over hers and looked down, not willing for her to see him as he was. Tears came to him and his shoulders shook with the emotion he felt.

"I waited for you, Finn, all these years, just as I said I would."

"You shouldn't have," he replied curtly and turned away from her. "I never wanted you to see me like this."

"Will you stand and look at me, Finn?"

"Ha!" he answered sarcastically. "With my one good eye and my face half melted? And you – you've hardly changed in all these years. Still the same open, sweet face. Still the same tender smile. Still the same tiny frame. I must be dreaming. You'd better go, Louise. There's nothing for you here."

"I will not go, Finn. After all these years of waiting and hoping, I will not go. I will not lose you again."

Finn stood, reaching with his right hand to palm her face. He looked her over from head to toe, turning his head to examine with his good eye her grey hair, her dress, and her legs. Louise, in turn, reached out her right hand, her fingers gently exploring the keloid marks of his burned face. Her fingers caressed every scar with tenderness. She wrapped her arm around him in an embrace. He had stood stiffly at first, as though he couldn't bear her touch. But when she lifted her lips and kissed his burned face, he broke down in heaving sobs and sat down instantly. Louise pulled a chair up close to his and sat next to him, reaching out for his hand. She lifted it to her lips and kissed it.

"I have found you at last," she said. "And I've brought you your handkerchief which you loaned me. See? I laundered and pressed it. I told you I'd return it to you. It just took me a while to find you."

Louise handed the linen handkerchief to him, reached up and ran her fingers through Finn's hair, once blonde, now grey but still full. She turned his head to her so that he could see her with his good eye.

"See, Finn? I've grown old waiting for you while you are still handsome."

"Never, Louise. No more of that talk. I thought you would be repulsed at the sight of me. I guess my pride got in the way."

"But why didn't you come back for me or at least contact me? I have lived in the same cottage all these years."

It took Finn a moment to take that in and gather his courage. He took a long drink of the water he'd been sipping before his guests came and set the glass down on the table beside him. Taking a deep breath, he started at the beginning, telling her briefly of sinking the U-Boat and of being gunned down by a machine gunner on the U-Boat's bridge before it sank. He told her sadly of how Hawk was killed. Louise began weeping as she remembered Finn's old friend and observer during the war. She looked in her purse for a tissue, but found none.

"Here, you can use this," Finn said, with his crooked smile, and handed her the monogrammed handkerchief she'd just returned to him.

Then Finn told Louise of the many plastic surgeries on his face he'd had to have as well as other operations following the downing of his plane. He told her shyly of the depression he'd suffered and the years of therapy it had taken for him to feel even a little bit normal again.

"I just didn't want to inflict all that on you. I didn't want you to have to be my nurse. You should have married and had children."

"I wanted to, Finn, with you," Louise replied sadly, shaking her head.

He told her of working for the Veteran's Administration in Norfolk and of his parents' passing. He shared that he lived now in a senior living apartment for retired military personnel nearby and was quite independent.

He had just asked her to tell him of her life on the Outer Banks when the six others of the party came back in, a little slowly, taking the temperature of the room. When they saw that Louise was holding Finn's hand and that they were smiling through tears, Astrid came up to her uncle on his right side, and kissed his cheek.

"We're hungry, Uncle Finn. Isn't it time to eat?"

Louise patted Finn's hand and stood, telling him they could finish their discussion after dinner. Birgit had prepared a delicious birthday feast of smoked salmon, with potatoes, carrots and broccoli. Louise had insisted on sitting by Finn, and he had demanded that she sit on his right side so he could see her. Birgit offered a blessing before the meal, thanking God for the reuniting of Finn and Louise and the new friends they'd all made. Finn and Louise held hands frequently during the meal and smiled as though they were the handsome Coastie and the pretty waitress they each remembered the other to be. All eight of the diners sat around the mahogany table in the dining room after the meal remarking about what a coincidence it had been for Astrid to have gone to work at Colony Books which led to her ultimate meeting with Louise and Della. It was as though God had planned it as an answer to their prayers.

Louise told about opening the bookstore after the war with books from her grandfather's library. Della added what a remarkable thing it had been for her to have come home and found a job at her aunt's bookshop. Louise inserted how remarkable the redo of the shop had been – bringing it into the future, thanks to the hard work of Della, Luke, Roy, Maxine, Luke's parents and so many others.

"I don't think we can forget to thank Biscuit for his part in bringing us together!" Luke said, laughing, bringing Della's hand to his lips for a kiss. He told the assembled guests about how Biscuit had jumped up on Della on the day they'd met. Everyone had a good laugh at that.

Finally Birgit brought in a huge chocolate cake and Astrid helped her light the birthday candles atop it. They all sang an unharmonious chorus of "Happy Birthday to You" and Finn successfully blew out all the candles though, with his malformed mouth, it took him two tries. He said he didn't need to make a birthday wish, though, because all his wishes had come true.

After coffee and cake, Roy stood and said, "I guess we better head back to the Outer Banks. No telling how bad the traffic will be."

Tears came immediately to the eyes of both Finn and Louise and they withdrew into the hall by themselves. Neither was ready to let the other one out of sight after so many years of being alone. They exchanged contact information and planned to get together the next day. Finn said that Astrid had told him during dinner that she'd drive him down to the beach anytime. He thought tomorrow would be a good time to take her up on that.

The entire group walked out to the driveway, Finn and Louise hanging back while the others got into their cars. In the dark, they looked up at the sky, its velvet blackness studded with stars.

"I thought of you every day, Finn."

"I thought of you, every day too, Louise. That's what saved me when I was bobbing about unconscious in the water. I don't want to let you go but I'll see you tomorrow."

He leaned down and wrapped her small shoulders in his still strong arms. Looking into her eyes, he could hardly believe she was next to him after all those years.

"Could I kiss you?" he asked, still a little worried about how his scarred lip might affect her.

Louise closed her eyes, nodded and lifted her mouth to reach his. Their lips brushed together tentatively at first. She stood on her tip-toes and leaned into the kiss which became deeper and more passionate. Finn crushed her to his chest and ran his fingers through her hair. It was a kiss that had been worth the wait.

CHAPTER FORTY - SEVEN

1994

Louise rode in the back seat with Luke and Della on their way home to the beach. She hardly said a word for the hour and a half that it took, focusing all her thoughts on finally seeing Finn again. When she was in her cottage, she went to her bedroom, and ran her fingers along the silk dresser scarf, remembering the day Finn gave her the parachute. She dressed in her nightgown and knelt in prayer beside her bed.

"Thank you, God, for returning Finn to me."

She slept that night more contentedly that she had in years.

In Norfolk, Finn was still in a daze at having been reunited with Louise after all those years. He drove back to his apartment and looked in his closet. He pulled his pants and shirts aside, and found one of his old Coast Guard uniforms that he'd saved somehow all these years. It brought a tear to his eyes to think of all the time he'd wasted. Nevertheless, he slept well that night, thinking of how he would see Louise in a few hours.

Luke brought Della back to her apartment, but was reluctant to leave. They'd both been enchanted by the love story of Finn and

Louise and somehow they wanted to extend that enchantment to themselves. So Luke suggested they take a walk on the beach. It was nearly 11:00 PM and the moon was full. They took off their shoes and left them on Della's porch, then walked around Louise's cottage to the path that led through the sea oats. The oats sat atop dunes which protected the cottages from the surf. It was low tide on the beach and the bright moon lit the sand so that it almost appeared to be midday. Luke took Della's hand in his, and they strolled down to the water's edge, the wet sand cold on their feet.

Luke looked out over the ocean and shook his head. The water was so calm, lapping against their feet. They stepped over a couple of broken shells and stopped to embrace. Luke was aware of his burning desire for Della and Della's heart was racing inside her chest. He looked at her with eyes that were smoldering.

"The day has been so wonderful, hasn't it, Luke?"

"Yes, seeing your Aunt's reunion with Finn was so moving. I hope they'll finally be able to spend some time together now. What time will Finn and Astrid be here tomorrow?"

"I think they are coming right before lunch. Aunt Louise said she'd fix some lunch for them but I told her not to bother – I'd get some takeout from the Ocean Tide Café and bring it home so she won't have to worry. Can you join us?"

"I'll try but I'm on duty at the station so it will just be for a bit. Guess I better get you in. It's beginning to look like it may shower. Have I told you today how much I love you?"

Luke grinned, wrapped his arms around her, and then picked up Della swinging her around on the hard packed sand. She squealed with delight and threw her head back. He put her down, and then looked at her eyes and grasped her chin with his hand. He pulled her lips up to his and pressed a kiss on them. Then he kissed her again and again and again and finally yelled,

"I love this girl!"

Someone in the cottage two houses down the beach yelled back. "Good. Now hush! I'm trying to get this baby to sleep."

Della and Luke looked momentarily embarrassed and then laughed. Luke grabbed her hand and they ran up the dune back to the cottage where he kissed Della once more. Then he dusted off his feet, picked up his shoes, and put them back on again.

"I'll see you at noon tomorrow, sweet girl," he said throwing her a kiss. Della caught the kiss with her hand and hugged it to her heart, waving goodnight.

The next morning, Louise was up early having washed and set her hair. She thought about wearing a pair of slacks but thought better of it as Finn never saw her in anything but a dress so many years ago. She wanted to please him and wasn't sure just what he'd like. She still had the slim figure of so many years ago, and wanted to be attractive for Finn. She found a pink dress with navy pinstripes that she thought he might like and wore that. Then she began looking around the cottage to see if everything was in its place. She and Della had decided to close the shop for the day so they'd be free to visit.

By lunch time when she had gotten everything shipshape, she heard the sound of a car arriving. She went out on the porch, but found it was Della bringing her the lunch she'd promised. Louise's hand went to her heart as she imagined all sorts of things that might have delayed Finn's arrival.

*What if he hadn't liked how she'd aged and decided he didn't want
to see her again? What if they'd had an accident? What if Finn had
had a heart attack?*

By the time she got through imagining all these scenarios, Astrid's
car turned into Louise's driveway, the wheels throwing up sand and
gravel. A huge smile broke across Louise's face and, seeing Finn in
the car, she waved from the porch. Finn was the first one out of the
car and he practically ran up to the steps.

"It still looks the same, Louise. It all looks the same…and so do
you," he said.

"Pshaw! You've been out in the sun too long. I was beginning to
worry. What took you so long?"

Astrid had gotten out of the car with her mother by this time and
told Louise of the usual traffic back-up. Birgit looked in between
the cottages at the Atlantic Ocean beyond and marveled at its beauty.
The sea was calm today and the temperature was mild. So it was a
perfect day to visit. Louise invited them all to come inside and they
sat in the family room with its lovely views of the ocean. Finn said
that the only things missing were the three-foot tall Philco radio and
the green velvet couch. Della laughed and told him they'd moved
the couch to the bookshop and Finn said he'd have to see the shop
after lunch.

Louise got up to set the table but Della told her to sit and visit. She
knew Luke was coming so she wanted to get things set out in case he
was short on time. He arrived as soon as Della had set the food on the
table and she called everyone into the dining room. Finn marveled at
the memories the old house called to mind. As they did the previous
night, Louise sat on Finn's right side and they looked frequently at
each other throughout the meal. Della asked Luke to return thanks

and he offered a prayer that was elegant in its simplicity – thanking God for family, food and friends. Then everyone began to dig in, the old house filling up with laughter, chatter and love.

After lunch, Luke had to go back to the station but he promised to see them later. Della walked him to the door where he wrapped his arm around her waist, drawing her to him. He planted a big kiss on her lips, smacking his lips afterward with a grin.

"Um Um! That's all the dessert I need."

"Well, here's a piece of cake for you anyway, in case you need a pick-me-up this afternoon," she said, handing him a Tupperware dish containing a piece of lemon pound cake. Luke took it, kissed her quickly and left her with a wink.

"See you later, sweet girl."

Inside Louise's cottage, Birgit was helping Louise clear the table while Finn sat on one of the porch benches, looking out across the ocean's waves. He was lost in thought, remembering the events which had changed his life so markedly, when Louise and Birgit came out followed by Della.

"Does it look the same to you, Finn?" Louise asked quietly. Birgit took one of the rocking chairs while Della stood leaning against the door jamb. Louise moved to sit beside Finn on the porch bench.

Finn thought a moment before answering," In some ways, when I look out at the eternal ocean, I can imagine that it's still 1942, when I saw you last, Louise. But a drive up and down Virginia Dare Trail has convinced me otherwise. I'm just glad you're still here."

A smile crossed Louise's lips and she said, "Why don't we go see the bookshop? You know I opened it after I lost you. It was a way to preserve my sanity, I guess, and it has become something of a Nags

Head tradition. I had a health scare a while back and I had to close it for a bit. Then Della here came back from Raleigh and made some amazing changes to it. It really looks wonderful now."

Everyone agreed that it would be good to see Louise's shop, so the five of them got into Astrid's car and drove the few blocks to the shop. There, Della was pleased to see that the chrysanthemums she'd planted after the hurricane damage were thriving. Louise unlocked the shop door and proudly ushered Finn and the others into the shop. She took him immediately to the place near the counter where the green velvet couch rested. Finn placed his hand on the arm, now a little shabby but still beautiful.

"Oh, how many memories this brings back," Finn sighed.

Louise pointed with pride to the picture hanging on the wall of Finn and her.

"Remember that day?" she asked him.

He told her that he had bought a copy of the photo for himself as well and he looked at it almost every day. Then Louise took him back to the office where the hidden closet had been discovered. She opened the safe to show him where the dress had been stored for so many years. Then they walked back to the front of the shop to look at the displays of books.

"Louise, you are an amazing woman," he told her, looking down at her with awe. "It was practically unheard of for a woman to be in business alone back in the war years. But you did it."

"I did it for us. I kept hoping you'd come back to me, Finn. And you did."

CHAPTER FORTY - EIGHT

1994

The happiness which surrounded Louise and Finn was contagious and everyone they met felt it. Luke and Della also seemed to be infected by their joy. So it was natural that all agreed that with the 50th anniversary of the bookshop coming up, a grand celebration should be planned. Finn came down to the beach as often as he could get away from his job, as he was still working part time for the Veteran's Administration. Luke came over to the shop frequently, as much to see his girl as to help out.

Della and Louise put their heads together and came up with lots of grand ideas to make the anniversary celebration a spectacular success. They were able to get several well-known authors to appear at various hours during the day of the celebration to do public readings and sign their current books. Louise rearranged her First Edition collection of books in the locked glass case near the counter and featured one of the special books or one of the classics in the shop each week in her new blog. She was becoming quite at ease on the computer and couldn't believe she hadn't thought to do this before.

Since leaving her job at Colony Books, Astrid Olsen had been spending a lot of time on the Outer Banks and had taken up her old hobby of painting. She'd done some really lovely pen and ink designs of the beach and the "Unpainted Aristocracy" and Della felt that they'd really sell. So she set up a corner table with some of Astrid's work. They were extremely popular, so Della felt that her friend ought to make greeting cards and book marks featuring her Outer Banks art. Maxine made space for the greeting cards in her coffee bar. It was, as Della had hoped, the sort of place where one could sit and enjoy the smell of fresh brewed coffee and read a book or do a crossword puzzle. It was a place to be with others if you wanted or to have a bit of peace and quiet if you liked. It was the sort of place where you could overhear the conversations of all sorts of people – fishermen, lovers, or friends gathering for a snack.

Through all the preparations for the anniversary celebration, Finn and Louise had been in constant contact, either by phone, or by visiting one another. In each of their visits or conversations, they revealed what their lives had been like over the course of the last 50 years.

Finally, the day of the anniversary celebration arrived. It was four weeks before Christmas and Della had decorated the shop in every corner. A tall Fraser Fir stood watch by the counter, its tiny lights reflected in the shiny brass of the restored cash register. The tree was hung with beads and baubles from Louise's extensive collection. She had inherited boxes of Shiny-Brite ornaments of all colors from her mother and grandmother, made in pre-war Germany. On a tiny faux fir tree at the end of the counter, Della had placed miniature knitted stockings made by Maxine. In each stocking, Della had placed a discount coupon to be used on purchases in the shop.

When Louise turned the sign on the door to "Open," she was immediately met with an influx of customers eager to take advantage of the sales. Older people who shopped brought memories of the shop in its early days and these especially pleased Finn, who was eager to know everything about his beloved Louise.

The UPS trucks had brought daily deliveries of more wonderful books, the beauty of their covers enhancing the warm glow of wooden shelves and countertops. Louise placed what she called "shelf-talkers" here and there about the store - little cards on which she wrote about her favorite reads.

On the morning of the celebration, Della hosted a story time for children and their parents, introducing them to her favorite Christmas books - *A Christmas Story, Two from Galilee, A Christmas Carol*, and of course, the Christmas story from the second chapter of Luke in the *Bible*.

As a special gift to the community, Louise announced that she was establishing the Finn Ingram Scholarship in honor of her courageous hero for Manteo High School students who were planning to join the Coast Guard after graduation. And Finn announced that he would be underwriting the donation of 500 books to Kitty Hawk Elementary School. L. Gates, Bookseller became so popular that it brought new businesses to what had been a fading business district – a new boutique, a gift shop and a surf shop.

Della was busy the entire day, ringing up purchases, talking to customers and authors, and making time to snag a hug from Luke when he popped in at lunch time. She told him of her plans to have writing workshops for local authors with opportunities to talk with agents and publishers.

As the day ended, Finn put his arm around Louise's shoulder, a look of amazement on his face. He couldn't believe how successful the event had been.

"You amaze me, Louise Gates. My time in the Coast Guard was very brief – it was important but it was cut short thanks to a U-Boat I met. But you – you've built this amazing business pretty much on your own. You've created the kind of store where you and Della seem to know the reading preferences of neighbors and newcomers alike. And you can guide customers to titles they might like. It's just the kind of bookstore I've always loved and it's all due to you."

"Finn, if I built this business, it was because of the hole in my heart when you went missing. I had to do something or I thought I would die. You were my inspiration all of these years. And really, I couldn't have completed it without help from Della and the rest of the family. I look around this room and know that I am so very blessed. I have everything I need – the warm sun on my back in the summer, a cozy cottage to watch the winter storms, a business which gives people a quiet place to read and enjoy good coffee and good books aplenty, and finally, Finn, finally after so many years, I have the love of my life by my side."

"And I'm never leaving again," Finn said, kissing the top of Louise's head.

CHAPTER FORTY - NINE

1994

As the month of December began, the weather turned unseasonably cold for the Outer Banks. A light snow had fallen and the mountainous dunes of Jockey's Ridge were covered with a thin dusting of snow. It made everything look festive and the bookshop had been decorated with boughs of evergreens, red plaid ribbons and Christmas baubles everywhere. Della had gotten the help of her father and Luke to hang swooping evergreen swaths over each of the bow windows out front.

Astrid was still unsure of her future plans, though Della was hoping she might consider opening a gallery of her work on the Outer Banks. Astrid's cards and paintings had become so well-liked that she frequently sold out and had to restock the revolving card rack which stood near Maxine's coffee bar. A small tee-shirt shop next door to L. Gates, Bookseller had gone out of business at the end of September and Astrid had been considering opening it as a gallery for her cards and art. She had talked with a realtor about the costs involved in rehabbing it for her purpose and found that it was a bit above her pocketbook.

At about the same time, Maxine was realizing that her coffee bar was beginning to overwhelm Louise and Della's bookshop. So, she called Astrid one day and inquired about the possibility of a joint venture between the two of them. Maxine said that Roy had offered to front the cost of renovations to the shop next door to L. Gates to make it work as both an art gallery and a coffee bar. And since the shop shared a wall with the bookshop, Roy felt that he could design an opening between the two shops to make for easier access to both places. All that would be required would be to purchase the building, something which Finn and Louise eagerly did. Astrid loved the idea and they set to work putting their plan into motion.

By three weeks before Christmas, a finished opening between the two shops had been created. Astrid had moved her artwork and cards into the new half of the shop and had been able to paint the shop's interior (with some help from Della and Luke.) Roy had begun work already on running plumbing into the new half of the shop and had built a counter for the coffee bar. Maxine had bought three art nouveau ice cream bistro glass-topped table and chair sets of French blue wrought iron. The chairs had sweetheart backs, metal seats, and looped feet. Maxine and Astrid ordered heavy polished brass curtain rods with café curtains of blue and yellow striped and floral fabric. As a final touch, Maxine ordered white coffee mugs and small plates emblazoned with the United States Coast Guard emblem on it, as a way to honor Finn. The coffee bar and art gallery proved to be as popular as the bookshop had been.

Louise was less involved in the shop's renovations and celebrations as she was more focused on her new relationship with Finn. In years past, before she found Finn again, Louise had always celebrated holidays with Roy, Maxine and Della. But this year, she planned to celebrate with Finn. Roy had driven her to Norfolk a week before Christmas to stay with Birgit. She was nervous about spending so much time with Finn's sister and with Finn himself as he planned to stay at Birgit's house as well. But Birgit was delighted at the possibility of the rekindled romance for her brother and so she was eager to plan an elaborate Christmas Day dinner.

On the big day, Louise dressed in her best ruby red two piece wool suit with a white jewel collar blouse and red pumps to match. Finn dressed in a navy blue suit and ruby tie while his sister wore a green woolen dress with a sweater to match. Their first event of the day was a breakfast of croissants and coffee, followed by the Christmas morning service at Birgit's church, St. Paul's Lutheran, a magnificent Gothic structure in downtown Norfolk. Astrid, Birgit, Finn and Louise sat on one of the garnet velvet cushions covering each of the pews and sang lustily the old carols they knew so well. The pastor told with great tenderness the age old story of the Nativity of Christ from the Gospel of Luke:

"[4] So Joseph also went up from the town of Nazareth in Galilee to Judea, to Bethlehem the town of David, because he belonged to the house and line of David. [5] He went there to register with Mary, who was pledged to be married to him and was expecting a child. [6] While they were there, the time came for the baby to be born, [7] and she gave birth to her firstborn, a son. She wrapped him in cloths and placed him in a manger, because there was no guest room available for them. [8] And there were shepherds living out in the fields nearby, keeping watch over their flocks at night. [9] An angel of the Lord appeared to them, and the glory of the Lord shone around them, and they were terrified. [10] But the angel said to them, "Do not be afraid. I bring you good news that will cause great joy for all the people. [11] Today in the town of David a Savior has been born to you; he is the Messiah, the Lord. [12] This will be a sign to you: You will find a baby wrapped in cloths and lying in a manger." [13] Suddenly a great company of the heavenly host appeared with the angel, praising God and saying, [14] "Glory to God in the highest heaven, and on earth peace to those on whom his favor rests."

Louise, as always, sat at Finn's right hand side, unable to believe that after all these years she was where she had always wanted to be. Finn held onto Louise's hand during the closing prayer and kissed her as they exited the church.

Dinner at the Olsen house was a grand affair as Birgit had ordered a catered meal from a nearby restaurant. She was an accomplished cook but she wanted to be free to enjoy the day with her family and Louise. The imposing dining room was hung with Christmas greenery and candles adorned the table. The assembled guests dined on beef tenderloin, roasted potatoes, green beans, and hot yeast rolls with French butter. For dessert, Birgit served her own chocolate cake which Finn admitted was his favorite.

After dinner, the foursome moved to the family room where a ten foot tall Fraser fir stood regally in the center of the room. Astrid and Birgit had decorated it with family ornaments brought from Norway. The lights on the tree sparkled and lit the mound of presents beneath the tree. They brought chairs to sit around it and began opening presents. Louise had brought Finn a volume of Coast Guard history. Birgit and Astrid exchanged sweaters and bracelets. They laughed when they opened their packages, revealing that the gifts were almost exact duplicates. Finally Finn reached under the low branches of the tree and brought forth a tiny box wrapped in gold paper.

"This is a little late, Louise, but the feeling behind it is the same as it was so many decades ago," Finn said handing the package to Louise.

Louise looked at the box and tears came to her eyes. She held the box close to her breast for a moment, and then unwrapped it carefully, preserving the paper as she did as a child of the Great Depression. Inside the gold paper was a green velvet box. She looked into Finn's eyes and he nodded, silently encouraging her to open the gift. She lifted the lid slowly and found inside a diamond solitaire of incredible beauty.

"Now I can finally replace this one," Louise said, taking the Cracker Jack ring off her finger.

Finn lifted the box from Louise's hand and got down on one knee, which creaked a bit as he did so. He pulled the ring from its slot in the velvet and carefully, tenderly placed it on Louise's ring finger.

"Will you marry me, Louise? I'll love you for as long as I have left and I'll always take care of you."

Louise expelled a breath, feeling as though the earth had finally settled into its correct position in space. She told Finn that now it felt as though all the planets and stars were in alignment. She looked at the ring on her finger, finally there after so many years.

"Well...will you?" Finn said impatiently.

"Yes, oh yes, Finn. I'll marry you and I'll love you for all the days of my life. And I'll take care of you, too."

"Now, then," Birgit said joyfully. "We have a wedding to plan!"

CHAPTER FIFTY

1994

The shop was closed for Christmas Day and Della was having Christmas dinner with the Howards. They'd invited Roy and Maxine as well and with the addition of Matt and his family and Gideon, the little flattop in Southern Shores promised to be filled to the gills. In their Southern Shores home, Luke's family Christmas was a simpler meal than the Olsen family dinner in Norfolk. But it was none the less joyful. Baby Grace had begun sitting up and Ann and Matt were especially proud of her accomplishment. On Christmas Eve, Gideon brought a new dinner companion to the meal, a classmate from college. He introduced Margaret Solomon to the family, indicating ahead of time to his brothers that they should go easy on her. Luke and Matt, of course, had no plans to do that very thing, bringing out all the old embarrassing baby pictures of Gideon with his diapers and pacifier, or in his clown Halloween costume. Margaret laughed good naturedly at all the jokes and seemed to fit right in, just as Ann and Della had. Biscuit couldn't decide which of the Howard women he preferred so he shared his licks with all three from time to time, plopping atop the feet of one or the other.

Christmas Day started with the annual Christmas service at St. Andrews-by-the-Sea. Its gray shingled exterior looked the same as always, but the freshly red-painted door bore a huge wreath of pine and shells with a bright red bow. As the Howard family entered the church, the bell rang out its chimes calling all to worship the birthday of the King. The pastor read the Christmas story from the Gospel of Matthew, his voice ringing to the rafters of the old building.

After the service, each of the couples got back into their cars, and headed for Southern Shores. Luke took the long way home, stopping by the bookshop as Della had requested. She had put her gifts for the family in the closet in the office and she wanted to retrieve them. In the darkened bookshop with only the lights of the Christmas decorations glowing, there was an air of magic everywhere. Luke looked outside the windows which were decorated with books of every description and evergreen boughs. The snow was still falling and it was getting a little heavier.

"Let's call Aunt Louise and see how she's doing in Norfolk."

So they called her and she described the Lutheran service she had attended with Finn and his family. The Olsen family were about to sit down to dinner, so Louise had to cut the call short. Scooping up the gifts she'd stored in the office closet, Della told Luke she was ready to go. He took advantage of the fact that her hands were full, and put his hands on either side of her face. Her cheeks were rosy from the cold outside and her mouth was ripe for a kiss. So he did just that, and then took the presents out of her hands.

They left for the Howards' house, just arriving ahead of Roy and Maxine. Della's parents had stopped by their house in Kitty Hawk after church to pick up a basket of homemade yeast rolls, one of Maxine's specialties, and some deviled eggs and jars of her homemade pickles.

The Howard's Christmas dinner was a simple one with turkey and dressing, mashed potatoes and gravy, butter beans and pecan pie in addition to the things Maxine brought. After it was over, May wanted to go right to the tree and open presents but the other women said it would be more fun to delay it a bit so they could get the kitchen cleaned up. Everyone helped. The women carried the dishes to the kitchen, except for Ann who was nursing baby Grace. The men rolled up their sleeves and washed, dried and put away the dishes. May tried not to look as Gideon was prone to juggle the coffee cups as he dried them, bringing shrieks of laughter from everyone else. Finally the kitchen was clean and a pot of coffee was put on to brew. Everyone made their way to the family room where a tall Balsam fir held pride of place in the corner by the door to the porch. May had hung all of her boys' handmade ornaments in prominent places on the tree, much to their embarrassment. But the glow of the Christmas lights on the tree was reflected in the happy faces of all gathered there.

Everyone exchanged presents with everyone else so there was a huge mountain of gifts under the tree. Chaos ensued as everyone ripped open their gifts at once. Della gave Luke a Helios rod and reel personalized with his initials. Luke had told her of his interest in fishing so she thought it might be a good choice.

"I don't know anything about fishing, though, Luke, so if this isn't right, maybe you can just hang it on the wall – for décor," she told him.

Luke thought it was a wonderful gift and immediately set up a fishing date with his brothers and father as soon as the weather warmed up. Then when all the gifts had been opened, Luke went to the pocket of his coat hanging in the hall closet and pulled out a small box wrapped in Christmas paper. To no one's surprise, it was a diamond solitaire, not quite as big as the one Finn had given Louise, but still quite a nice size. There in the presence of so many loved family members, Luke slipped the ring on Della's ring finger and dipped her, giving her a long, passionate kiss. Everyone laughed and clapped and finally, Della came up for air.

"Welcome to the family, Della," all the Howards shouted.

CHAPTER FIFTY - ONE

1995

Within a month, Finn and Louise were married. They said they'd waited long enough and they didn't intend to wait any longer. They were married in St. Andrews by-the-Sea with all the Gates, Olsen and Howard families present. There were also quite a few friends and neighbors as well as other shop owners along Virginia Dare Trail who came – enough to fill all the pews of the church. Even Louis Murdock came, bringing a ten dollar gift certificate to the R & R as his wedding gift.

Louise had taken her parachute wedding dress to the local dry cleaners who had remarked on its amazing condition after being stored for so many decades. They cleaned and pressed it and repaired a tiny rip in one seam. The dress was slightly yellowed from age but was still quite beautiful. So Louise decided to wear it for her big day. She was still slender enough to fit into it and it brought back such happy memories of those days during the war when she and Finn had fallen in love. She knew that there were probably a few people who thought it was ridiculous for a woman in her seventies to wear a long gown for a wedding, but she didn't care. Louise carried a small bouquet of forget-me-nots as a testament to her love for Finn. Roy walked his aunt down the aisle and Della, Maxine, Birgit and Astrid were her bridesmaids. Louise and Finn were deliriously happy after being denied their bliss for so long. Finn still fit in his Coast Guard dress uniform and he wore it to marry his bride. They made a magnificent couple and newspapers from Norfolk, Richmond and Raleigh sent journalists and photographers to cover the story. After an extended river cruise in Europe, they settled down in Louise's Nags Head cottage and continued to work in the bookshop whenever the mood struck them. For the rest of their lives, they never had a cross word, realizing how precious time was to them.

Luke and Della decided to wait for six months to marry, but they did marry, also at St. Andrews by-the-Sea. Della wore a gown of ivory satin, the bodice of which was embellished with lace overlays. The long sleeves were made of the same lace which cascaded down the long gown. She made a breathtaking bride and carried a large bouquet of white sweetheart roses. Luke wore a black tuxedo with black bow tie. Astrid was her friend's maid of honor and Luke asked his father to be his best man. His brothers and one of his friends from the fire station, a tall drink of water named Buck Harrison were ushers. When the minister pronounced that they were husband and wife, Luke gave Della a deep and lasting kiss and the audience erupted in cheers. Matt and Gideon whistled and yelled "Attaboy, Luke!" but later denied that they could ever do anything so crass. At the reception after the ceremony in the church's social hall, Buck asked Astrid for her telephone number. She gave it to him with a shy smile. While the reception was going on and the bride and groom were busy greeting their guests, all the groomsmen were busy tying empty soup cans to the back of Luke's getaway car and writing "Just Married" all over the windows.

The happy young couple took a brief one week vacation to Bermuda, but came back to the bookshop and to Luke's work at the fire station. They found a very small oceanfront cottage for sale in Kitty

Hawk near Roy and Maxine's house. It was an old house but was on a fairly good sized lot so there was room to expand. They would need the extra room since within the next five years, they added two children to the mix with another one on the way.

"L. Gates, Bookseller" continued to thrive as did Maxine and Astrid's gallery now named "Coffee and Culture." Astrid started dating Buck Harrison who seemed like the kind of guy she could bring home to Birgit. Louis Murdock eventually bought the R & R and installed self-service check-out aisles because he could never find enough help.

Finn fell in love with Louise all over again and loved living with her in the cottage by the ocean where they had made so many memories so long ago. Finn often took walks along the sands in front of the cottage and looked out across the ocean. On days when the sea was calm, and the sky was blue, he looked eastward to the horizon, imagining the U-Boats that once terrorized the coastline. He could hear again the sound of the bombs as they exploded. He could see once more the fiery clouds that rose from the vessels that had been torpedoed. He felt the scars on his face and realized once more that he'd lost an eye. For a few moments as he stood on the shoreline, these things became very real to him again.

And then he heard the sweet sound of Louise calling him to dinner, and the dark days faded away in his memory. Then it was that he saw only the sweet present and the hopeful future ahead of him. He walked briskly up to the cottage porch, grabbed Louise around the waist as though they were the young lovers of 1942 and kissed her long and hard.

2014

I t was after eight o'clock on Saturday and time to close "L. Gates, Bookseller" for the weekend. Della walked over to "Coffee and Culture" to say goodnight to Astrid. Their joined shops had continued to be wildly popular with tourists and locals alike and kept both women busy and successful.

Luke now headed the Outer Banks Fire Department. He'd been promoted to Chief about five years before and luckily had not had any more accidents like the time the shed wall fell in on him. He'd led the department in modernizing its equipment and recruiting more trainees as the Outer Banks population swelled. Buck Harrison was made Assistant Chief and had married Astrid a couple of years after Luke and Della's wedding. The Harrison's had one child, a bright and loving boy, and had been surprised with a pregnancy when Astrid was 35. Their daughter was born healthy and was the apple of her father's eye.

Luke and Della had three children – two boys Samuel and Lucas, Jr. and one girl, all born in the first five years of their marriage. Their daughter was named Maxine after her grandmother, but everyone called her Maxie. They still lived in the Kitty Hawk cottage, now greatly expanded, next door to Della's parents who were in their mid-seventies and still living independently.

Finn and Louise were still alive and had just celebrated their 90th and 92nd birthdays jointly. They lived in an apartment in an assisted living facility which had been built in Manteo around the year 2000. Though both were mostly confined to wheelchairs or walkers, their minds were still quite agile and they took joy in life. They read lots of books (hard covers, naturally, which they got from L.Gates, Bookseller,) ate whatever they wanted, worked the *New York Times* crossword puzzle in ink and enjoyed visits from their families. Life, which had kept them separated for so long, seemed determined to give them as many years together as possible to make up for the earlier mistake.

Luke and Della's youngest child, Maxie, was inordinately interested in history and genealogy. She was fourteen and had inherited her father's dark brown hair and dimples. She frequently helped out in the shop as she loved to read.

One day, as she was dusting in the office, Maxie looked at the small closet behind her mother's desk. It was an odd thing as it had no doorknob, only a keyhole which didn't look like any keyhole she'd ever seen. She'd recently been reading *The Lion, the Witch and the Wardrobe* and fancied finding such a portal through that unusual closet. She called her mother to the office from the bookshop.

"Mom, I've never paid much attention to your office before. But this closet interests me. What's in it?"

Della drew her daughter to her in a warm embrace. She raked her fingers through Maxie's long curls and sighed.

"Oh, Maxie – the secrets that closet held for fifty years. Come sit beside me for a minute."

Maxie pulled a chair up next to her mother. Della reached in the bottom drawer of her desk and extracted a skeleton key on a black grosgrain ribbon. Without another word, she inserted it into the keyhole and pulled out a small tin money box containing seven Buffalo nickels and a small Victorian era cast iron safe on wheels. Della pulled the safe out and turned the dial to a set of numbers she had memorized. Soon the final click was heard and Della turned the handle to open the door. Maxie was disappointed to find only an old yellowed dress, a handkerchief and an empty Crackerjack box.

"Oh, phooey. I was hoping there'd be some secret treasure or a magic doorway to another world in here," Maxie said, disappointment dripping from her words.

"Oh, child," said Della. "There is treasure here and this is indeed a doorway to another world. Sit down and let me tell you…"